Table of C

MW00938492

1. Tag Tea

2. Peer Pressure 5

3. Age Ain't Nothing but a Number 9

4. You Got Served 15

5. Bonnie and Clyde 19

6. Candy Man 21

7. Laser Focused 25

8. Set it Off 31

9. Georgia Peach 39

10. Fake It Until You Make It 47

11. Salty Daddy 67

12. Room Mates 77

13. Résumé Submission 85

14. Check Mates 101

15 The Secretary's Secret 111

16. Help Wanted 121

17. No Twerk Experience 133

18. Paid Attention 143

19. Home Twerk Assignment 151

20. Conflict of Interest 163

21. EntrepreNewHer 165

22. Celebrity Crushed 171

23. Guns and Roses 185

24. Robbing the Hood 189

25. Peace of the Pie 203

26. 21 Questions.. 207

27. Hot, New, Single 211

28. Mr. Big Shot.. 217

29. Stupid Cupid 221

30. Baecation.. 227

31. Idols become Rivals.............................. 251

32. Surprise Party 263

33. Touchdown in the DMs 269

34. Connect. Calls. Collects........................ 281

35. Ebony Envy... 285

36. Kiss of Death 291

37. Favor for a Felon 295

38. Side Peace 301

39. Too Legit to Quit 311

40. Leader Shift 327

41. Ride or Die... 341

42. Fed Up 345

43. Pursuit of Happiness............................. 359

1. Tag Team

Pittsburgh, Pennsylvania

They were jealous of Latoya. All of the girls at her school hated her guts. Being the best-looking girl at school was tough. They talked about her clothes every day at lunch because she didn't have name brand attire. Her sneakers had yellow stains. They would point and laugh and ask her where she bought them. Her clothes were never ironed and the kids said that they smelled like burnt bacon. Most of her clothes were from the thrift stores like Goodwill and Salvation Army. Martha, her mother, didn't have a steady job so that's all she could afford. Guys used to laugh and talk about her clothes too, but they still wanted her, quietly. She knew that because guys would still ask for her number all the time when no one was watching. She was a freshman in high school, 14 at the time. The first time she got jumped was by this girl named Shantel and her two friends in the bathroom, just because a kid named Corey Stackhouse, who Shantel had a crush on, didn't like her but he was infatuated with Latoya. So, just for that, Shantel and her friends caught Latoya in the bathroom stall all alone. Latoya opened the stall thinking that there were three random girls in the bathroom just hanging out. One girl grabbed Latoya from behind and slung her to the ground. Not prepared for the ambush, Latoya didn't fight back. Instead, she braced the thud to the ground with her arms but protected herself as she balled up in a fetal position. Blows to the head and ribs came next. After the longest 15 seconds that Latoya had ever endured, she was left lying on the cold tile of the bathroom floor with a busted lip, bloody nose, and a bruised ego. Shantel and her friends were suspended for ten days. The second time Latoya got jumped, she actually won the fight. Latoya was next up to get food in the long lunch line when two girls walked up talking amongst themselves and stood directly in front of her in line.

"Excuse me," said Latoya.

The girls ignored her, still talking to each other.

"Excuse me!" Latoya repeated.

The girls finally looked her way.

"What are y'all doing? Umm. I was here first. I'm next," said Latoya.

"Oh. I'm sorry, we're in a rush. Is it ok if we hop in front really quick?"

Latoya was fed up with the nonsense of being disrespected and belittled. "No, you can wait just like everyone else. Get to the back of the line."

They rolled their eyes.

"Who's next?" said the cafeteria lady waving her hands for someone to come forward.

The girls turned to the cafeteria lady and began to order.

"I'm next!" said Latoya stepping between the both of them slightly bumping shoulders with them while she made room.

One of the girls grabbed her and pulled her away from the line. The girl swung and hit Latoya in the back of the head. Latoya closed her eyes and began to fight back, even though she was outnumbered. Then she heard a loud smack and a thud. She thought she had gotten knocked out. She opened her eyes and saw that one of the girls was on the ground, defending herself in horror. Little did they know, a girl named Sandy Booker was standing behind Latoya and saw the whole interaction and sucker punched one of the girls to the ground. Then, Sandy clocked the second girl off balance. Both girls looked confused. Shocked, but excited that someone had finally helped her, Latoya started throwing and landing punches with the help of Sandy. Latoya and Sandy beat those two girls up so bad that no one ever wanted to fuck with them again at that school. Ever. Before that fight, she didn't know Sandy, but after that, her and Sandy became best high school friends. Latoya and Sandy got suspended for 10 days for fighting, even though they were defending ourselves.

2. Peer Pressure

Latoya admired Sandy. To Latoya, Sandy looked like a grown woman and carried herself like a grown woman. She stood kind of tall at 5'6". She always had her makeup done and she always had her nails done. On Fridays, she would wear heels to school, religiously. She was a freshman but she was 17-years old. She got held back a couple of grades. But she was super popular. Everyone knew her and respected her because she always had the nicest clothes. She always had on clean Ralph Lauren outfits.

Latoya started hanging out with Sandy outside of school when they were suspended. Sandy had an old beat-up Toyota Corolla, so she would come pick Latoya up from her house every day that they were suspended. Sometimes, they would go hang out at Pheasant Park. Sandy would go see her boyfriend Niko up there. Niko was 28. Latoya had never really been around older men before. But she liked hanging around them because it made her feel grown. Latoya's body was fully developed, she had double-D breasts, a round booty, a coke bottle shape with a shimmering golden-brown complexion... all at the age of 14. The older guys on the block loved when she came around.

Niko would hang out at the park all day and all night with a bunch of guys. They called themselves the Wild Side Gang. All they would do is roll dice, smoke weed, and sell drugs. All day. Occasionally, he would give Sandy money to go to the mall.

She would tell Latoya, "I get what I want from these niggas. They buy me whatever I want, whenever I want. That's why I don't fuck with those lil boys at school. I like older men because they can take care of me. Plus, they not about games like these little broke boys at school."

The more Latoya hung with Sandy, the more she started skipping school. She would just leave school and go to Pheasant Park and hang out with the Wild Side Gang. She liked being up there because it made her feel like a grown woman. None of the guys talked bad about her clothes or made her feel inferior. The guys would actually give her compliments and make her feel good. They would say things like, "You fine as hell lil brown skin." Or they would ask who her boyfriend was or if she was fucking with anyone in the Wild Side Gang. She would always turn them down, and tell them no.

But Latoya secretly had a huge crush on one of the guys in the gang. That's why she didn't mind hanging out. His name was Scooter. Scooter was 26. When she first saw him, she liked that he had swag. He was always fly. Name brand everything. He was definitely the best dressed out of the bunch. When his pants sagged, you could see that he had on Versace underwear. He always had on the new Jordans and they were clean like they were fresh out of the box. He had neatly dreaded locks down to his shoulders. Latoya loved when his dreadlocks hung over his face and he would jerk his head backwards sending the dreads flying back. She thought that was so sexy. He had six gold teeth on the bottom. He reminded her of Lil Wayne but to Latoya he was way cuter. He was very quiet, he didn't talk much. She also liked him because when he spoke, everyone listened. He was the leader of the Wild Side Gang.

While hanging at the park, Niko always had a blunt of weed rolled up and he would give it to Sandy to smoke. She would smoke it, then try to pass it to Latoya, and she would say no. "More for us then," Sandy would always say shrugging her shoulders. Then Sandy would continue smoking. Eventually, Latoya started hitting the blunt too. She started coming home high almost every day. Latoya never knew her dad, so the only parent in the house at the time was her mother Martha and she didn't notice Latoya's glassy red eyes and marijuana-scented fragrance because, most of the time, she was high too.

Martha would smoke weed and do other drugs. Not in the house though. She would never do it in front of the kids, but Latoya knew the truth. Martha probably would do whatever drug you put in front of her. She didn't work anywhere, she just collected government assistance. Food stamps were the family's best friend. She tried to work, but she would always quit her job or get fired within weeks. Latoya and Martha didn't get along so she stayed out of her mother's way most of the time. Latoya hated when she would have random men come over and stay the night. Sometimes,

Martha would leave the house late at night once she thought Latoya was sleeping and she wouldn't come back until the morning when it was time for Latoya and her little sister Leah to go to school. That's why, every time Latoya got home, she would go straight to her room and close the door. Her little sister Leah, however, loved their mother to death. She looked up to Martha, she was only five-years old. She didn't know any better.

Leah was the opposite of Latoya and their mother. She was super smart. She always got good grades and loved to read. Latoya knew she was going places. Latoya's goal in life was to mentor Leah and make sure that she doesn't make the same mistakes that her or Martha did. She always stayed on top of Leah because she knew that Leah would be the golden child of the family.

3. Age Ain't Nothing but a Number

One day, Sandy called Latoya and said that Niko had a hotel room and she wanted her to come chill and smoke with her. She agreed and then Sandy picked her up. Once Latoya got in the car, she asked who would be at the hotel with them.

"Just Niko and Scooter," Sandy said.

Latoya's face lit up.

When Latoya got to the hotel room, Niko opened the door. The room was dimly lit but they could still see into the room and the two queen beds. The television was on but muted. There was an auxiliary cord connected to the hotel room's speaker and they were playing a Gucci Mane song. The room smelled like straight marijuana. Scooter was sitting on the bed rolling a blunt. He didn't look up once to see who was at the door. There were little plastic bags of drugs everywhere. There was a pistol on the nightstand.

"Y'all ready to get fucked up?!" Niko said pointing to the bottle of gin on the table.

"Yep," said Sandy. Sandy looked at Latoya, "You drinking with us?"

"Girl. I never drank before. I thought you said that we were just going to smoke?" Latoya said.

"We got smoke too! Whatever you like, we got it," said Niko.

"Just take a shot with me. Don't worry, you won't get drunk off a shot," Sandy said.

"Ok. Just one," Latoya responded.

Niko got two of the plastic complimentary cups that the hotel provides and poured them each a shot. Holding the shot in her hand, she put her nose in the cup and the smell hit her like a Mike Tyson punch.

"Oh my God! It smells like rubbing alcohol!" said Latoya fanning at the smell.

"That's what it's supposed to smell like. Just take the shot and don't think about it," said Niko.

Latoya held her nose, tilted her head back, and threw the shot in her mouth. It was one of the worse things that she had ever tasted.

Niko smiled. "Now that's what I'm talking about! Turn up! Now we can smoke. Scooter has the blunt rolled up and ready."

They all gathered around Scooter as he lit the marijuana filled blunt. He calmly puffed the blunt multiple times, then passed it to Niko. They each puffed and passed the blunt around the circle. Latoya was feeling woozy, but she liked it.

After a couple of rounds of passing the blunt, Niko whispered in Sandy's ear. She giggled and they both went to the other bed and got under the covers. Scooter and Latoya sat on the bed alone.

There was silence between Scooter and Latoya until she broke it.

"Why are you always so quiet?" she asked.

"Because I like to just watch and listen. I like to analyze everything. You can't do that if you're always running your mouth," said Scooter not looking at her.

"Oh. ok. I was just wondering. You never spoke to me, out of all the times that I was at the park, you never said anything to me."

"Because I was waiting on you to speak to me. Plus, I been watching you trying to figure out if you're my type of chick or not."

"Your type of chick? What's your type?"

"A chick that stay to herself. That just got a cool vibe about her. A chick that's gone hold a nigga down," said Scooter as he puffed the blunt and blew smoke out of his nose.

"Oh. Well, do you like what you see?"

"I don't know yet. I'm trying to figure it out now." Scooter reached over to his left and grabbed a tiny plastic bag. He put his fingers in it and pulled out a tiny ball of white powder. "Here," Scooter said.

"Here what?" Latoya said.

"Take this."

"What's that? And what do you mean *take it*?" she responded.

"Just call it, Snow White. And all you do is sniff it up your nose. Like this," he put it to his nostrils and sniffed it up smoothly. Then he wiggled his nose and his mouth a little. "Ok. Your turn. Try it."

She looked over her shoulder to talk to Sandy about it, but her and Niko were under the covers moving around. Then she heard Sandy softly moaning, so she didn't want to bother her.

"If that's cocaine, I'm not doing that. Hell no."

"Cocaine sounds so evil. Don't call it cocaine. Call it Snow White. I sell this stuff, I know all about it. I promise after you take it you will feel better than you ever felt. You will feel smarter. You will feel like you can take over the world. You will feel like superwoman. Just try it once. I do it all the time and I'm fine. Does it look like anything is wrong with me?"

Latoya looked him in his eyes. He looked confident. He looked brave. She trusted him. She wanted him to like her so bad, that she would do anything for him. Plus, he looked healthy, he didn't look sick, or like a drug addict.

"Ok. Just a small tiny pinch. And just one," she pinched a tiny bit from the bag, she looked at it for a second, then snorted it. It felt like her brain had been shocked.

"See, it wasn't that bad," Scooter said.

She looked square at him but she didn't say anything. She was super alert and energized. She felt happy. Scooter began speaking, she could hear his voice, but she was just so focused on how good she was feeling that she wasn't paying attention. She bravely leaned forward. Next thing she knew, her lips met Scooter's lips.

Scooter started taking her clothes off. Everything was moving so fast. She was worried that he would find out that she was a virgin and she had no idea what she was doing. What if she had sex with him and he hated it and he would never talk to her again. Her mind was racing. They both got naked and under the covers. Scooter started caressing her vagina with his two fingers. He tried to force his fingers inside and she winced. It was super painful. Then he gradually forced his fingers in and out of her. Then it started feeling better but it still hurt. Then he put his tongue down there and started licking her vagina and her clit. She kept jumping in fear every time his cold and wet tongue touched her. It was a weird feeling, but Latoya liked it.

He finally tried to put his dick inside her. It was the most painful thing that she had ever felt. She tried her best not to be loud but she couldn't help it. She cried. Scooter turned the music up louder to mask her shouts. She kept pushing him away because it hurt so bad. He started going, slow, and steady, not going deep, just easing the tip of his dick in and out. Eventually, she was comfortable enough for him to go halfway in so he could get a quality stroke. He nutted in five minutes. She lost her virginity to her biggest crush.

4. You Got Served

After that night, Scooter became her boyfriend. Now, just like Sandy and Niko, every time she asked him for money, he would give it to her. Sometimes he would give her a couple of hundrod depending on the mood that he was in. Then her and Sandy would go to the mall and buy Ralph Lauren and Christian Dior. After awhile Scooter started coming to her house. He met Martha. Sometimes he would spend the night. Martha knew he was 26 and Latoya was 14. She liked Scooter so she was cool with it. They had a really good relationship.

After Latoya started dating Scooter, she started skipping school more than ever. She didn't show up to school much but when she did, she was the best dressed. Now, everyone knew her for being fly. She had on name brand clothes. No one could talk shit anymore. She was untouchable, the boys couldn't afford her and the girls wanted to be her. She eventually became the most popular chick at the school.

She was infatuated with Scooter. Just crazy about him. Their relationship was very strong. One day, she woke up in the morning and she heard her house phone beeping. She went and checked, and it said that she had a missed call from Scooter at 3:00 a.m. Scooter would never call her house phone, because she had her own cell phone. There was no reason to. Her cell phone had no missed calls from him. So, she called him back. She was worried that something had happened.

"Hey is everything ok? Did you call me last night?"

"Yea everything is ok."

"Why did you call then?"

"I was returning someone's call."

"Returning who's call?"

"Look Latoya. I don't want to get between you and Martha."

"Get between us?! What are you talking about Scooter?! Did she call you?!"

"Yes, she called me."

"What the hell is going on?! Are you fucking my mama or something?!"

"No girl! She need to be served so I brought her some Snow White, that's all."

She immediately hung up the phone. She ran to the living room where Martha was sitting on the couch.

"Martha! What the hell are you doing calling my boyfriend at 3:30 a.m. in the fucking morning?!"

"Who are you yelling at?! Have you lost your damn mind?! I pay the bills around here. This is my house and I can call whoever the hell I want in my house, and on my phone," Martha didn't look her in the eye.

"Your broke ass can barely pay the bills because you're too busy calling my nigga to buy drugs!"

"You know what? Get the fuck out of my house, and don't come back either!" She finally made eye contact and pointed at the door.

Leah crept around the corner.

"I'm gone. I don't want to stay in this shithole anyway. And Leah is coming with me. Come on," Latoya said motioning her way.

"You're out of your damn mind if you think you're going to take my damn daughter with you. Go!"

Latoya left and called Sandy to pick her up and take her straight to Scooter's house so that she could get to the bottom of everything. He apologized for serving her mama. Although she was mad at Scooter, she forgave him. Then she moved in with him.

5. Bonnie and Clyde

When Latoya moved in with Scooter, she barely went to school. If living with Scooter taught her anything, he taught her how to be a crook. He told her that she had to use her good looks to get what she wanted. When times were hard, Scooter would have Latoya and Sandy go on missions to find money. They would go find other drug dealers, flirt with them. Go home with them have sex with them and rob them. They would talk them into having threesomes, and while one of them would fuck the guy, the other would change out his cocaine for baking soda. They were making thousands of dollars at age 14 and 17.

Although she had moved out of Martha's place, she would eventually stop by to see Leah. For one, she really missed her and she would always give her money, toys, and clothes. But two, she wanted Martha to see her looking good in her name brand outfits. She wanted to show her that she didn't need her and that she was actually doing better than ever without her. She noticed it too. One night, Leah was asleep so Latoya came and slipped $50 under her pillow. Martha had something to say.

"So, you're living with Scooter now?"

"Yes. Why do you care?"

"Ok. Well I don't appreciate you coming in here trying to show off and give Leah money."

"You don't give her shit. Why shouldn't I? If I don't who will?"

"She doesn't need any of your drug money. Please stop it! And the principal of your school called and said that if you have one more unexcused absence you're getting kicked out. Whatever you're doing with Scooter is going to fuck your life up!"

"Don't worry about my life. And what Scooter and I have going on is none of your business."

She walked out not wanting to hear anything else from Martha.

The next night, around 11:00 p.m., Scooter was bagging up some of his drug shipments in the bedroom while Latoya was laying in the bed and watching old episodes of *Martin*. She got a call from Martha. She answered.

"Latoya, I just wanted to let you know that I love you, and that this is for your own good. I'm saving your life."

"What are you talking about, Martha?"

The next thing she knew, she saw red and blue lights circulating around Scooter's apartment. Scooter ran to the bathroom flushing drugs down the toilet as fast as he could. Latoya ran to the closet and just hid. Latoya told herself that she would never date a drug dealer ever again. And she was ok if she never spoke to her mother again either.

6. Candy Man

The cops raided the place and they both were arrested and taken into custody. Scooter already had a serious record. He was a felon, with a lengthy rap sheet. He already had a warrant out for his arrest. He had pounds of cocaine in his apartment. He was sentenced to life in prison. Latoya was convicted with three felonies. She was sentenced to be in the juvenile center for a minimum of three years at the age of 14.

She was back to square one at the juvenile center. All the girls hated her just because she was pretty. They all wore the same clothes so she couldn't stand out like high school. No more fancy clothes. But this time she refused to be bullied. She had to fight multiple times to earn respect. And eventually she did.

Juvenile detention was super boring, and she felt like she was wasting her life away. But she did have plenty of time to reflect on her life. She wrote down her goals and what she wanted to accomplish with her life when she got out. Although it seemed so far away, she still wanted to graduate high school. And maybe even enroll in college. Her goal was to just become successful. She didn't talk to her mother while she was locked up. Didn't want to. Her little sister Leah would call her and tell her how good she was doing in elementary school. She spoke to her Grandma Betsy from South Carolina as well. Grandma Betsy told her that it would be better if she just moved down to stay with her and left Pittsburgh all together. She said that she would take care of her and look out for her. She agreed. The first step was to earn her freedom again.

The only interesting part of being locked up was when she used to flirt with this guard named CJ. She knew he liked her by the way that he would look at her. He was mean to all the other girls, but he was nice to her. She would use him to get what she wanted every time. Food, blankets, and sometimes he would smuggle her in some liquor. One day, CJ and Latoya were alone in the hallway. CJ had some Reese's Pieces in his hands. Latoya jokingly said, "CJ, I know you're going to share."

"Share? Maybe. What are you willing to do for it?"

"Anything for some Reese's Pieces," Latoya said.

"Ok. Come here then."

She followed him to a closet. Secluded from the main hallway. He locked the door behind her.

"Hurry up. Pull your pants down," said CJ.

"Pull them down? Why? We're not having sex for Reese's. Plus, aren't you married?"

"That's none of your business. And I never said we were having sex, just pull them down," He grabbed her pants and began to pull them down. She grabbed his hands. "I just want to play with it. Relax," he said.

Latoya thought about the situation and realized that it may be her way out of the juvenile center. If she played her cards right, she would be free in no time. She let his hand go and he began to caress her vagina. He stuck two fingers in it gently then pulled them out. He did this a couple of times. His hands were cold and dry.

"That's all I wanted to do. Here's your Reese's," he said as he handed the candy to her.

"Whatever, CJ," she said.

They left the room and one of the girls saw them. Latoya was sent back to her cell. The next day she approached the girl that saw them leave the closet. Latoya told the girl everything that happened. She told the girl to tell everyone, because she was afraid to tell everyone herself. The girl did just that.

The rumors spread quickly. It was a huge scandal that gained the attention of many news outlets. Based on the sexual scandal between CJ and Latoya, instead of facing three years in the juvenile detention center, she did just one and she was set free. CJ was charged with sexual assault and molestation.

7. Laser Focused

After getting out of juvenile detention, she was determined to make a better life for herself. She decided to move to South Carolina to live with her Grandma Betsy. She waited patiently outside of the 20-foot tall barbwire fence for Grandma Betsy to pick her up. Her grandma arrived in an old-school Cadillac and gave her the biggest hug. Latoya told her to take her to her Martha's house one last time so that she could pack her clothes and so that she could say one last goodbye to Leah before she moved to South Carolina.

"Big sister! I missed you! I'm so glad you're home!" Leah rushed Latoya and gave her a big hug as she walked into the house.

Grandma Betsy stayed in the car and waited. Martha was in her room with the door closed.

"I missed you too! You're getting so big, girl! How's your report card looking?"

"Straight As, and one B!" said Leah proudly.

"Good job, girl! Keep it up! Hey I wanted to let you know that I'm moving to South Carolina with Grandma Betsy!"

"Why?"

"So that your big sister can get a fresh start somewhere else and so that I can get good grades like you!"

"Can I go?"

"No. Mother is going to keep taking care of you. Now, when you graduate high school, maybe you can move down there with me!"

"I'm going to go to Spelman College in Atlanta." said Leah with her hand on her hip.

"You can go anywhere you want, girl. Just keep getting good grades and stay out of trouble."

"I will!" yelled Leah.

Latoya gave her a big hug and kissed her on the cheek.

After all of her bags were packed. She was walking out of the house when Martha came out of her room. They looked at each other.

"Good to see you," Martha said.

"Good to see you as well," said Latoya clutching her bags.

"Look Latoya, I'm sorry for turning you in—"

"Ma, you don't have to apologize. Save your breath. I'm over it. I'm sure Grandma Betsy told you that I'm moving to South Carolina to stay with her."

"Yes, she told me. I think it would be good for you. You need some new scenery. And you damn sure need to be around new people."

Latoya glanced at Leah. "I agree. But I was thinking, maybe Leah can come live with Grandma Betsy too. We can find her a good school in South Carolina or something where she can really do well."

"No! Hell no! Leah is staying here. She ain't going nowhere. She's doing just fine."

"But Ma, let's keep it real. You're not going to look after her like Grandma Betsy and I can. Especially, if you're always high all the time."

"Latoya, you don't know what you're talking about. That's in the past. You've been locked up for a year. I'm 100% sober. I haven't touched no damn drugs in so damn long. Plus, I got a job working at Walmart. A lot has changed. Leah needs me and I need her."

"Ok. Just promise to look after her please."

"That's my baby. Of course, I will. I promise," she said.

Latoya nodded. They hugged each other and Latoya left.

Columbia, South Carolina

Grandma Betsy was working her butt off to get Latoya back into school. She went from county to county, school to school trying to get Latoya enrolled. High schools would not accept her at first with her poor grades and her criminal record. But thankfully, after so many "*nos*," someone finally gave her a yes. She enrolled at Richland High School.

Latoya remembered the promise to herself while she was locked up that she would succeed and graduate high school. So, she was more focused than ever. She went to school every day and gave it her best. She went straight home after school. No after school extracurricular activities. She was 100% sober and she did not mess with any boys. She would just get home and talk to Leah on the phone and keep giving her words of encouragement. She didn't want to let Leah or Grandma Betsy down. Latoya wanted to be successful.

After three full years of hard work, discipline, and sacrifice Latoya graduated from Richland High School with a 2.9 GPA. Walking across that stage was the best day of her life.

"Latoya Ashley Robertson!" The announcer said as she walked across the big stage with 6-inch heels tapping the stage like a true boss chick. It was the best feeling ever. Neither her Grandma Betsy nor Martha graduated high school. She was the first from her family. Latoya grabbed her diploma with pride as she strutted across the stage. Her smile was a big as the state of Texas.

After exiting the auditorium, she was greeted with a big hug by Leah. Leah and Martha had flown down for the graduation. Martha gave her a hug and said congrats, then Grandma Betsy did too.

"So, what are you going to do next?" asked Leah.

"I don't know lil sis. Hopefully go to college."

"What college are you going to?" Leah asked.

"I don't know. I applied to some schools: Spelman, Georgia State, Georgia… but they didn't accept me. I'm waiting to hear back from FAMU. We'll see."

Grandma Betsy rubbed her back. "It's ok, baby. Keep your head. By the way, I got you a graduation present." She handed Latoya an envelope.

"Thank you, Grandma! Should I open it now?"

"Sure. Why not?"

Latoya started opening the envelope. She pulled out a letter. It was an acceptance letter to FAMU. She screamed. They all grabbed each other and began to jump up and down in joy. It was the happiest day of Latoya's life.

8. Set it Off

Tallahassee, Florida

Latoya was a proud member of the new freshman class at Florida A&M. She didn't know anyone at all. She was pretty anti-social. She had her "resting bitch face" on at all times so that boys would leave her alone. And it seemed like all the girls had already cliqued up and found groups of friends so she really just stayed to herself. The first person that she met and connected with was Tina Prescott.

Tina was a junior at the time. They literally met on the set at FAMU. The set is where all the students would hang out on campus and on Fridays, there was usually a DJ there playing music. People danced and had fun, and the fraternities and sororities strolled. It's a festive, cultural experience that Latoya thought was super dope.

She was sitting there watching the sororities stroll on the set. She loved the Deltas. They were these chicks that had on all red. They just looked like confident, smart, bad bitches, and she liked that. This girl, Tina, who was a pretty-ass Delta, saw Latoya staring. Tina came up to Latoya and asked her name and where she was from. Latoya wasn't used to that. Latoya thought Tina was gay and trying to hit on her at first. She wasn't used to people being so friendly. But later she realized that Tina genuinely wanted to get to know her. Tina became Latoya's mentor. She always respected Tina because she was always on top of her shit. She had good grades, she was gorgeous, and she was just the most confident and put together person that Latoya had ever met. Tina saw potential in Latoya, so she took her under her wing.

Tina was Latoya's only real friend in college. Wherever she went, Latoya went. She was her protege. Latoya met all the cute fraternity boys while she was with Tina because they partied a lot. She had sex with a couple of the cute ones too, she would admit. One was a handsome dark skin Alpha named Terrance, but she would eventually regret having sex with him. Tina made college fun for Latoya. Latoya loved everything about Tina and her Delta organization. Tina knew that Latoya wanted to eventually become a Delta and that's why Tina would stay on top of her even though they had a good time together. She saw potential in her, and Latoya appreciated that. Because of Tina, Latoya believed that she had lived her college life to the fullest. The parties, the liquor, the fine guys. All of it was the best experience, ever.

The spring semester of Latoya's sophomore year, the Deltas came out with a new line full of girls. Latoya wasn't one of them. Latoya stood shoulder to shoulder in the crowd full of people watching the new Deltas do their line show. Everyone screamed the girls' names and their line numbers in excitement. Crimson and white balloons were floating everywhere. Latoya's stomach was all knotted up as she watched their probate coming out show. She believed she looked better than all of those girls. Most of the girls were in her freshman class.

During their coming out show, Tina came over and gave Latoya a big hug. "Don't worry, we'll be coming out with another line really soon. If you apply yourself, you'll be on it for sure. I'll make sure of that. And either way, you're still my girl no matter what," said Tina.

That didn't make Latoya feel any better. Latoya's grades weren't good enough to become a Delta. She had a 2.5 GPA and the grade requirement was a 3.3. She felt like she had let Tina down. That semester, Tina graduated and moved to Atlanta, Ga.

After missing the Delta line, she had no more real motivation for school. Becoming a Delta became way more difficult because Latoya didn't respect the new Deltas and they didn't think much of her either. Plus, Latoya's grades still weren't up to par, and with Tina leaving her in Tallahassee, Latoya became lonely. She didn't know many people in school. Didn't want to know many either. She became depressed. She started smoking a lot of weed and she would be drunk almost every other night. She enrolled in classes every semester, just to get the financial aid money and then drop the classes. She started taking trips up to Atlanta to visit Tina. She would stay at her apartment for the weekend and they would hit the city hard together. She would get so inspired by being around Tina and her young successful girlfriends. They all had good jobs, made good money, and they were all confident black women. Latoya was inspired but she also was a bit envious of them too because she felt like she couldn't relate to their success at the time. She was a broke college student that was flunking out of school.

Latoya started meeting a lot of new people when traveling to and from Atlanta. She loved it. She would meet these ballers that would offer to take care of her all the time. Pro athletes, business owners, doctors, you name it. She told Tina that she wanted to finish school then move to Atlanta. It got to a point where she would go to Atlanta just to see some of her male sugar daddies without even letting Tina know she was in town.

One day, while in her dorm in Tallahassee, Latoya got a call from Grandma Betsy. She had a crack in her voice.

"Latoya, where are you right now?"

"I'm in my dorm."

"Are you alone?"

"Yes."

"Brace yourself. I have some bad news. Your mother was intoxicated while driving, and she got into an accident while Leah was in the car."

"What?! Are they ok?"

"No. Your mother survived. Leah passed away."

Latoya couldn't believe what she was hearing. She immediately started tearing up her room. She threw sheets in the air, she threw school books, and she dropped to the floor on her knees. She yelled and cried in sorrow for hours until she cried herself to sleep.

Latoya woke up still in disbelief and continued crying. With so much grief in her heart, she didn't care if she lived or died at this point. So, she looked on her bed and grabbed her roommate's medication and put five pills in her mouth. She drank water, closed her eyes and laid on her bed and prepared to die.

She woke up in the hospital. Her suicide attempt had failed. Her roommate found her and called 911. Latoya remembers waking up and having the worst headache. The nurse mentioned to Latoya, "An angel must've been with you because you're supposed to be dead. You must be here for a reason."

Latoya stayed at the hospital for a week until she was cleared to go home. Her body was so weak that she left the hospital in a wheelchair. She could barely walk.

Latoya's mother ended up going to prison for involuntary manslaughter of her own daughter. She was sentenced to seven years in prison. Latoya flew up to Pittsburgh for the funeral. Seeing her little sister in a casket made her hate her mother more than she ever did before. Latoya was now heartless.

Grandma Betsy approached her after the funeral. "You holding up ok?" she asked.

"As best I can, Grandma."

"Well. Just know that Leah was just an angel. God blessed us with her presence before he called her back home."

"Yea. I know. I still can't make sense of any of it, Grandma. She should've just came to live with you, like I did."

"Hindsight is always 20/20. Everything happens for a reason. Now she's just looking down on us all. We have to make her proud. Speaking of making someone proud, when are you supposed to be graduating from school?"

"Probably next spring."

"Ok. Well, let me know so I can come down there. I'm counting on you to make me proud. To make your whole family proud."

"Ok Grandma. I will let you know."

Latoya was a aware of the complete lie she had just told. She had no idea when or if she could even graduate. She flew back to Tallahassee feeling like she had let Grandma Betsy down. She hadn't been to class consistently since her freshman year and she had been in college for five years now. All the people that she had come to school with had already graduated. She had no more financial aid. She was living off of student loans, which she had maxed out every single year for a total of $100K. With all this being the case, she told herself that she needed to go see if she could re-enroll in school and to see if graduation was still a possibility. She had to do it for Leah and her grandma.

She sat in the hallway in line waiting for the dean to call her name. She wanted to make her grandma proud. But she figured she would have to face reality. She hadn't been to her guidance counselor in over a year and a half. But it was worth a try to see what she actually needed to do to get this diploma to keep her grandma off her back.

"Latoya Robertson!" said the counselor as she waved her into her office. She got up and proceeded. "Ok. Sooo Latoya, what questions do you have for me?" she said sitting down and looking at her computer.

"Well, I wanted to know how many classes I need to take to graduate. Like how far am I? And all that good stuff."

"Ok. Well, let me look you up really quick, what's the last four of your social?" she said as she got to typing.

"6754."

"Ok. Ummm. Ms. Robertson it looks like you are no longer a student here."

"Really?! How is that?!"

The counselor looked her in the eye. "Come on. Let's not act lost here. You've dropped every class that you had registered for. Except for one, in which you got in F in."

"So, I can't re-enroll? There has to be a way."

"Latoya you have a 0.8 GPA at this point. Your scholarship and grant money is depleted. You have been on academic probation for awhile now. I hate to be the bearer of bad news, but it looks like you've dug yourself in a hole that is pretty impossible to get out of. I'm sorry. There's not much that I can do."

She looked at her. "Welp. That's all I needed to know. Thank you."

She wasn't surprised. She knew what the counselor was going to tell her. Who was she fooling? She had mentally checked out of college a long time ago. Latoya knew she wasn't a dummy. But she just can't get into studying and learning shit that doesn't interest her. Her freshman year's major was Biology because she said she wanted to be a doctor. That lasted for two weeks until she found out that her and science go together like peanut butter and spaghetti. Then she switched her major to accounting, which was the biggest mistake of her life because accountants actually need to be pretty good at math. Then she figured, maybe she should study English, which wasn't that bad at first but eventually her procrastination would leave her missing due dates for all of her literary assignments. So, that department kicked her out. She really tried to study and keep up, for all of two weeks at a time. But then eventually she'd just get bored and stop. Latoya spent most of her time partying, and smoking weed.

9. Georgia Peach

Atlanta, Georgia

There was no reason for her to stay in Tallahassee anymore. She had overstayed her welcome. She was ready to get out ASAP. Plus, she was dead broke. She needed some money. With $150 to her name she caught the Greyhound bus to Atlanta.

Now she was very familiar with Atlanta at this point. Actually, she was way too familiar. While she was in school, Atlanta was her second home. She knew she had a couple of sugar daddies that would look after her. One was a basketball player for the Atlanta Hawks. His name was Dexter Sabir. He would do whatever she told him to do. He was fresh from Africa and he barely spoke English. She met him one time at the club in Atlanta. Since then he had been begging her to come back to Atlanta. He even sent her $500 once, just to go shopping.

She told him that she was coming to Atlanta and that she needed a place to stay. He told her that she could stay at his place in midtown Atlanta. Free of rent. That's exactly what Latoya needed.

When she got to his house, she was surprised. The condo was super nice. He didn't even try to have sex with her. She basically had her own spot. Free of rent. He was barely there. He would come and stay the night, probably twice a week. He would bring over some of his NBA friends. He would introduce her as his girlfriend. She didn't care because she was living rent free. She started going out to the clubs a lot with him. Going out with Dexter everywhere. She didn't have a job. Dexter would just send her money every week or so to go shopping; $1000 here, $2000 there. She would just wake up, work-out, go shopping, then eventually go to the club that night. She never paid for anything. She believed that she had made it. Even when she went out with Dexter, all these guys would be spitting game and trying to get her number. She was the shit. Since Dexter wasn't around much, sometimes she would go out with guys and have them pay for everything. She would have them buy her clothes. When Dexter had not sent any money in awhile, she would finesse her way into other guys' pockets. That means occasionally she would have them pay her to have sex. Typically, it was the older married guys that knew they didn't have a chance with her any other way. She didn't care how they looked. As long as they would pay. At one point, a guy named Mr. Freddy would pay her $8K a month just to hang out with him and to have sex with him every once in a while. All of her sugar daddies had money.

In Latoya's point of view, she was no different from the average girl. Girls do that shit all the time. They let guys take them out and spend all of this money on them, and they eventually have sex with the guy. Most of the time, the guy never really had any intentions to marry the girl or take her seriously. All they really wanted was the sex. All she was doing was speeding up that process. She didn't have a job and she didn't need one.

Latoya had been in Atlanta for months before she reached out to Tina and told her that she had moved there. She wanted to make sure that she was pretty secure in her situation because she knew Tina would be in mentor mode trying to make sure that she was handling business. She had a fly crib. The nicest clothes. She had money in the bank. She was living it up.

She told Tina to meet her at her condo in midtown. She wanted Tina to see how she was living. She wanted her to see that she had made it. She knew she would be proud. Especially once Tina found out that she was dating someone from the Hawks. She wanted Tina to realize that she wasn't a failure after all.

Latoya opened the door for Tina to come into the condo.

"Toy! What are you doing here?! You didn't even tell me you were coming in town."

"I wanted to surprise you," said Latoya.

"Girl, I guess. Whose place are you staying at. This is nice," Tina said looking around.

"I live here. This is my place."

"Since when?"

"I've been here for three months now."

"And you didn't tell me. Since when have you not told your mentor about big moves like this? I thought you loved me."

"I do love you. That's why I'm telling you now."

"Wait a minute. I didn't get an invitation to your graduation, when did you graduate from FAMU."

"Oh. Umm. I didn't graduate yet."

"You didn't graduate?!"

"Yes, because I transferred to Clark University."

"Ohh ok. I see. So, you're still in school. I was about to say. When are you graduating?"

"Next semester in the spring."

"Ok. Well, let me know so I can be there," Tina was looking around. "But seriously, who do you share this with?"

"I didn't tell you that my boyfriend is Dexter Sabir."

"Dexter Sabir?! The basketball player for the Hawks?! Damn, girl you are winning!"

"Not like you! You're the one that is still winning. Got the corporate job at PWC, making good money. You still inspire me."

"Girl, you'll get here, just knock that degree out so that you can get into the real world so you can get this corporate money."

"Hey. What are you doing tonight? Dexter and some of his NBA friends are supposed to be going out tonight. I want to introduce you to them."

"Now that you said that, I won't be doing shit tonight. I'm coming with you!"

That night. Latoya and Tina went out and met with some of Dexter's friends. They were in the VIP room popping lots of bottles with them. Tina was having a ball. Bending over shaking her ass, everywhere. She didn't have a care in the world. Tina even hooked up with one of Dexter Sabir's friends for a one-night stand. Tina wasn't used to this life, she wasn't built for it. She was googly eyed for the players. The player that she hooked up with was Tory Bishop, another big star on the team, but Latoya would never have imagined Tina doing something like that. Although Tory was a fine man. Tall, light skinned, nice teeth with tattoos, any girl would fall for him. But she didn't think that Tina was just any girl, until that night. It showed her that even Tina was vulnerable with the right circumstances. Latoya looked at Tina in a different light. But she still respected her.

Tina then started bringing Latoya around her other friends: Lisa and Wanda. Latoya respected them as well. They all had their shit together. They all had great careers and were very smart and ambitious. They all were FAMU alums. They were all under the impression that Latoya had transferred to Clark University. Latoya didn't know Lisa and Wanda while they were at FAMU although they mutually knew Tina. Now this was new to Latoya. She never really hung out with a group of girls. She realized how different she was from the other girls. Very different. Different upbringings. Tina, Lisa, and Wanda, all graduated from college. Latoya was a dropout. Tina, Lisa, and Wanda had full time jobs, Latoya was unemployed. To a certain extent, Latoya was ok with it because she was inspired by them. Latoya played her part in the group though. Latoya was known as the friend that had all the connections with the ball players, the celebrities, and the clubs while allegedly still being enrolled in college.

Lisa was the most uppity chick out of the bunch. She was the politically correct friend that acted as if she could do no wrong. When Latoya first met her, she knew that their personalities didn't quite mesh and they would eventually bump heads. She was right.

The first mistake that Latoya made to hurt her relationship with Lisa was actually an attempt to help Lisa. At the time, Lisa was mad at her boyfriend because she had found out that he had cheated on her back in college with numerous women. Lisa was heartbroken, shocked, and disappointed to the extent that she decided that she wanted to test the dating waters again, in Atlanta. So, Latoya, with all of her connections, thought it was a great idea to introduce her to Tory Bishop, the same guy that Tina, had freaked on the first night. Big mistake. The second misunderstanding started when Lisa eventually found out that Latoya was one of the chicks that her boyfriend cheated with. Terrance, was an Alpha that Latoya occasionally freaked while back in college.

Latoya knew he had a girlfriend at the time but she didn't know his girlfriend was Lisa, nor did she know that she would eventually end up being friends with her. So, one day, Lisa put two and two together and tried to fight Latoya while they were all at this restaurant. Lisa was going through a lot of shit at the time with Terrance and with the basketball player, Tory Bishop. Not long after Lisa and Latoya's spat at the restaurant, Lisa then found out that Tina was freaking Tory Bishop all along and was actually pregnant from him as well. Everyone knew except for Lisa. Tina eventually had a miscarriage but that didn't stop Lisa from leaving the group. So, Lisa eventually stopped hanging out with Latoya, Wanda, and Tina. Latoya really didn't care because she didn't like her much to begin with.

10. Fake It Until You Make It

At first Latoya didn't think much of Dexter. She was just using him for a place to stay. A nice place to stay at that. But eventually she started to fall for him. It was serious. Serious enough for her to cut off all of her sugar daddies, including Mr. Freddy, her main sugar daddy. Mr. Freddy was upset but she didn't want anything to interfere with her and Dexter. The fact that Dexter was so selfless. He was not arrogant even though he had every right to be. He was easy going and didn't just use her for sex. It was deeper than that. And he was the most consistent thing in her life at the time. She knew that she could count on Dexter in the time of need. He bought her a car. They started falling for each other more and more as the months went by. He even told her that he was planning on kicking his fiancée out of the main house and moving Latoya in. Then he would propose, eventually. Dexter told Latoya that he was prolonging his wedding with his fiancée because he knew that Latoya was really the one that he wanted to marry. She just had to be patient. She believed their bond was impeccable.

Latoya called Terry. He was a club promoter.

"Hey you got any VIP sections still available for tonight at Club Destiny?"

"Yea. I have one. How many people?"

"Just me and my two home girls."

"Alright. Well, I got you. Hit me up when you get here."

"Ok. I'm on the way."

She called Tina. Latoya had been home all day thumbing through Instagram and Facebook and watching Netflix. She needed to get out the house. She called Tina, she figured that if she could get Tina on board with coming out Wanda would follow suit.

"Hey girl. Get dressed. We bout to go out."

"Go out where?"

"To Club Destiny."

"Toya. Not tonight. I had a long day at work. I need rest."

"Come ooonnn. Come out with me. I got a section reserved. We're going to pop bottles tonight like some boss bitches!"

"YOU have a section reserved? I don't believe you. And that doesn't change me from being tired."

"It's a celebration. I'm graduating tomorrow. Are you not going to celebrate with me?"

"Holy shit?! Are you serious?"

"Yea. You coming out with me tonight or what?"

"Well, since you're finally graduating... I'll come turn up with you."

"Good. Call Wanda and let her know," Latoya said.

"Clark graduation is at 9:00 a.m. Are you going to wake up?"

"Yep. I'll be fine."

All of the men around them were drooling. They were drooling at Tina and Latoya. Not so much Wanda. Their VIP section was right on the floor. Right in front of everyone, just like Latoya liked it. There was a two bottle minimum so they got two bottles of Patron. Guys were still trying to lean over the section and buy the girls drinks. Latoya let the guys buy extra drinks and she would just give them to Wanda. Wanda could drink the most out of all of them.

They were turnt up. Latoya was dancing to every song, shaking her ass like no one was looking, all three of them were. At 2:05 a.m. Latoya felt someone tap her on the shoulder. She turned around.

It was a waitress with a receipt in hand. "Whose card are we going to use to pay?"

"Ummm," she reached in her cleavage to get her debit card. "Here."

The waitress went away. Latoya went back to partying.

Ten minutes later. Latoya felt another tap on her shoulder. She turned around. It was the waitress again.

"The card declined. Do you have another?" Latoya's heart dropped.

"That doesn't make any sense. I for sure have money on that card," she replied.

"Well, I tried like three times. It declined each time."

"Hold on."

She pulled out her phone and logged into her Bank of America app. She was going to prove to her that it was money in her account. And. Oh shit. Negative $175. Latoya knew better. Those damn overdraft fees. That $1200 that she had gotten from Dexter, she spent it all that fast. Again. She was broke. She tapped on Tina's shoulder and she turned around and she handed her the receipt.

She looked at it. "$650. Are we splitting this?"

"Yea, but my card isn't working," Latoya replied.

"Card not working? Toya, you reserved this booth. You dragged me out tonight. Don't pull this shit on me today. Did you even tell Wanda how much we had to pay? I'm only splitting this three ways."

"Tina, just take care of my share for me. I'll pay you back."

Tina shook her head. "You know what. Don't worry about it. I'll take care of it. I'm only doing this because your graduating and I'm your mentor. I love you, but if it wasn't for that, I wouldn't have paid a dime."

"Thank you, Tina." Latoya gave her a hug.

"That's what friends are for!"

Latoya Ashley Robertson! The announcer said as she walked across the big stage with 6-inch heels tapping the stage like a true boss chick. It was the best feeling ever. The first person to graduate from both high school and college. Yep, first generation student! She grabbed her diploma with pride! She had a smile bigger than Texas. Looking in the crowd to find her Grandma Betsy.

"I'm an official graduate of Clark University!" they hugged as they finally saw each other outside of the ceremony.

"You're a big girl now! I'm proud of you Toya!" Grandma Betsy said.

"Thanks Granny!"

"So, what are you going to do now?"

"I'm going to find a job like everyone else I guess," she rebutted.

"You don't have one lined up yet?"

"No, I don't have one yet."

"Didn't I tell you that you needed to be applying while you were in school, so that you would get a head start."

"You're right Granny, I just wanted to finish so bad that I was just focused on my exams and stuff."

"Ok, baby. I just want to make sure you're making all the right decisions that will help you succeed that's all,"

"I know, Grandma. I get it."

"You're 24-years old now with a college degree. So, it's time to be more responsible and more disciplined. It's time to learn how to take care of yourself."

"Ok, Grandma."

"It's time for you to wake up. Toya."

"Ok."

"Wake up!!"

"Ok!" Latoya said as she jumped up and sat up from her bed. Her phone was ringing, it was Grandma Betsy.

"Aren't you supposed to be going to graduation? Clark is graduating today and I haven't gotten any type of invitation. You told me that you were supposed to be graduating in the spring."

The dream seemed so real. She had been lying to her grandmother for the longest. Telling her that she was on track to graduate. But this time she had went too far. All the way up until the actual day. She had gotten so far that she couldn't even keep up with her own lies. Five years in school, $120,000 in student loans. And still she wasn't even close to getting a diploma.

"Grandma, I'm sorry, but I was wrong, apparently they pushed my graduation back. I need to go to my counselor again..."

"Stop it! Stop it right now! Stop with your lies! This is the third time you've told me that you were graduating."

"Ok, Grandma. Fine, I lied. I dropped out of school. I don't attend Clark, I'm just in Atlanta looking for a job."

"Dropped out of school? After all that I had invested in you, and this is how you repay me? I know that Leah's death was hard on you but that didn't mean you had to give up."

"College ended up not being for me, Grandma. And plus, I'm doing fine in Atlanta. Everything has worked out. I'm living with my boyfriend now and he's rich. He doesn't want me to work. But I just might get a job to bring in some extra income."

"Latoya. I just want the best for you. I just want you to be better than your mother and I. I'm worried. I'm praying for you."

She hung up.

Latoya was supposed to meet Tina and Wanda at the Cheesecake Factory in Buckhead at 3 p.m. but Latoya was running late. She still had to do her makeup and get dressed. It took way longer than she thought. She was Ubering there because her car was at the repair shop. The engine in her 2002 Camry was acting up because she had forgot to get her required oil changes. She was going to pick it up from the shop soon but not right now because money was tight. She was waiting for Dexter to pay for it, or he may just pay for a new car all together. She could've easily just got one of her other sugar daddies to pay for it, but she had cut them off. She wanted to be faithful to Dexter now. So, she was carless for now. But she didn't mind Ubering everywhere...because Uber was attached to Dexter's credit card.

The energy was different about her friends when she walked into the Cheesecake Factory. It was 3:45 p.m. when she got there. She could tell something was up. She could tell that they knew.

"You sobered up yet?" Wanda asked as she pulled up the chair.

"Yea I'm fine now," Latoya said.

"Good. Because we need you to have a sober head for this sober heart to heart that we're about to have," Tina said.

"What are you talking about?"

"LaToya. For once, can you be honest with me. Were you really supposed to graduate today?"

"Yes. Like I said I overslept because I was drunk. What part do you not understand?"

"Ok. It's just funny how your name wasn't on the pre-printed graduation program," said Wanda holding a folded program.

"Let me see," Latoya grabbed the program. "I told them that I didn't want to be on this shitty program,"

"Please Toya! Why do you have to lie to us! We're your friends! Just tell the truth!"

"What is this? A meeting to bash me or something? This is why y'all wanted to meet?"

"Toya, Please don't take this the wrong way. We are your friends. We care about you. We wanted to meet because we're concerned. As your friends, we're concerned about your behavior recently."

"Behavior? What have I done?"

"Where do we start. Toya you're in the club three times a week. You lie to me about the silliest things. You lie to us about graduating from school? You've been in school for over 5 years. Plus, let's face it, you're broke. Every time we go out somewhere, we're paying for you."

"I always eventually pay y'all back though."

"Yes. With a married man's money. Not yours," Wanda replied.

"Oh, you're going to bring my man into this?"

"That's not your man! He's married!" said Tina.

"Dexter is not married calm down Tina. He's engaged. You know I met him at the club during his bachelor party, we've been in love ever since. That's why he's been pushing his wedding back."

"That's what he tells you? Toya you can't be that gullible. What makes you think he's going to be faithful to you if he's cheating on his fiancée now? If you take her position, that means your position will open up," said Tina.

"He won't. He loves me. I love him. He doesn't love her, and he's just trying to figure out a way to end shit with her. Listen, Dexter and I have been out of the country together numerous times. I can't count how many times we've been out together. We pretty much live together. We've been dating for two years now. It's impossible for you to understand what we have."

"Tina, I'm not going to lie, That's a fine man right there. I don't blame Toya. 6'5", African, chocolate brother. NBA player. Rich as hell. I wouldn't mind being his side chick either," Wanda said with a smirk.

"Don't call me a side chick Wanda, I'm his lover."

Wanda and Tina laugh.

"You're his lover alright. He loves-her, not you," said Wanda.

"This must be gang up on LaToya day. Neither of y'all should worry about me because I'm going to handle my business. So, save your concerns."

"I just want the best for you LaToya. That's all."

"I won't be needing anything from either of you. But thanks for the offer. And as far as college and graduating, I didn't tell the whole truth about that. I'll admit that. But I'll figure it out. Don't worry about me. I got this. As a matter of fact, I'm not really even hungry anymore. I'll talk to y'all later," Latoya pushed away from the table, got up and started walking towards the exit. Tina and Wanda looked at each other.

"Come on. Latoya come back! Don't be so sensitive! We're just keeping it real," Wanda yelled across the restaurant.

"Let her go. Don't chase her. She's hard-headed. She's going to have to learn the hard way."

They both watched her walk out the door.

Latoya was angry but she was still hungry. She ended up going to the nearest Chick-fil-A. She was sitting at Chick-fil-A minding her own business, eating a chicken sandwich, brainstorming on what the hell she was going to do with her life. Contemplating her next move and trying to figure out how she would prove both Wanda and Tina wrong. Then someone walked up to her table. She could not believe her eyes.

"Long time no see," Lisa said.

It was Lisa Smith. The old friend that used to hang with her, Tina, and Wanda. The last time she saw Lisa was a year ago, and that was when Lisa was trying to give her a black eye. She didn't know what to expect. Latoya was not prepared to fight today.

"Oh, hey Lisa," she said awkwardly.

"Something told me to come to this Chick-fil-A today. Do you mind if I sit?"

"Um. Yea girl go ahead," Latoya shrugged.

She sat.

"So how have you been?" Lisa asked.

"I'm ok. But check this out. Let's be clear. I don't want any problems. I just want to let you know that I'm still sorry for what happened with Terrence and I."

Lisa looked at Latoya and began laughing hysterically.

This bitch must be crazy, Latoya thought to herself. "What's so funny?" Latoya asked.

"Girl. I am sooo past that whole situation. I've grown so much, spiritually, since then. If anything, I hope you forgive me for my actions. The way that I acted that day at that restaurant was just a reflection of my level of consciousness at that time. I wasn't mentally strong. I'm just here to say hello and to catch up."

"Oh ok. Well, all is well with me. I'm still hanging out with Wanda and Tina. I just left them actually. They're doing well. How are you doing?"

"I'm better than ever! You know I had to break away from everything and everyone to do a little soul searching. I left corporate America. Well, I didn't voluntarily leave, they fired me after the sex tape incident between Tory and I. I hated everyone after that. You, Tina, Wanda. Everyone. I hated the world. But now, things are different. I forgave myself. I forgave you all. I'm at peace now. I'm a fulltime life coach, and I started my own non-profit TEA CUP which stands for: Tribulation, Embarrassment, and Adversity, Creates Unprecedented Power. I started it to mentor and uplift battered women ages 14–35 and it has been taking off. I have over 100 women actively in the program now."

"That's good for you. Seems like everyone is making something happen. I'm happy for you. I'm not doing much of anything new right now. Nothing as exciting as what you have going for yourself. Just focusing on getting a job. Probably will be working in healthcare as a nurse or something. I'm not sure yet."

"Was that your major in school?"

"Ummm. Honestly, I don't want to talk about school right now. I didn't finish school. I'm doing whatever I have to do without a degree," said Latoya.

"I understand. Don't worry, your time is coming too, girl. Just stay focused on yourself and God will create a way for you. He has something special in store for you, I can feel it."

"I'm sure he does. Thank you for that."

Lisa pulled out her business card and handed it to Latoya. "Well, I'm going to let you finish your food in peace. Remember that I'm a life coach so if there's anything that you need to talk about, feel free to reach out to me, free of charge. Remember, whatever you're going through, you're not alone. Somebody has been there, and someone can help. Just ask. It was good seeing you, especially since the last time we saw each other I was trying to kick your ass. This may sound weird but, I feel like God wants me to look out for you. I will keep you in my prayers. As a matter of fact, what's your number. I'll do a better job at keeping in touch."

Latoya hesitated for a second but she gave Lisa her number. As soon as Lisa left, Latoya threw Lisa's business card in the trash. That was the most awkward interaction ever. She said "free of charge" as if Latoya would ever consider paying for someone to tell her about her life. She wouldn't pay a dime for her services. Girl please. That was a joke. Plus, she didn't want Lisa calling her and trying to mend whatever friendship that she thought they had before. That ship has sailed. She didn't care what type of spiritual journey she has going on. She didn't want any more friends in her life. Especially if they're just going to judge her like Tina and Wanda were doing currently.

She finished her Chick-fil-A and just sat there in the restaurant. She began thinking about what Tina and Wanda said about her relationship with Dexter. Feeling some type of way, she figured that she would call him and express herself.

"Hey you," Dexter answered.

"Sooo. I haven't heard from you in awhile, where you been?"

"I told you that I had been busy. Schedule has been crazy. We've been practicing a lot to get ready for the playoffs, but what's up, what do you need?"

"You know my car is still in the shop. I haven't had my car for a week now. Are you going to pay for it to get fixed or are you going to buy me a new one?"

"Oh yea. About that. I have some other finances I have to take care of first. It's going to be awhile before I can pay for that."

"Other finances? This must have something to do with April huh?"

"Not at all. Nothing to do with her. And if it did, why would that matter anyway?"

"It matters. Because, it would mean that you would be choosing her over me. Again. I see where your priorities are. Where are you anyway?"

"I'm headed home. Why?"

"Well I'm coming over," said Latoya

"Where, to the main house?"

"Yep,"

"What are you talking about!? You know that coming to my main place is off limits."

"Is April there?" Latoya asked.

"Yes. She should be. Why?!"

"So, what are we going to do? Remember you promised me that we'd be together after a couple of months, And that you'd be kicking her out. Well what happened? I want us to live together, I'm getting restless over here..."

"Well, I still need time. This is not an easy process for me Toya."

"Well what can I do to make it easier for you? Because I'm tired of waiting. I'm tired of getting strung along, Dexter, like some puppet."

"Toya. Stop it. You have to know your place in this whole thing."

"Huh. Know my place? The side chick? Right? That's what you really wanted to say."

"You know I didn't mean it like that."

"Oh, I know what you mean. Trust me. I'll show you my place." The call ended. Latoya hung up.

Upset. Latoya called an Uber to Dexter's main house. That was the most forbidden action that she could ever take. She knew that, but she didn't care. Her and Dexter had an agreement for her to never show up to the main house where his fiancée lived.

Latoya's Uber pulled up to the brick paved driveway that led to the mansion. The Uber driver looked at the mansion, then looked at Latoya. "This is your residence?" he asked.

"Yep. It's mine," said Latoya with no hesitation.

"Impressive," The Uber driver nodded.

There was a BMW in the driveway. Latoya strutted up to the front door. *Ding Dong Ding Dong Ding Dong!* She waited. Still no answer. After two minutes, she heard someone come to the door.

"Can I help you?" A short cute girl opened the door.

"Yes, you can. Is Dexter home?" asked Latoya looking past the woman and inside the house.

"Um no. He should be home in a bit. What do you need with him?" asked April looking Latoya up and down.

"You're April, right?"

"Yes. Why?"

"I've heard so much about you. Well, not to bust your little bubble but Dexter and I have been talking for 2 years now and we've been trying to figure out a way to kick you out. He wants to dump you but he doesn't know how. He's going to be looking to have me as his fiancée."

April chuckled and smirked.

"Ummm. What's amusing about what I just said?" Latoya was baffled.

"So, you're Latoya?" April asked.

"Yep. So, he told you about me?"

"Yes. He actually did. He told me all about you as well," she said folding her arms and leaning against the door entrance.

Latoya was more perplexed. "What did he tell you? Did he tell you that he comes over late at night? Did he tell you that we have dinner dates quite often? Did he tell you that he met my grandma?"

"Listen, Latoya. See, if you had any type of sense you would be able to see who's really getting played here. Dexter and I have a unique relationship. I know all about you. I know that you're fucking him. I know that he tells you any and everything that you want to hear. He and I have an agreement that lets him do what he wants as long as he doesn't lie to me. So, the fact, that you showed up here today just lets me know that you have gotten a little too bold. You are out of line, sweetie. You're supposed to be on your back, and not on my doorstep." April winked.

No, this bitch didn't. Latoya lost it. She saw red and she attacked. She pushed April through the doorway and onto the floor. She got two punches in before Dexter's car pulled up behind them.

"Stop it! Stop it!" said Dexter.

She felt his big hands grab her shoulders and lift her off of April. He pulled Latoya away from the house.

"I'm pressing charges! Dumb-ass bitch!" yelled April from the house.

Dexter held Latoya back. "Go home Latoya. Please! Before I call the police!"

"Are you serious, Dexter! Is it true that you've been lying to me! I thought I was going to be Mrs. Sabir! You promised that we would be together forever no matter what. You told me that you would leave that bitch!"

"I lied Toya, ok. I did. It was a mistake. Our relationship is over. Go get your shit out of the second house. I will have the locks changed tomorrow. It's over." said Dexter.

Latoya said nothing for a second, until she internalized what Dexter had said. Then she lost her cool and started swinging at him.

"Liar! I hate you! You played me like a fiddle!" she said as she kept swinging for Dexter's head until she heard police sirens. She then ran away from the property.

Latoya was speed walking on the side of the road. Fist balled up. Looking over her shoulder for the police. Fuck Dexter. She needed to make Dexter jealous ASAP. She needed to get even. But now she was officially homeless. She didn't have a penny to her name. She needed to bounce back quick. Her pride would not let her hit up Wanda or Tina for help. She didn't want to hear them saying, "I told you so." Not right now at least. She would probably fight them too, she was furious. She had a better idea. She was going to hit up one of her guy friends that would die to have her company. One that would do anything for her and won't want anything in return. She needed a place to stay, and some money in her pocket so that she could get back on her feet. And she knew exactly which guy would be perfect.

11. Salty Daddy

The next day, Latoya had all of her stuff packed and she was ready to leave the condo behind for good. She had no choice because Dexter had the locks changed immediately upon her departure. Now, she just needed to implement her game plan. She made a call to an old friend.

"Hey, Kwame!"

"What's up, shorty? What's good with you?"

"I'm good. What you doing right now?" asked Latoya.

"Nothing important, now that I'm talking to you. I haven't heard from you in a loooong time. I guess it takes 25 text messages to get you to respond to one, huh shorty?"

"Kwame, you know I'm always busy. I'm sorry, I'll do better. Let's hang tonight if you got some free time."

"Let's do it. You want to get dinner somewhere?!" asked Kwame.

"Ummmmm. Why not. Where at?"

"It's going to be a surprise, just wear your finest shit."

"Oh no Kwame. I don't have any dress up clothes right now. I'm in the process of moving so everything is packed up. Plus, I'm not home."

"Don't worry. I got you! We'll go shopping. We'll find you something. Where are you right now?"

"Kwame, you don't have to do this…"

"Baby girl it's nothing. I'm coming to pick you up right now. Send me your location."

Fifteen minutes later, Kwame pulls up in his BMW with the top down. He gets out and opens the door for her.

"Toya, good to see you baby girl. Looking good as always," he says and hugs her.

"Hey Kwame! Good to see you too!"

"Go ahead and get in. Let me put these bags in the trunk for you," said Kwame ready to assist.

Kwame is Jamaican, originally from Queens, New York. He has a very strong New York accent. He would say, "Ma or Shorty" when referring to Latoya all the time. He's about 38, has some money but really doesn't know what to do with it. He's a schemer. She met him at this day party awhile back when he and his buddy was popping mad bottles in their section. She was there drinking all of their liquor so she gave him her number just because she felt bad. He does credit card scams and identity fraud to get money. Hangs out with people younger than him. He was dark skinned with a large head, heavy acne, and a gap between his front two teeth. He's super reliable and he has money.

"You know how long I've been waiting to take you out! When did I get your number? A year ago, right? It's been a year since I met you at that day party!"

"Yea, I guess it was a year. I've just been so busy."

"Nah it's cool, it's cool, ma. That's why we gone do this right. We going to the mall," said Kwame.

As soon as they stepped foot in the mall.

"Go get you a nice dress for tonight."

"Ummm. Ok. You're not going to give me a price range?"

"Go get what you want, ma. I'm serious Toya. Get something that you like. I got you."

"Ok," said Latoya right before she wandered off into the Gucci store.

After thirty minutes, she found a nice dress that was on sell for $750. It was the best deal ever. It looked like it was worth at least $1500. She really didn't feel bad because she knew he had the money. She tried it on and came out of the dressing room?

"What do you think?!" she asked posing for him and looking in the mirror at the same time.

"You look amazing! If you like it. It's yours, ma."

"Thank you, Kwame!" She gave him a kiss on the cheek.

Ruth's Chris, 7:30 p.m., Buckhead, Atlanta

"Damn! Kwame you are the best! This is so nice! The food here was amazing! You popping bottles of champagne. I'm really impressed right now, I'm not going to lie," said Latoya sipping a glass of champagne.

"See you could've been my shorty a long time ago if you just would've responded to my texts!"

"You're right! But I'm here now. Let's not focus on the past. Let's focus on the now."

"You're right! And right now, I'm full and this champagne got me feeling right! You ready to take it in for tonight? We can go watch a movie at my crib. A little, Netflix and Chill?"

"I'm ready when you are."

They got to his place. It was the ultimate bachelor's pad. It was a sprawling loft space with big-screen TVs, imported handwoven rugs, and original artwork on the walls.

"Nice place you got here. Did you decorate?"

"Thank you. And yes, I decorated it myself."

"You have great taste."

"Well I chose you... so that should tell you something right there," said Kwame.

"I guess. Do you have a T-shirt and shorts that I can put on? I'm about to take a shower so that I can take this dress off."

"Yep," he reached in a drawer.

"Here you go."

"Ok. I'll be right back."

"I'll be waiting," he said smiling.

After the shower, she laid in his bed and started watching Kevin Hart's stand up on Netflix. An hour in she was very comfortable and just about to go to sleep. Until she felt his hands rubbing on her back.

"You want a massage?" he whispered in her ear.

"Ummmm. I'm good baby. Thank you though."

"Well I want one," he whispered.

"I'm tired. I had a long day. Maybe tomorrow."

"Ok. I respect that."

It was back to silence when she felt his hard rough hands rubbing around her inner thigh, getting close to her vagina. She moved his hand. He then leans and starts kissing on her neck. She could feel his coarse, acne and razor bumps scraping against her cheek. She slightly elbows him away.

"No kissing, baby."

"Damn, like that?" Kwame says.

He eases his way down to the foot of the bed and starts touching on her inner thighs again. This time, a little more aggressively. Then he starts kissing down there. She tried to ignore it until he tries to finger her with his dry index finger. She moves it and she pushes his head away.

"No touching and feeling, baby. Let's just go to sleep."

"Go to sleep?! No, ain't no sleeping. I'm not going to sleep."

"Well we're not having sex tonight, that's for sure," said Latoya firmly.

"Oh really?! We're not?! After all the shit that I bought you today? $750 Gucci dress? $250-dollar dinner at Ruth's Chris?! And you won't let me touch you, you got me fucked up, ma!"

"I didn't tell you to buy that Kwame! You bought all that on your own! You think I'm going to fuck you just because you bought me some shit?! I'm not that type of girl."

"Not that type of girl? You lying bitch! I know a couple of niggas in the city that you let hit with no strings attached. Don't act brand new. You've been ignoring my text messages with the read receipt on ever since you gave me your number, and you think that you can just come up in here spend all my money, lay up in my bed and not fuck something, you got to be out of your goddamn mind. Get up and get out of my damn house!"

"Are you serious right now?!"

"Does it look like I'm playing? Get your broke, free-loading ass out of my house! And take off my T-shirt and shorts." He got up and pointed at the door.

Baffled. She took off his clothes. Kwame grabs her luggage and all her belongings and throws them outside his door.

"You can change outside. And I'm keeping the dress,"

"Go to hell," she said.

She got up and walked out the door. Bra and panties on. He slammed it behind her. She shivered as the wind chill hit her naked body. It was 2:30 a.m. She unzipped her bags to find clothes to fully dress herself.

Before contacting Kwame, she was determined not to call her friends for help. She didn't want to prove that they were right about Dexter all along. The only thing she wanted to prove was that she was independent and that she didn't need them. But, at this point, she had no choice. She called Wanda five times, no answer. She called Tina five times, no answer. Wanda stays 45 minutes away in Fairburn and Latoya has no idea where Tina stays because she just moved in with her new boyfriend. She tried to use Uber but apparently Dexter had disconnected his card from her Uber account.

Luckily, she had a free Lyft coupon that she had never used before. That was God looking out for her. She caught a Lyft to the nearest 24-hour gym. There was an attendant at the gym. She knocked on the door. He opened it.

"Yes, can I help you?"

"Ummm. I need a favor."

"What's that?"

"I'm kind of stranded right now. I am in a very sticky situation and I just need a place to lay my head at for a couple of hours until the sun comes up and until my friends answer their phone."

"Absolutely not. Bums come here all the time looking for a place to sleep. If you don't have a membership, you cannot come in, especially to sleep!"

"Listen, I'm not a bum! Do I look like a bum? Do you know who Dexter Sabir is? That's my ex. I just moved out of a condo suite downtown. And, I understand your policy, but I'm begging you. Please, just give me a couple of hours to rest. I'll be out of here before you know it."

"Lady. I'm not trying to lose my job over this."

"I promise you won't lose your job! If you lose your job, I promise you that I'm going to be so rich one day that I'll buy you your own Anytime Fitness. Please! Just make something up and say that I'm a member that got so tired that I fell asleep!"

"Ok. You have until 5:45 a.m. when my shift ends."

"Thank you so much!!! You're the best person in the whole wide world!"

She laid down on the matted floors. She could feel the dirt on it. There was a small roach, laying on his back, still kicking his feet as if he was still alive two feet away from her. It was at that moment when she told herself that she would never be homeless again. Never. And she would do whatever it took to never feel as low as she did at this very moment.

Latoya opened her eyes when she felt someone tap her on the shoulder. She looked up and saw the gym worker, Tina, and Wanda.

"How did y'all find me?"

"We called your phone and the gym worker answered it since you were crashed out and told me you were here. What the hell is going on?! You had us worried sick!" said Tina.

"You don't even know the half," said Latoya embarrassed.

"You have a lot of explaining to do. Right after we stop by Waffle House because I'm hungry!" said Wanda.

12. Room Mates

The three friends sat at the Waffle House. Latoya was cold, so Tina gave her a blanket from her car to wrap around her.

"Sooooo. Now that I have my breakfast. What the fuck is going on with you Latoya?" says Wanda while she stuffed scrambled eggs in her mouth.

"There's so much to say right now. I don't even know where to start. Just know that I've been going through a lot lately. I've been really depressed. And I apologize for the way that I walked out on y'all the other day. I appreciate you all being honest with me. I know y'all just want the best for me."

"That's what we're here for. You just can't keep omitting the truth from us. We're your friends," said Tina.

"I know. Just seeing you all graduate and have successful careers while I'm sitting here still trying to figure my life out is nerve racking. Imagine being surpassed by your friends in all aspects of life. I just see myself as a failure right now. I can't do shit right."

"Girl, that's not true! Comparison is the thief of joy, don't compare yourself to us. Everything is going to be ok," said Tina.

"Plus, Dexter kicked me out last night. So, technically, I'm homeless right now. I tried not to tell you all because I was so embarrassed. My pride wouldn't let me. I'm so broke right now, I didn't even have enough money to pay for a hotel. I'm broke. I have a criminal record that dates back to when I was 14. I couldn't finish college. Everything has been shitty. And I don't know what to do with my life right now. I can't believe that I let my life get so off track like this,"

"Latoya, don't ever feel like you can't be honest with us. We're your girls, you know we got your back," says Wanda.

"And girl, you can stay with me. I have plenty of room in my new spot. You can stay in one of my guest rooms," says Tina.

"Guest rooms?"

"Girl you know Tina's new boo is rich. She hit the jackpot with this one. He got room for all of us," said Wanda not looking up from her food.

"Thank you, Tina! You're the best."

"Plus, you know he owns a construction company, he's always looking for good talent. He may be able to get you a good position paying pretty well."

"Damn. Are you sure? He can do that for me?"

"Of course! I talk to him all the time about stuff like this. I know he can hook you up," said Tina.

"See, that's why I love having people in my circle that actually care about me. I really love you both," said Latoya, and they hugged.

"Yea. Because to be frank with you, Toya, you're not going to find a good job with no college degree. You need something to get your resume up. I'll set up a meeting with y'all ASAP," said Tina.

Latoya had not been to Tina's house since she moved in with her boyfriend, Marvin. They moved in together about six months ago. Wanda had been, but Latoya hadn't. It was way up in Alpharetta, Georgia so she never got a chance to check it out. Wanda told her it was gorgeous.

Latoya was in an Uber XL with all of her bags when she road through Tina's neighborhood for the first time. The houses were bigger than she expected. Two and even three story houses. They were mansions. Estates. Huge lawns. Huge gates around the properties. It was a very upscale, wealthy neighborhood with not that many blacks. She pulled up into the driveway. She texted Tina and told her that she had arrived.

Latoya stood at the front door with two of her packed bags in hand.

"Welcome to mi casa," Tina said as she opened the door.

"Hey girl. Thank you. This shit is amazing," Latoya said.

"Yes. It's pretty nice. Come on in, let me help you with the bags," she said as she grabbed a bag from her grasp.

She followed Tina inside the house and to the room where she would be staying. The inside looked even more attractive than the outside. Super high ceilings. Chandeliers. Fancy art. Clean and crisp furniture. Latoya was thoroughly in awe. Tina helped her bring all the stuff in. Then they both flopped on Latoya's soon to be bed and looked up to the ceiling.

"Woooo! Girl, you have more junk than me! These bags are super heavy. What'd you have in them, bricks?!" said Tina.

"I know. I have too many clothes. It's ridiculous…That's probably why I'm broke now. I have too much of an expensive taste for clothes and bags."

"Yea, you and me both," said Tina.

Latoya looked towards Tina. "But Tina, I really can't thank you enough for this. You didn't have to open up your place for me, but you did. I appreciate you."

"Spsssss. Girl, it's nothing, we have plenty of room. We have to look out for each other. We have five guest rooms, we probably won't even see each other that often."

"Yep. I'll be as quiet as a mouse. You won't even know I'm here. This property is so big we'll have to use walkie talkies to communicate. It's really inspirational though. You are really doing it big! I knew you were living, but I didn't know you were living like this!"

"Well, you know I make pretty good money at PWC… but I don't make THIS much. You know I can't afford this house. This is all Marvin."

"That's what I'm saying. You hit the jackpot with him. I'm just hoping I find a man of this caliber."

Tina blushed and held her hand to the sky, "Well I am blessed. I'm not going to sit here and act like I'm not. You know it ain't all about the money with him… I really love him regardless. He's just a solid man that handles his business. That's all. Very humble. Very generous. Laid back. You'll meet him, soon. You'll like him I'm sure. He'll be home any minute now."

"How'd you meet him again?" asked Latoya.

"He was one of my clients at PWC. Usually my clients are old white men. But I got assigned to Marvin and there was just chemistry immediately. We started meeting outside of work then the rest was history."

"Well, find out if he got some rich friends. Shit. I'm single and ready to mingle," said Latoya.

"Ha ha, I'll ask when he gets here. I don't think so though. If so, I haven't seen any good looking ones," said Tina.

The front door open alert came on.

"Speaking of the devil. Let me introduce you," said Tina walking towards the front entrance.

Marvin had on a brown suit jacket with black dress pants. He was on the phone. He was talking on some type of Bluetooth headset. He had a briefcase in hand. Bald. Dark brown skin. With a small mustache. He stood at about 5'8".

"Let me call you back. I just got in the door," said Marvin.

"Hey hun, we were just talking about you..." said Tina going up to him and kissing him on the lips.

"I hope it was something good," he said smiling.

"This is Latoya. Well, we call her Toy. My friend that I told you about that's going to be staying with us for awhile, until she gets back on for feet."

"Nice to meet you," he said holding his hand out.

"Same here. Thank you for letting me stay."

"Anytime. If you're Tina's friend then you're like family to me. Plus, we have plenty of room here that we never use and we're never home," he said.

"Oh, and baby I told her all about what you do and how you may be able to help her find some work. Maybe y'all can set up a meeting or something soon," Tina suggested.

"Yea we can meet in a week or so. Actually, how's next Monday 9:30 a.m. at Starbucks?"

"Well, I don't have a job right now so it works for me," says Latoya jokingly.

"Alright. I'll put you on my calendar," he looked at Tina. "Baby, I have to hop back on this conference call with some business partners, I'll be in my office. I'll speak with you all later," he said walking towards another part of the house where his office was.

"Go handle business," Tina shooed him away. She looked at Latoya. "So, what do you think?"

"He seems like a nice wholesome, guy. But like I said, if you loved me you'd hook me up with one of his rich friends."

"I will, girl."

Seeing how Tina lived was very inspiring. It made Latoya really want to get her life together. Not only did Tina have a great job working in accounting at PWC, her man was a multi-millionaire business owner. Not to mention that he was named on Atlanta's top 40 under 40 list for the most successful movers and shakers in the city. Latoya didn't think she could land a good, wholesome man like Marvin, because her resume wasn't good enough. A good successful man wouldn't want to wife up with a college dropout that was jobless. In Latoya's eyes, Tina had won in life. Tina and Latoya are almost the same age. But sometimes it doesn't feel like it to Latoya. She just felt like Tina was so far ahead of her in life.

13. Résumé Submission

Monday 9:15 a.m.

The baristas were swift on their feet as they took customer orders and prepared to pour the strong liquid goodness in everyone's cups. People were anxious but patient as they waited in line for the typical morning boost. The strong smell of crushed coffee beans had Latoya alert in Starbucks. The place was so crowded she barely could find an open seat. People were doing everything from reading newspapers, to having business meetings, to doing college coursework. Latoya had her padfolio in hand. But no resume. She just had a notepad. And she had a suit on.

"Latoya?" said Marvin as he walked towards her table.

"Nice to see you again. I barely see you around the house," Latoya said.

"Yep. Because I'm always, working. But. Wow. You look...great," he said while taking a seat across from her.

"Thank you. I guess you haven't really seen me dressed outside of house clothes."

"No. You look great in house clothes as well. Tina should've warned me about you before you moved in," said Marvin with a chuckle.

"Thank you, I guess she should've." She felt awkward.

"So, I hear that you're looking for a job?" he asked.

"Yes I am. I'm looking for work."

"Ok. Well, what do you know about my company?" Marvin asked.

"I don't know much. To be honest, I just know that you own your own construction company."

"Oookay. So yes, that is true. It's called M&M Construction. It's an exciting time to be in construction because of all the new developments that are happening in Atlanta. Right now, I'm looking for an assistant project manager."

"This all sounds great Marvin. But I do want to let you know that I don't have much of a construction background. Like, at all."

"Of course, I knew that. Most people don't. That's why it's an assistant project manager. You'll learn from the project manager for a year or so. Helping them with all of their contracts. You'll have firsthand on-the-job-training. And you'll make pretty good money doing it too."

"Ok. What's the pay structure, if you don't mind me asking?"

"75K. "

"Damn. I'd love that. So, what else do you need from me."

"It's pretty much your position. So, all that you have to do is fill out an application. We will do a quick verification to confirm our minimum requirements which are a bachelor's degree, no felonies, things of that nature."

"Wait. Background check? To verify what? My degree? My word isn't good enough?" she asked.

"Well, although I'm the owner, I can't just throw you on the payroll and give you a hard hat. There is still a process that you have to go through to be hired officially. We have over 100 employees, that all go through the same application process. This is a big operation here."

"Well to be honest, when I was younger I got in a little trouble and ended up with a felony. And what if I don't have a bachelor's degree?"

"Then you don't have a position. That's a minimum requirement. You do have one, right?"

"I thought Tina told you, that I didn't officially finish."

"Oh, well in that case there's nothing that I can do for you. I was already sticking my neck out a mile to give you this position, but that's just something that I can't do," said Marvin attempting to get up.

"Wait. So, what can you do? Can you change up the requirements?"

"Unfortunately, No. You're already unqualified as it is with no experience. There's no way that I can take you. I have a board of directors and stakeholders that I have to answer to. There's no way that I would be able to give an explanation on why I have a degreeless, felon as an assistant project manager."

Latoya grabbed his arm, "Marvin, please. I need this position. What do I have to do? I'm desperate at this point. I'm begging you," she said looking at him in his eyes.

Marvin stood there. He said nothing. He looked at her hand grabbing his. He then took a coat.

"Ok. I will make you an offer. But you have to be an open-minded individual and you have to promise me that you can keep a secret."

"I'm very open minded and I can definitely keep a secret," said Latoya.

"Ok. If you want this position, give me one night with you," he said looking her in the eye.

"What do you mean one night with me?"

Marvin looked away. "You know exactly what I mean. One night. You come to my place, and handle your business and then, the job is yours."

Latoya couldn't believe her ears, "Are you blackmailing me? For sex? Did I just hear that right?"

Marvin leaned forward. "Latoya. This is not a blackmail, this is the price of me jeopardizing my whole career, and everything that I have built for you."

"You are fucking sick. The answer is a hell no. And I'm telling Tina."

"Latoya, Think about this. Who is going to really be the loser? Not me. Tina wants me more than I want her. She loves me. I'm rich, ok. She'll never find a dude as rich as me that she truly loves and loves her. She wants a wedding ring. So, you going to her with these allegations are just going to complicate that. She'll choose me over you. Then you'll just be homeless again. Believe me. Plus, you have no degree, no skills, and you're a felon, so no one on this green earth is going to hire you and give you the experience and the pay that I am willing to offer you. So, here's my card. I'll give you a week or so to think about it," Marvin said as he winked and left.

She was dumbfounded. She thought about calling Tina immediately as Marvin walked out the door. She had her phone in her hand, dialing in her number. But she stopped. She was afraid. She didn't know why. The coward in her didn't let her call. She didn't want to create that drama between them at the time. She would just complicate things even more. Her anger and disgust for Marvin made her apply for every job opening in Atlanta. She was going to do this to show him.

She was in her room minding her business when Tina walked in.

"Soooo. How'd it go?!"

"How did what go?"

"The meeting, girl! With Marvin."

"Oh. Oh that. Yea it went good...I'm not sure if it's going to work out though because of my experience. Plus, I technically still don't have a degree so I think I'm just going to apply for other jobs,"

"Ugh. I knew he was going to say something about that. I'll talk to him for you."

"No. It's fine Tina, I'm sure I can find a good paying job, I just have to look harder."

"No. Toya, I'm telling you. With just a high school diploma, it's going to be tough. With no skills, few people are going to hire you. I'll talk to Marvin about maybe getting you a paid internship or something. He owns the whole damn company. He can do what he wants. I'll drip on him a little, he'll eventually turn around. But in the meantime, go ahead and start applying."

"Tina… I have a something important I need to tell you."

Beep. Beep. Latoya heard the front door alert. Marvin was home.

"What's up?" Tina asked.

"Ummmm. Nothing. I'm just glad you gave me the opportunity to stay here. I'm forever indebted to you for this. Thank you again for caring."

"Anytime girl. That's what friends are for."

It had been three weeks since her meeting with Marvin. She felt like she had applied for every job in Atlanta. She felt like she had gotten every rejection letter that was ever sent out, too. Her email was full of, "We regret to inform you, or we are considering other candidates." Most legitimate jobs required a bachelor's degree. Others, didn't and they still weren't interested. Jobs paying $12 an hour weren't even returning her calls. It was because she had never really had a job. Ever. Not in college, and not even in high school.

Cafe Circa

Latoya was at a bar. She didn't have enough money to buy a drink. But she damn sure needed one. She waited patiently for a guy to offer her one. She sat there trying to figure out her life. Time was winding down.

An older guy with a drink in his hand comes to sit next to her.

"Hey! What's your name?"

"Toya. And you?"

"Robert. Nice to meet you. What's with the long face? You're too beautiful to be sad."

"Oh nothing. I'm ok. Just a lot on my mind right now."

"Well, let me buy you a drink, that's the least I can do."

Finally. She said in her head. "Yes, that's fine."

"Bartender, let me get four shots of tequila," said Robert.

"Wait. Four shots? I meant just a drink."

"What type of drink do you want?"

"Ummm. Sex on the beach."

Robert got the bartender's attention again, "Sex on the beach on top of those shots please."

"Are you taking all of those shots?"

"They are for both of us. Two for me, two for you. You look like you need them."

"I guess I do," said Latoya.

Robert and Latoya took the shots together. Then she started on her sex on the beach. She was feeling good.

"Robert. You ever had to make a hard decision?"

"All the time."

"But I mean like a really hard decision. That could possibly jeopardize a friendship forever. Like a make or break decision."

"Sometimes, you have to do what you have to do. Life is all about taking chances. You just have to be able to live with those decisions after the fact," said Robert taking a sip of his drink.

"Right. Because, sometimes we have to put our pride to the side. We may have to do things that we may regret. But say fuck it."

"Yea. Sometimes."

She pulled her purse out. She looked through it. She pulled out Marvin's card. She looked at it for a second. She texted his cell phone.

"I'll accept your offer. But it has to be tonight before I change my mind."

She sent the text message.

"Two more shots Robert? Two for me, two for you."

"Of course. Bartender! Four more shots of tequila, please."

"Thank you."

"So, you're going to give me your number, right?"

"Is that the cost of you buying me drinks?" asked Toya.

"No. I did that out of the kindness of my heart. But I mean I bought them because I want to get to know you outside of this bar."

She heard her phone go off. It was a text message.

"Ok. Just meet me at the W downtown. Be there at a decent time please," the text read.

The bartender brought the shots out. She grabbed both shots and Robert grabbed his.

"Let's make a toast to tough decisions and taking risks in life," she held the shots up with both hands. Robert nodded then they downed them together.

"Wooohooo!" they both said as they finished.

"Ok. So, about that number?" said Robert.

"I'm sorry, Robert. I have to go. I don't give my number out. Find me on Facebook. Latoya Robertson."

Latoya texted Marvin to send her an Uber to take her to the W. She was drunk. Really drunk. But she needed to be. This was the only way that she would be able to do what she was about to do.

The Uber driver came and she was on her way. The drive felt like she was on a roller coaster. With all the turns. As they were pulling up to the W driveway she received a text from Marvin.

"755"

Latoya was so drunk that she almost didn't recognize what it meant. But it was his room number. She was on the elevator, feeling nothing but numbness. She liked it that way.

She got to the floor. Every step that she took, felt heavy as if her legs were turning into tree trunks. She got to the door. *Knock knock knock!* The door opened.

Marvin stood there. Fully dressed, as if he had just got in the room. He motioned her in.

"So, you finally came to your senses," he said.

"Please... don't go there, I still can change my mind."

"You know what, you're right. Let's keep this professional."

"Let's be clear, If I do this, I will have a job making 75K a year, at your company, with the same position that you presented."

"Yes. Just as I proposed."

"Let's shake on it," she held her hand out. He held his hand out and shook it.

"Ok. Let's get this over with," she said as she walked to the bathroom to undress.

"You need something to drink?" he said.

"Nope, I'm already drunk," she said as she closed the door.

She slipped her dress off. She took her heels off. She took her bra and panties off. She looked in the mirror and took a deep breath. She wrapped a towel around herself then she came out.

He had gotten naked under the covers. He looked at her.

"Take that damn towel off. Get comfortable."

She rolled her eyes. "You got some more liquor?"

"I thought you were drunk?"

"Not drunk enough."

He poured her a glass of Dom Perignon. She downed the shot. After she finished, Marvin pulled the towel off of her. He looked her up and down.

"MMmmmm. Damn, you look even better naked."

"Shut up, just hurry up and do whatever you need to do," she said annoyed.

As drunk as she was, she was still not attracted to him, not one bit. She was extremely uncomfortable. He laid her on the bed. All she tried to think about was having a job. Having money to pay for her own place. Having a career. Anything to make sense of her current situation.

He spread her legs. He started kissing on the inside of her thighs, then he came up and started sucking on her nipples. He came up to try to kiss her. She moved her head immediately to the right.

"Ahem. No kissing," she said.

He went back down to sucking on her breasts. Rubbing them and caressing them. Then he eased down to her pussy. His tongue started licking her clit. He started doing tricks with his tongue like he was in a circus. That felt pretty good to her. She tried not to moan, so she just took a couple deep breaths. After a satisfactory job of giving head for like five minutes. He lifted his head up.

"Are you going to return the favor?"

"Fuck No. I will not. Just keep going."

Not wanting to ruin his stride. He returned his head down there and went even harder. At this point, she put her hand on his head to give it a little guidance. She figured that she had already crossed the line so she might as well enjoy this part. He then got up. The part that she had been dreading had finally come. He started licking on her neck. She could feel his penis ease inside of her simultaneously. It hurt. So, she let out a slight screech. He chuckled. Then he replaced his mouth on her neck with his hand grabbing her throat. Loose enough for her to breath but firm enough for her not to move. He laid directly on top of her. Face to face.

"You work for me now," he said as he pumped slowly.

She closed her eyes.

"You hear me?"

"Ok," she said softly.

"Say, 'I work for you now, Marvin!' Say it!" he said as he started pumping harder.

She obeyed. Just because she wanted him to hurry up and finish. "I work for you now... Marvin," she said.

"Who's the boss?"

"You're the boss, Marvin," she said with a fake sexy voice.

He smiled. Then gave her a peck on her lips and a wink.

He stroked and stroked, working as hard he could to please himself. While she laid there. He stayed on top and he had his way with her for all of six minutes... Until he nutted all over the hotel sheets.

Some of it got on her inner thigh and her stomach. He flipped over and laid on his back, panting.

Latoya immediately hopped up. She wrapped the towel around her, disgusted with herself and went into the bathroom. She hopped into the shower. The shower was like a symbol of her washing away all of what just happened. She scrubbed every inch of her body, hard. She wanted to dump every remnant of recollection that she had for the last twenty minutes. After the shower, she put all of her clothes on. Her dress, her heels, and made sure that her hair was fine, trying to look as normal as possible. She came out the shower ready to leave. She was hoping that he was sleep and she could just slip out the door. But he was wide awake.

"I'm headed home," she said.

"Ok. You sure you don't want to stay and relax for a second, why rush out?"

"I just fucked my friend's boyfriend. What is there to talk about?" she said walking to the door.

"I'm just saying. We're going to be working together so I don't want there to be any bad blood between us. We have to be natural friends and just act like this night never happened."

"Believe me, I will most definitely act like it never happened," she said opening the door and walking out.

She caught an Uber back to Tina and Marvin's place. She quietly wept in bed. She was praying that she wouldn't see Tina anytime soon. There was no way that she could look Tina eye-to-eye after what she had just done. The house was so big that it was a possibility.

14. Check Mates

The next evening, Latoya was in her room in her bed watching an episode of Atlanta Housewives when someone knocked at her bedroom door. Latoya jumped in fear.

"Yes?!"

"Girl open up, its Tina."

Latoya's body grew cold. She tried not to shake from her nervousness. She got out of the bed and went to open the door.

"Congratulations on the new job!" said Tina walking in.

"Thank you," said Latoya with a sense of relief.

"Marvin told me that you accepted the job and that you should be starting soon."

"Yea. That's what he told me too."

"You don't seem excited girl. What's wrong?"

"Nothing. I am excited. Just a little nervous, that's all. I'm new to construction, don't know much about it, but I'm ready to learn."

"You'll be fine. I'm not worried about you. Marvin said he pulled a lot of strings to get you this job."

"I'm sure he did," said Latoya, cringing inside.

Two weeks on the job felt like it was two months. Why did it feel like it was two months? Because she had no idea what she was really doing there. Her job was really to just play along, as if she would eventually know what she was doing. She would sit with the project manager, Andy, and watch him work. Andy was a fat, middle-aged white guy that always wore his shirts too small. The smell of sweat, cigarettes, and bologna seeped out of his pores. Latoya knew nothing about construction. But Andy was very helpful and he was super nice to her. Most of the time she would be so quiet that Andy would forget that she was there. She stayed quiet so she didn't sound ignorant. Her job was to shadow him for awhile until she was trained enough to possibly be a project manager herself. Thankfully, Andy didn't quiz her on anything because she knew she would fail miserably. He just did what Marvin told him to do... let Latoya shadow him. Latoya knew Andy was probably wondering how this young prissy black girl barely out of school got the opportunity to shadow him. She did learn some things though. She learned how to be confident, even when she was clueless.

Friday

It was payday. Latoya was excited to finally get her first paycheck for the job. Apparently for her first check, she had to pick it up from the main front office. Direct deposit kicks in on the second paycheck. That's what Andy told her.

After her shift, she made her way to the front office to pick up her check.

The secretary was at the front desk with her head facing the computer, as if she was typing. She was a pretty dark-skinned girl with long hair, she looked like she was about 22.

"Hi, my name is Latoya Robertson. I'm here to pick up my first paycheck," said Latoya.

"Ok. Hold on..." She opened her desk drawer and started looking through some envelopes. She looked through a couple of times. Then she looked back up.

"What's your name again?"

"Latoya Robertson."

"Oh!! Yes. Your check is with Mr. Maples."

"Mr. Maples/ Who is that?"

"The owner of this whole thing. Mr. Marvin Maples. He said that you have to report to his office for your check."

Latoya's heart dropped. "Why do I have to report to him?"

"I don't know. He didn't say. He's in his office, it's all the way down the hall and to the left," she pointed.

At first, she wanted to curse and just walk away. But she had to go so that the secretary didn't think anything.

She walked down the very long hallway to his office. There were no surrounding offices, just his. On the door it said CEO Marvin Maples in red letters. His office door was halfway open. She took a deep breath and knocked slightly. She could hear that he was on the phone. She peaked in. The office was huge. It had a conference table. Coffee table and coffee maker. Refrigerator. There were pictures of him on the wall with the mayor of Atlanta, celebrities, other business owners. He had on a tan colored sports coat with a red tie. He sat in his chair and motioned her to come in. He was speaking on his Bluetooth that was stuck in his ear. He motioned her to sit down in the chairs in front of his desk, but she just stood. He then got up and closed the door behind her.

"Hey Barry, I'm going to give you a quick call back, someone just walked into my office. Ok. Call you right back."

"Ms. Robertson, how have your first two weeks gone?" Marvin said sitting down and loosening up his tie.

"They've been fine. Andy has taught me a lot."

"Good! Andy is a great guy. He's very good at what he does."

"The secretary said that you had my paycheck?"

"Paycheck? What paycheck?" he said with a serious face.

"Don't fuck with me Marvin," Latoya said sternly.

"SHhhhh. Relax. I was just playing with you. Yes, I have it, right here," he said holding up the envelope.

"Ok, so can you give it to me, so I can leave?" Latoya held her hand out.

"Not so fast. You have to earn this check."

By his desk he had a small safe cemented to the ground. He put in a code then threw the envelope into the safe and then closed it and mixed the numbers up.

"What are you doing?! I already earned it Marvin. I came to work every day. Please just give it to me. Why did you lock it up?"

"I'll give it to you under one condition..."

"No! We made an agreement Marvin. I will not do anything that you are suggesting."

"So, you're going to walk away from your first $3400 check? Because of your pride? You worked hard for this money. If it wasn't for me, you would not be employed nor would you have a place to stay. I'm like your boss and your daddy."

"Marvin. I will tell the whole world what you're doing to me!"

"Tell them what? That you agreed to have sex with me? I never put a gun to your head. Don't forget that you have a record. You're a felon. Yea, I looked you up. I know everything. You can't find a real job. No one will I hire you. No experience. Plus, you don't have a degree. I have connections all over this city, I can make your life a living hell if I really wanted too. But, I'm too nice of a guy to do anything like that. You fuck this up and you'll be broke and homeless, again."

"What the fuck do you want from me Marvin?!" she said.

He smirked. "Come here, for a second and find out."

"No." she said standing there.

"Well I'll come to you..." He stood up and walked around his desk. He walked over and grabbed her neck firmly.

She quivered. His hand was rough, dry, and as cold as a glacier. He pulled her shirt down with the other hand. Then pulled her bra down to the top of her stomach. And he began to suck on her breasts while standing up. She shook her head. Rolled her eyes. In anger. In disgust. In fear. She looked around on his desk to see if there was anything sharp, that she could pick up and stab him with. She wanted to murder him. But she was a couple steps to far away. The pen was the closest thing. She stood there and didn't move. He had a firm grip around her neck. Tears fell down her cheeks. She just stood there and did nothing. He then grabbed the back of her head and guided her to the chairs in front of his desk. He grabbed her shoulder and pushed her back to bend over. He unzipped the back of her skirt and pulled it up.

She tried to turn around. "No! Please Marvin! Just give me my check. Please! Why are you doing this!"

He held her back and neck down. "Shhhh. Hush...! Be quiet. My secretary is still here. It's going to be quick, just let it happen. Get it over with."

He adjusted her panties to the side. He pushed himself inside of her. It hurt because she was so dry, so forced. She grimaced with pain. She whimpered like a puppy. He jerked her to keep her quiet. She tried to play with her clit to get wet, just so that it would hurt less. He started thrusting back and forth. He let out a quiet grunt. She closed her eyes praying that he would finish soon. After about three minutes, he was done. He zipped up his pants. Wiped his forehead. He walked over to his desk and handed her the envelope. "I'll see you at the house."

Latoya didn't call an Uber yet. She just sat in the parking lot crying. She had her phone in one hand, her paycheck in the other. She was ready to call the police. She couldn't stop crying. She was angered with herself more than anything.

She dialed the number.

"911, how can we help you?" they answered.

She hesitated. Not knowing what to say. She looked at her paycheck.

"Hello, is anyone there?" they continued.

She hung up.

Something was holding her back from telling. Fear. She wasn't even sure what she was afraid of. *What if he tries to harm me?* she thought. What if it backfires and she ends up losing and taking the blame. Should she tell Tina? Just the police? Or both? Or no one.

The first thing she wanted to do was move out. She called an Uber to go home. She got to the house and went straight to the room and started packing.

"Knock, knock, knock."

She turned around in panic. It was Tina standing in the doorway.

"Oh shit! You scared me," Latoya said.

"Everything ok? Why are you packing?"

"Wooo. Tina. I need you to take a seat next to me. I have something to tell you."

Tina took a seat. Then Latoya heard the front door alarm go off and the door open and close.

"What's the problem? Talk to me?" said Tina.

"Ummmm." Latoya muttered.

"Tina. Baby, where are you?" says Marvin from the main room.

"I'm in Toya's room, come here for a second. Something's wrong with Toya," she yells.

A dark shadow approaches from the hallway. Marvin walks in.

"What's going on in here? Everything ok?" Marvin comes in with a concerned face.

"Latoya has her bags packed. And I'm trying to figure out why," said Tina.

Latoya sat there silent with her head down. Not knowing how to respond with Marvin there.

"What's bothering you Toya. Whatever it is, we can fix it. But we have to know what it is," said Tina.

"It's nothing," said Latoya.

"I think I know what it is," said Marvin. "Work has her stressed out. The job can be very demanding. Especially in her position. There's a lot of responsibility. Being new to this industry and getting over that learning curve can be tough. That's the problem, isn't it?" He looked at Latoya with a straight face.

Latoya looked at Marvin and she couldn't believe what was coming out of his mouth. She was so astonished that she didn't say anything. She was just witnessing his evil devilish con artistry at work. She nodded in agreement. Just for the sake of being in the moment and not knowing what to say. She felt cowardly for backing down again.

"That's what I thought. The last thing we want is for her to leave here and quit the company because of the stress level. So, as the owner, I'll pull some strings. I'm going to up her salary from 75K to 100K... That's the least I can do."

Tina's eyes got big. "Wow! See! All you have to do is speak up! Let him know what you're struggling with and Marvin will fix it. He's good for it."

"The only way that I'll stay is if every check from here on out is direct deposit...and I want 115K," she said to Marvin looking him in dead in his eyes.

"It's done," he said quickly.

"Well with that being said, I'm going to sleep, I need time alone please," Latoya said.

"Let us know if you need anything," Tina replied.

15. The Secretary's Secret

It had been a month and Latoya was getting the hang of the job. People at the company respected her and thought highly of her. Especially Andy. She hadn't had any new issues with Marvin and receiving her money. She barely saw Marvin at all anymore, so that made her feel a lot better. She had made enough money to buy a new car. Additionally, she had been in talks with a realtor because she had planned on moving out and finding a nice condo in Buckhead. Or maybe even a house. She could afford it with the money she was making.

She was just clocking out of work when she got a call from Tina.

"Meet me at Sivas Hookah Lounge tonight. 8 p.m.," said Tina.

"What's wrong with you? Everything ok?"

"Just come," said Tina as she hung up.

She had never heard Tina with that type of worried tone. Something must really be wrong. The first thing that came to her mind was that she found out about her and Marvin. This couldn't have come at a worse time. Everything was going fine at work. She tried her best to get her story together in her head. There was no right way to tell her. But she was ready for it. She was ready for a beat down from Tina. She wondered if she should tell her over the phone before they met up. Or should she could call Marvin to see if he knows anything about her finding out? Maybe he's at the Sivas Lounge too and she's going to interrogate the both of them? She decided just to show up.

She got to Sivas Hookah Lounge. Worried like hell. Her mind wondered. Her heart rate had sped up. She looked around to see if Marvin was anywhere. No sign of Marvin. She turned to the right to see Wanda and Tina there. They both looked at her. Wanda was rubbing Tina's back. Tina looked at Latoya. She looked like she had been crying. Wanda looked at her concerned.

"What's going on, ladies, sorry I'm late," she said sitting.

"Why didn't you tell me," said Tina looking at her with piercing eyes.

Latoya froze. She looked at her in her eyes. She was caught red handed and there was no lying to get out of this one.

"I'm sorry Tina. I was just desperate and I needed a job so."

"Fuck your job!" Tina interjected. "Why didn't you tell me that Marvin was fucking his secretary?"

"What?!" Latoya said confused. Looking at both Wanda, then back at Tina.

"You knew all along, didn't you? Everyone knew except for me."

"Ummmm. No! I assumed. But. I had no clue, I'm not just going to accuse your man of something if it's not definitive."

"She's right, Tina. She can't just say something if she doesn't know for sure," said Wanda.

"Well, apparently, everyone at the job knows. The VPs, the managers, and I'm just sitting here looking liko a fool."

"How did you find out?" asked Latoya with a bit of relief.

"One of the lower level guys named James that works there told me. We go to the same gym together. He has a crush on me. He doesn't like Marvin as his boss so he told me."

As big of a relief as it was to know that she didn't find out about her and Marvin. This was still a problem. If Tina and Marvin have problems, or break up, that means Latoya doesn't have a job. Marvin only gave her a job as a favor for Tina. Once he has no obligation to her, Latoya knew that it was over for her.

"How do you know he's telling the truth?" asked Wanda.

"I didn't believe him at first, so I started asking other lower level workers, and apparently everyone knew. They would leave for lunch together, he would take her home after work. Obvious shit like that."

"I didn't pay any attention to that Tina. I'm just working, trying to learn my position," Latoya replied.

"You're right, Latoya. I'm sorry. I'm just paranoid. I love this man so much. I don't know what to do."

"I know what you can do. Get back at his ass! Get even. I would fuck the worker, James..." said Wanda.

"No! Don't do that. That's only going to make matters worse. Tit for tat never works," said Latoya.

Tina chuckled. "That would kill him inside. That would tear his pride apart. James is kind of cute too. Hmmmmmm."

"Tina, you're not thinking straight. What about your morals? Just fucking for revenge will not make you feel better. Plus, you have no concrete proof," said Latoya.

"I have enough proof," said Tina holding up a picture with the secretary laying down in the bed with a man sleeping. "I pulled this from her Instagram. You see that tattoo of those praying hands on his chest. That's Marvin. I ain't stupid. And this bitch has the nerve to say in the caption, *he's the cutest when he's sleeping*. He's going to learn not to fuck with me."

Latoya shook her head. " I just don't think it's a good idea."

Wanda looked at her, "Latoya, are you saying this because you don't want to lose your job and place to lay your head? Because usually you'd be on board with something like this. You're the queen of petty."

"I just don't want Tina to do something that she'd regret."

"I'm sorry you have to be in the middle of all this, Latoya. Really, this should have nothing to do with you, this is between me and that cheating, lying, punk. Your job shouldn't be jeopardized because of this. We'll live with Wanda if we have to. I'll make sure you're fine."

"I have plenty of room," said Wanda. It would be a huge slumber party every night. I'm down for that. No men are allowed! I don't get dick to visit me anyway so it won't be anything new for me."

The next day, Latoya was home contemplating on if she should up and move in with Wanda before shit hit the fan. She just didn't know what to expect. The front door alert came on.

Latoya cracked her bedroom door to see who it was. It was Tina.

She looked a little disheveled. Her hair, was a bit frizzed. Her outfit was wrinkled. Her lipstick was gone. But her facial expression was relaxed.

"Hey, you ok?" she said.

"Yep. I fucked James," she said with a smirk.

Latoya stood up. "You did not!"

"I sure did. And I liked it," said Tina shrugging her shoulders.

"Oh shit," Latoya said putting her palm to her face.

"Latoya, relax. I'm not worried. Why should you be?"

"I just. I just didn't sign up for this shit," Latoya said.

A minute went by. Then they heard keys jingling at the door. Marvin entered. They both looked at him. He looked at them in suspense.

"Ummm. Well good evening to you all too," he said as he closed the door behind him and begin walking to put his coat on the coat hanger.

"Marvin do you have a minute? I need to talk to you," said Tina.

"Not tonight. It's going to have to wait. Long day, I need to rest," he said heading to his room and rolling his eyes.

"This can't wait, it's urgent," Tina urged.

"Y'all I'm going to head to Wanda's for a bit so that you all can talk," Latoya said.

"No. You don't have to go anywhere Latoya, because like I said, I don't feel like talking right now," said Marvin undoing his tie and looking at Tina.

"So, when are you going to tell me about your little secretary? Or are you going to keep lying?" asked Tina.

"There's nothing to tell you. I have no idea of what you're talking about," said Marvin.

"Have you had sex with your secretary? Just tell the truth Marvin and I won't get mad."

Marvin laughed. "Who, Kayla? That's the stupidest thing I've heard all day. Who's putting these lies in your head. Latoya did you tell her this foolishness?"

"I did not," Latoya replied.

"So, who told you that lie?" asked Marvin.

Tina took out her phone and held it up. "No one told me, I just found this on your secretary's Instagram."

Marvin looked at the phone and said nothing. He continued heading to his room and undressing. Tina ran in front of him and blocked him from walking.

"Why can't you just tell the truth?!"

"The truth is she's just a worker. That will be fired tomorrow for posting that shit. That picture doesn't mean anything. It's a picture of me sleeping. So, what? It doesn't mean we had sex."

"So why the hell would you be sleeping with your secretary?! Stop lying!"

Marvin turned to her, "Ok. You want me to admit it, huh? You want me to admit that I fucked my secretary? Maybe. Ok. Maybe we fucked once. I was drunk, it was an after work function, and we may have got a little frisky. You happy?"

Tina backed up. And smiled. "That's all I needed you to do. Admit it. Now I can admit that I fucked James from your morning shift."

Marvin turned around. Dumbfounded. "You what?!"

"You heard me right. I fucked James. I was drunk, it was an after work function, and we got a little frisky," said Tina with a little smirk.

Marvin picked up a vase and threw it at Tina. She ducked, the vase hit the wall and shattered, missing Tina. Tina screamed.

"You put your hands on me and I'm calling the police and I'll have you put under the jail! I have Latoya here as a witness."

Marvin put his hands on his head in disbelief "Ahhh!!! You hoe! You stupid hoe! You dumb bitch. You fucked big mouth James?! He's going to tell everyone! I'm going to be the laughing stock of the whole organization."

"You put this on yourself Marvin! You cheated on me first!" said Tina.

"Get the fuck out of my house! It's over. Forever. Both of you, get out! You fucking slut!"

Latoya's stuff was already halfway packed. So, she quietly started getting it all together.

"That's okay, James dick was better than yours," said Tina with a smirk.

"And that's why Latoya's pussy was better than yours!" said Marvin.

Latoya felt like her insides had just exploded.

"So, what! Wait what?!" said Tina looking at Latoya.

"Yep. I fucked Latoya. So, we're even. " Marvin said winking.

"Go to hell! You're the weakest fuck boy that I've ever seen. I swear you're going to pay for this," said Latoya.

Tina looked at her, "Latoya, what is he talking about?"

"Tina... I made a huge mistake."

"Please tell me that he's lying?!"

"This was the worse decision that I've ever made...very bad judgement on my part... let me explain."

"Hush! Don't say another word. To me ever. You and Marvin are made for each other," said Tina as she ran out of the house crying.

Latoya looked at Marvin, "I fucking hate you, you little dick, bitch-ass fuck boy!"

Marvin looked at Latoya with a childish smirk on his face and pointed towards the door. "You're fired. Get your worthless ass out of my house."

Latoya ran outside looking to try to make amends with Tina. Knowing that it would be a failure. She was walking towards the street headed to Wanda's car. She got to the car and hopped in the passenger's seat.

"Tina! I was blackmailed," Latoya yelled.

"You fucked my man! And you had the audacity to stay under my roof and soak up my utilities?! Rent free?! After all that I had done for you ever since undergrad. You are a hoe! A straight-up no good slut. I should've known better! You fucked Lisa's man, you fucked April's man, and it was only a matter of time before you fucked my man. The only thing you're good at is hopping on dicks that don't even belong to you! You are a broke-ass, worthless piece of shit. You rotten coochie bitch!" she said as she rolled up her window.

Latoya was going to respond but she stopped. To say that her feelings were hurt was an understatement. Cutting deep into her heart like a steak knife. She trotted to the driver side to see if she could get Wanda to sympathize with her.

"Wanda. Listen. Please," said Latoya as tears started to roll down her face.

"Latoya, I have nothing to say to you right now. There's no way to make this situation better," she said as she rolled up the window. Tina and Wanda pulled off.

16. Help Wanted

Latoya had enough money to get a hotel. She stayed at the Marriott downtown. She had stayed in the hotel for two days straight and she didn't leave. She couldn't eat anything. She didn't know how she was going to mentally survive this situation. A couple of weeks back she had gone to the dentist to get her tooth pulled and the dentist had prescribed her Percocet for the pain. She had plenty left and she was prepared to numb the pain that she was having for good, even if it meant that her life would be over.

She sat in her hotel room. Everything was dark. Thinking about everything that Tina had said. About how she was worthless. Worthless was a strong word. But she agreed with her. She thought about her grandma and how she had let her down. Latoya always wanted to pretend like she would end up better than her mother, but in the grand scheme of things, she was no different. Maybe even worse. At least her mom had made it to her 40s. All the while, Latoya was ready to end her life before the age of 30. She saw herself as a loser. A worthless piece of shit. She sat on the edge of the bed and poured eight pills in her left hand, and in the right hand she had a cup of Patron ready to wash them down. All of a sudden, the phone rang. It scared the hell out of her.

She did not recognize the number. But something told her to answer it anyway.

"Hello?"

"What's up, girl?"

"Who is this?"

"It's Lisa."

"What? Lisa! What do you want from me?! Are you calling to crucify me too?"

"Not at all. I was calling to check up on you, just like I said I would. Are you ok?"

"Of course, I'm not Lisa! Do I sound ok?!"

"Toya, talk to me, hun, tell me what happened?"

"You wanna know what I did?! I fucked Tina's boyfriend while living with her. Everyone hates me! I'm worthless. I've never been good at shit my whole life. I'm a fuck up. Why should I not just put myself out of my own misery right now and make everyone's life much easier?"

"Toya. That is the last thing you should be thinking about. You have a purpose on this earth. DO NOT take your life prematurely. So what? You used bad judgement. You can and will bounce back from this. You're strong. Just pick yourself up and dust yourself off. God has a plan for you, you remember?"

"Easy for you to say! You're out here living your dream. Doing what you love! While I'm here just fucking everyone's life up. I know God has forgotten about me because I ain't shit and I ain't never going to be shit."

"Toya. You must have forgot! I got fired from my job because of a sex tape! I was humiliated, and I was clueless about what I was to do next. I was suicidal, too. But I didn't give up on my life. That embarrassment and humiliation was exactly what I needed to find out what my purpose was on earth. As I look back and connect the dots, everything happens for a reason."

There was a long pause of silence.

"You're right. My grandma would kill me if I killed myself. She'd hunt me down in hell and kill me again."

"Just don't give up. I didn't give up. Do you need me to come keep you company?"

"No, thank you, Lisa. I need some time to myself right now. But I appreciate you talking me through this."

"Anytime, love. From here on out, just look at me as your spiritual teacher. If there's anything you are going through, please feel free to reach out."

Latoya hung up with Lisa. She sat there, eight white pills in her hand. Liquor in her cup. She looked at the pills and she swore they looked like little devils. How could something so small and innocent looking be able to take a life. She busted out crying, thinking about everything that was happening. Trying to figure out if she had a future or not. Or if she was willing to take on the future. She thought about her grandma. She pictured her grandma looking at her in a casket. She pictured Grandma Betsy shaking her head in disappointment. That vision of her made her realize that she didn't want to give up on life, not yet at least. She knew her grandma thinks she can do more. It then dawned on her that Lisa had saved her life.

A couple days after her brush with suicide, Latoya agreed to meet with Lisa at a coffee shop. They were officially friends again. But most importantly, Latoya let Lisa become her life coach. Lisa wanted to do a friendly consultation.

"Have you read the book called *The Alchemist?*" Lisa asked.

"No. Never heard of it. You know I hate reading. What's it about?"

"Whenever you get a chance check it out. It's my favorite, but it's basically about a little boy on this journey in the desert, looking for this treasure. So that he can become his personal legend, the ultimate version of himself. What would the ultimate version of yourself be?"

"A super rich bitch that everyone envies," said Latoya.

"Ok. Well, you have a lot of work to do then. Do you know your purpose in life?" Lisa asked.

"Girl, I don't know. My purpose is just to be rich."

"Ok. Why do you want to be rich?"

"Because I know how it feels to be dead broke," she said laughing.

"Oh Lord. This is going to be fun," she said sarcastically. "There has to be something else that drives you."

"Hmmmm. My little sister, Leah. My sister is in the sky looking down at me right now. Hoping that I lead by example. She wouldn't want me to give up. And my grandma drives me. My Grandma Betsy wants me to succeed more than I want myself to succeed. She wants me to turn out better than my mom. My mom's a drug addict. That's why I went to live with my grandma. My mother killed my little sister Leah when she was driving while on drugs."

"Wow, what a story Toya. I had no idea. Do you think you can ever forgive your mom for what she did?"

"Fuck no. Martha is the reason why my life is so fucked up now."

"Do you think you can ever help Martha, try to change her life for the good?"

"No! There's no chance. And I'd rather not talk about her at all. Ever. Can we move on to the next question?"

"Ok. Fair enough. So, every time you feel like giving up, think about your grandma. Think about Leah. Think about how you don't want to walk in your mother's footsteps. Think about how you've failed all of those times and let that be the reason why you strive to win. Now answer this, What are you good at?"

"Not a damn thing. That's why I'm at where I'm at now. I'm just good at looking good. That's it."

"Well what interest you?"

"Make-up and clothes maybe. I love shopping. And partying. I like to dance. That's about it."

"Well that's a start. And actually, I have a great relationship with an executive at Sephora name Sarah Hamilton. Sephora is a partner with my non-profit and she's the one who writes the checks. It may take awhile, and it may be a stretch, but I may be able to get you a solid position at Sephora. Would you like that?"

"Girl, I love Sephora. They get all of my money. Of course, I would work for them."

"Good! That way you will be doing something that you love. If you do well, you will move up in the company in no time. In the meantime, we just need to help you get a quick job to get you some income.

"Yea, I'll start looking and applying now," said Latoya.

"Good. Now Latoya, my name is all I have. I'm vouching for you. Sarah is a big time donor to my organization. If I get you this interview, please don't let me down."

"Girl. I got you. And Lisa, Thank you for everything. I am truly grateful."

She was on her way home from the meeting. She was on I-75, about to send Lisa a text to let her know how much she appreciated her. Boom! She felt a jerk. Yep. She'd just hit someone's back bumper. It was a Porsche. A new one at that. 2017. She had never got into a car accident before. No insurance. No money. She started shaking. She pulled over behind the Porsche. She waited for the other person to get out of the car first. She was so embarrassed. A woman got out of the Porsche. She looked about Latoya's age. She looked foreign. Long hair, Glamorous. She had some expensive shades on with red bottom heels. She had on a red dress. Latoya was impressed. Latoya stepped out of her car after her.

The woman examined the back of her car. Then she looked at Latoya.

"Girl, you almost broke my neck," the woman said.

"I'm so so sorry. I was..."

"Texting and driving? Don't lie I do it all the time," she responded.

"Unfortunately, yea I was."

"Well, The good thing is that my car looks fine. Your shit is a little fucked up. You have a dent."

She looked and saw the dent the size of a football on her front bumper.

"Yea. Well I don't even have insurance."

"You're a pretty girl. I know you have money. What do you do?" said the woman.

"Well, I'm in between jobs right now. Hopefully, I start working at Sephora sometime soon. Maybe I can pay you after I start there."

"In between jobs? hold on." The woman started walking back to her car. Latoya didn't know what to do. She reached in the car and grabbed her purse. She started walking back.

"Here. This is probably how much the damage is worth." She pulled out a wad of cash. About $1,000 plus a little more.

Latoya looked at the woman like she was insane. "But, I was in the wrong, I hit you. Why would you pay for my damage?"

"Because, you need help more than I do girl. I know you can't really afford it, so here," the girl said.

She was still baffled. "How do you know?! I'm a grown-ass woman. I can take care of myself."

"Listen! What is your name?"

"Latoya."

"Ok. Latoya! Either you take this money for the damage or I call the police to report that you rammed me from the back and that my spinal cord hurts like hell, your choice."

Latoya looked down at the money. She looked up at her. She couldn't see her eyes through the shades, but her face looked like she meant business. So, she took the money from her hand.

The girl smiled. "See, that wasn't so hard. In life, if someone offers you an opportunity, you take it. Don't let your pride get in the way and don't overthink it."

Latoya couldn't say anything. So, she just nodded. She had never seen a girl her age talk to her as if she was a child. The woman was bold, and super confident.

"Thank you. Thanks for this," Latoya said holding up the money.

"Anytime girl. My job brings me plenty," she said as she turned and started back to her car.

"Wait, I'm sorry, I didn't get your name?" she asked as she walked behind her.

She turned around and lifted her shades up. "Farren."

"Thanks, Farren! And you said that your job gives you plenty of money? Are y'all hiring?"

"We're always hiring. I work at Dreamville."

"So, you're a strip…"

"I'm a dancer. Yes," the girl interrupted.

"Ohhhh ok."

"But I wasn't talking about hiring for dancers. We're hiring for waitresses. And you look good enough to be one. You can make some pretty decent money as a waitress there. Here's my card. The owner's name is Biscuit. Give him a call," she went in her purse and pulled out a card and gave it to Latoya.

"Thanks," Latoya said as she pulled off.

Latoya looked at the money and counted. It was more than $1,000. Then she looked at the card.

That same week, Latoya set up an interview with the Dreamville owner, Biscuit. They met at Dreamville. Biscuit showed up to the interview 25-minutes late with a huge plate of Jamaican food. The place was empty. They sat at one of the many tables that were in the middle of the floor. Biscuit sat directly across from Latoya as he unwrapped his food and started eating. The loud smacking and slurping that ensued while he devoured his food was a bit much for Latoya, but Biscuit didn't seem to care. He was a short chubby brown-skinned fellow. He wore a falcons hat turned to the side. He had a commanding voice.

"So, Farren told you about this position huh?"

"Yes, she just said that y'all were hiring."

"Do you have any serving experience?" asked Biscuit.

"No. Not really."

"Ok. Well, what I can tell you is that you need to learn the menu like the back of your hand. Take your time and make sure that you get everyone's order. Make sure it's right. You're fine and stuff but that's not enough. If you want to make some real money here, you need to be all about customer service. You have to work hard."

"Ok."

"Also. This is an entertainment club. Guys are coming to be entertained by beautiful women. Beautiful naked women first. Give the dancers their space. Don't interfere with their business. When can you start?"

"Ummm. As early as possible."

"Good. I'll see you on Thursday. Bring a black shirt and some black shorts," said Biscuit as he continued enjoying his dinner.

17. No Twerk Experience

Thursday 11:30 p.m.

Thursday was a handful. Latoya learned a lot on that day, because she was the only waitress that was working. The other two waitresses called off for some odd reason. It was her, the bartenders, and the chef. The only good thing about the day was that she looked cute with her all black leather top and leather shorts.

"What's your name again?" the man sitting at the table asked as Latoya bent down to take his order.

"Latoya. But you can call me Toy," she said.

"Ok. Toy. You must be new here. I have never seen you before."

"Yes. Today is my first day."

"How long you going to be here? You gone quit like the other waitresses or are you going to stay for awhile?"

"Well. We'll see."

"Excuse me! Waitress! Excuse me!" yelled a man to Latoya's left.

"Yes?"

"When is the food going to come out?! I've been waiting for a long-ass time. What, are they backed up or something in the kitchen?"

"They shouldn't be that much longer."

"Ok. Tell them to hurry that shit up. Please. And you haven't brought out the lemons. Remember I said water with lemons."

"Ok. I'm on it, sorry about that."

She left table two. Then table four called.

"Ma'me. I said I ordered my burger well-done. This burger is definitely not, well-done. It doesn't even look like it's cooked all the way." The guy holds his burger up. "You see all that red in there, it looks like it's blood. Does this look well-done to you? You can take this back, I don't want this," the man handed her his plate.

"Ok. Sorry about that. I'll check back in the kitchen," Latoya walked off with her hands full.

"She ain't getting no damn tip," they mumbled as she walked off.

Another table waves their hand…

"So how long have you been working here? I've never seen you here before."

"Because I'm new here."

"Ok. Well my name is Mark. What's your name?"

"Toya."

"Nice to meet you, Toya, I always come to this spot. And you're the finest waitress I have seen here yet? Where you from?"

"I'm from Pittsburgh."

"As fine as you are I know you got a boyfriend."

"I actually don't but hey I have to get back to work, I'm sorry. We can talk later."

"Alright, just right your number down when you bring me the receipt. Can you do that for me, gorgeous?" said Mark with a smile.

"I'll think about it."

The DJ got on the mic. "Next up we got Red Kisses. One of my favorite dancers! Get ready to experience the sexiest piece of light-skinned ass that you'd ever see! And she's single fellas so don't be afraid to shoot your shot. But remember, if you want to make her holler you can't be scared to throw them dollars!"

Latoya never really looked at the dancers but something told her to look up this time at the stage. Out walked Farren, the girl that she had hit in traffic. Walking slowly with red lingerie on and a red wig. Everybody turned their head to watch. Her body was banging. She strutted across the stage. Dancing seductively. Money started flying in the air like it was a tornado. Then she bent down low and started twerking. Even more money started flying, to the point where Latoya couldn't even see her anymore. Latoya turned to pick up her customers receipt. She saw that he had given her a 0-dollar tip. Latoya was furious.

The manager, Dara, who works directly over Latoya, calls her over towards the back of the restaurant.

"Latoya. What's going on? Are you ok?"

"I'm fine."

"No, you're not fine, I can see it in your face that you're not fine. You're sitting over there daydreaming looking at the dancers and not working. Plus, we had a customer complaining saying that he asked you for some lemons 30 minutes ago and you still haven't brought them. I'm concerned."

Latoya snapped. "Concerned about what?! These shitty-ass customers. They are rude and annoying!"

"Latoya. Watch out. Please don't do this in front of the clients."

"Fuck these customers, they wouldn't know good customer service if it bit them in the ass."

"Ok. Looks like your work is done. You can leave and don't come back. I'll tell Biscuit you quit."

"That's fine. I won't make enough here to deal with demon customers anyway. It won't be hard to find another server job."

"Not with that attitude. And I'll make sure that no other restaurant in Atlanta makes the mistake of hiring you," Dara said with a smiley face.

The club was closing and everyone was leaving. Depressed and angry, Latoya waited out back to catch Farren as she went to her car.

"Hey, Farren, I wanted to know if you were available to talk for a second."

"Wait, you look familiar. Where do I know you from?" said Farren walking towards her car.

"Latoya, I was the girl that hit your car. And you gave me the money. You told me to come work here."

"Oh. Yea! So, you talked with Biscuit and got the job. How was your first day?!"

"It was miserable. The waitress life is not for me."

"So, what are you going to do then?"

"Ummm. Well that's what I wanted to talk to you about..."

"Well it's going to have to wait. Meet me tomorrow at Starbucks at 2 p.m. on Howell Mill Rd. if you're serious," she said as she got in the car and closed the door.

Starbucks

Farren walked in looking fabulous. Her hair flew in the wind. She had on shades again with a nice dress that hugged her shape. She was on the phone. She showed up at 2:05.

"Ok. I'm going to call you back. I'm going to call you back, I'm about to have a meeting, bye," she hung up.

"So, what's up? Talk to me," she said taking off her shades.

"First off, thank you for meeting with me, I know you're super busy."

"Girl, you're fine, I'm chilling today, I just don't like to waste time you know. So, cut to the chase."

"Well. I wanted to ask you about your career."

"What about it?"

"Ummm. How long have you been dancing?"

"Two years, since I was 22," she replied.

"Wow. So, you're 24? Me too."

"Good for you," she said with a fake smirk.

"So, what made you start dancing?"

"I was broke, and I needed money. And I liked dancing," said Farren.

"Wow. Just that simple huh."

"What else do you want me to say? Yes, it is that simple. Why are you asking these elementary questions? Tell me what you are looking for. Be upfront."

Sigh. "Ok. To be honest with you, I am desperate for change in my life. I have been homeless. I'm lost. I just don't know what to do anymore. It seems like I can't do shit right. I dropped out of school. I can't keep a job. Everyone has turned their backs on me. I'm a fuck up. I have no friends or family that fuck with me. Sometimes, I don't even understand why and how I exist. And I'm broke as fuck."

"Ok. So, why are you coming to me, the dancer?"

"When I met you, in the weirdest way, I think you were God-sent. I had never seen someone my age so confident, so bold, with such a presence about them. You don't care what people think about you. You are about your shit. And I just felt like I could learn something from you."

"Well. Thank you for sharing that. Some people don't have the guts to express themselves like you just did. But I understand. I was in your shoes before. I actually can see a lot of myself in you. That's why I gave you the money that day. It's time for you to stop playing victim. You have a bright future ahead of you. Starting today. I'm going to hold you responsible for that."

"That's fine with me. I need all the help I can get it," Latoya replied.

"See, I was homeless at one point in my life too. I had just moved to Atlanta from Ohio. Lived with my mom who was on crack and my brother who sold it. Dad nowhere to be found. I had to get away from that shitty situation. Shit, At least you went to college. I never stepped foot on a college campus. When I first got here, I found a 9-5 that was paying me minimum wage. Could barely live off that shit. Then I got fired. After that, I told myself that I would never depend on anyone else to take care of me. I was going to do it on my own. The first step towards that was to become a dancer."

"What did your family and friends say?" asked Latoya.

"I have no friends. I had no family here. But if I did, what could they say? If they aren't taking care of me themselves and they can't offer other alternatives, then the hell with them."

"See, that's a problem that I have. I always worry about what others will say about me. I used to lie to hide things from people just to fit in."

"They are going to judge and talk shit regardless. You might as well do good for yourself. I made over $150K last year. You think I care about what other people think? I'm self-made, self-paid. I'm a boss bitch."

"I'm just scared to try something new, I guess."

"Latoya, since no one helped me coming on. I'm going to help you. I'm going to help you make money on your own."

"I appreciate that. I'm looking forward to it."

Farren was serious. The next day she called Latoya and said that she wanted Latoya to meet her at Dreamville.

They went in through the back entrance. It led her to a small office room where a round guy was sitting down and speaking on the phone.

"You met Biscuit. He's my Boss. And the Owner here."

"Why do they call him Biscuit?"

"Because he loves dough," she said with a chuckle. "Literally and figuratively. He's fat as hell."

Biscuit finished his conversation.

"Hey Biscuit, you remember Latoya. She's interested in becoming a dancer."

"Yea, the one that quit on me the other day? Dara told me what happened."

"She said that serving isn't for her. She wants to make some real money," Farren interjected.

"Do a 360 for me, right now," Biscuit said.

Latoya looked confused and felt violated but she turned anyway.

"Oh yea, you're going to make a lot of money here. Can you start tonight?" asked Biscuit.

"No, I'm not ready," she blurted.

"This is a learn-as-you-go job. Throwing you into the jungle is how you learn how to survive," he said.

"Maybe she can just come as a guest to watch me first, Biscuit, then she'll figure out if this is what she really wants to do," said Farren.

"I guess. Well be here tonight around 11:00 p.m. Have your pen and pad ready. Take some good notes. Because what you learn here at Dreamville can change your life forever. You can be as rich as you want to be," said Biscuit playfully spinning around in his chair.

18. Paid Attention

She got to the club at 11:00 p.m. She looked up at the lights on the building. *Dreamville. Where fantasy meets reality.* Biscuit told her to just come and shadow a dancer. Similar to like an intern. There was a line so she went straight to the door and saw two big security guards.

"Twenty for women," one of them said.

"I'm here to see Biscuit and Farren. I shouldn't have to pay to come in."

"Alright, hold on." He went inside.

The other security guard looked Latoya up and down.

"You about to work here?" he asked.

"Umm. I don't know, I'm just checking it out. Maybe?"

He laughed. "Checking it out? You'll be dancing by next week."

"Why do you say that?" asked Latoya.

"Because you'll make more money than you've ever dreamed of here. You won't be able to resist. Just don't get caught up in this life. It will take a toll on you. Be careful." he shrugged.

The other security guard came back out, and waved for her to come in.

She walked in behind the guard. Different lights flashed in and out. She smelled, perfume, oil, and marijuana smoke. She looked around and saw guys locked in on every woman. She followed the guard and he took her to a back room. Then they opened another door and they saw Biscuit counting money with another older woman.

"Ms. Toya, you ready for a quick tour?" said Biscuit not looking up at her.

"I guess,"

"You guess? You better act like you want to be here," he looked up at her.

"Ok, I'm ready."

"This is my mama, Rosie," he said pointing to the lady helping him count money.

"So, you the new dancer huh?" Mama Rosie said as she stood up and put both hands on her hips.

"Ummm. I haven't committed to nothing yet," said Latoya.

"You'll like it. See, I take care of all the girls here. I'm like a mother to them. They call me Rosie. I'm part owner here. If you ever have any girl problems that you can't talk to my son about, you come to me," Rosie said smiling. She had two front gold teeth. She looked like she was about 50-years old.

"Ok. thank you. I will."

"Alright, come with me. This room here is the business room. This is where we count money, we strategize, we create partnerships, this is where we build."

She nodded and then followed Biscuit down a dark hallway then they walked into a dressing room.

"So, this is where you'll be spending most of your time. Girls come here to relax and get dressed of course. They come here to vibe, do makeup. Shit like that."

A couple of girls where there putting on lotion and oil. They looked Latoya up and down and then continued whatever they were doing.

"Alright, follow me," Biscuit kept walking.

They walked into another small little walkway. Then they went into another room.

"Ok, this is the private room. We call it the Heaven room. If you ever have a client that wants to spend big money, you'll take him here."

The room had small sectioned off areas.

"So, just private dances, right?"

Biscuit turned and pointed at Latoya. "Yep, private dances. But no sex or no shit like that. If girls want to take it further they need to take that shit elsewhere. This ain't the brothel. You get caught doing something like that you won't ever dance at Dreamville again. I promise you that."

"Oh, you don't have to worry about that ever with me," Latoya said.

"So that's really it. Three back rooms, Heaven room, the business room, and the dressing room. And then the main room, we call that the big screen. You have any questions?"

"No. Not right now."

"Well, that's pretty much it. Listen to me Toya. I want you to work here. Girls come to me all the time. I turn a lot of girls away because they just don't have that "It" factor. But when I first met you, I saw that you have it. You don't know it yet, but I see it. The sky is the limit here. You'll make more money than you've ever dreamed of, if you work hard enough. I have girls that have left here that own businesses, restaurants, properties, boutiques, all of that. All I need from you is to be believe."

"I understand Biscuit. But I'm scared. I mean, stripping was like the last thing that I thought I would do. Everybody frowns upon it."

"Forget everybody! People are going to talk shit about you regardless! Whether you're doing good or bad! You might as well start doing good. Making yourself some real money. You came to me because you wanted the opportunity, the opportunity to change your life. This is it. Is it the conventional way? No. But who the fuck cares. Get your money and live your life. Be free. It's the naked hustle. Doing whatever it takes to make a better life yourself."

"I know. I'm so shy though. And self-conscious. It's going to be hard as hell for me to get naked in front of all those people."

"You'll be fine. All the girls that come to me are afraid at first. Until you get a couple dances under your belt, you'll feel that way, but after that, you'll love it. The money is going to make you forget about all that shit."

She nodded. "Ok."

"Alright, come watch some of the girls go to work."

They walked out into the big screen. More people where there. There were a couple of girls on the stage, and a couple of girls were on the floor. She saw one girl giving a lap dance, she was completely naked. She looked so comfortable. The girl was smiling and looked like she was having fun.

"That chick looks comfortable as hell," she said looking her way.

Biscuit looked that way. "Who Lilly? Oh, she's been here a couple of years. She does that to make her clients happy. The more fun you have, the more money you'll make. The easier it will be."

The song changed, and the DJ came on the mic. "Next to the stage, one of my favorite girls, Red Kisses!"

Farren came out. She had on just a bra and a thong. This was Latoya's first time seeing her naked. She was amazed by how nice her body was.

"See, you know her as Farren, we know her as Red Kisses. She's probably one of our best dancers, if not the best. But if you do what you're supposed to, you'll definitely be number one. And she knows that. But she's not jealous though because if you come and bring more clients to the place, you'll bring her more money. We're all in this together."

Farren started dancing and people started easing up to the stage. One guy, with a plain black T-shirt that wasn't throwing money before pulled out a huge wad of money. He started throwing money in the air, it trickled down as Farren danced in front of him. She shook her thighs and started taking off her thong. She bounced in sync with the beat. The harder she went the more money the guy threw. The guy started touching on her legs. She let him. The more Latoya watched her, the more she realized that she too could dance. And considerably better than Farren.

"You said that Farren is the best dancer?"

"Yea. One of the best. Give or take."

Once Farren was done, she picked up all the money that she had made. One of the security guards came and helped her gather it into a huge pile.

Latoya looked at Biscuit. "All of that is for her?"

"Most of it. I get a small percentage. but that's it."

Latoya followed Farren back into the dressing room.

"Hey, girl!" Farren said as Latoya came in.

"Hey! You were amazing!" said Latoya.

"Thank you. One of my main clients was there. So, I had to go a little harder," she said while wiping the sweat from her forehead.

"Yea, That guy. He pulled out a ton of money when you came on. It looked like he was waiting on you. I would've never known he had that much money. I would've walked right past him if I was dancer," said Latoya.

"Oh nooo. Lesson number one. Never make assumptions. Never assume someone doesn't have money by how they look or dress. There's guys that come in looking dirty and dusty and they will be throwing 100 dollar bills. Then there's guys that come in here with big chains, Rolexes and with all name brand shit that won't throw a dime. You have to just go hard no matter what. You'll eventually find out who's willing to spend and who's not. That client out there that made it rain like that. He's a drug dealer. His name is Watson. He spends a lot of money on me. After he leaves the trap, he just comes and balls out here. He cashes out on me."

"Ok. I'll never make an assumption like that again. So, Biscuit said that you're the best dancers here. What's your secret?"

Red Kisses smirked. "Well, it's pretty simple. In my eyes, there's two types of dancers. There's strippers, and then there's entertainers. Strippers shake their ass naked for money. They do the bare minimum. But I consider myself an entertainer. Entertainers, we give you a show. We go all out. We create an experience that will wow the clients. We make clients want to come back for more and tell all their friends to come spend money. We want to change your life. It's not easy, If you learn how to be an entertainer, the sky's the limit."

"I'm taking notes. How much money did you make just now?"

"Probably a grand."

"One thousand dollars, for five minutes of dancing?"

"Ahhhh. Yes."

"Shit. Well. I've made my decision. How do I sign up?" Latoya rubbed her hands together.

19. Home Twerk Assignment

Latoya had three days until her first day at Dreamville. She probably watched every YouTube video ever created on exotic dancers. She loved dancing so the twerking and shaking her ass part was easy. It was just the pole that was the challenge. She bought a stripper pole for her room. She had been practicing for three days straight non-stop. While practicing a spin around on the pole, she loses her grip and falls on the floor. Thump! She lands on her back and almost on her neck. "Ouch!" She yelled. Then her phone rings. "Ugh!" She said rubbing her neck while getting up and walking to her phone. It was Lisa calling. She answered.

"Hey, girl! What you doing?" said Lisa.

"Oh nothing, just watching this HBO series that's all," she said trying to hide the wincing in her voice.

"Oh. You ok? You sound like you're in pain."

"Nope. I'm just doing a little. Um… Doing a little stretching that's all."

"Ok. Well I just wanted to give you an update on the Sephora job. I spoke with Sarah and we were able to get you an interview!"

"That's awesome!" she said with fake enthusiasm.

"Yep! It's going to be for the product consultant position! You'll be making a bout 48K a year. Which is great starting off!"

"Great! When is the interview?"

"It's going to be 8:30 a.m. Thursday, January 26th, at Lenox Mall. Will that work for you?"

"Yep. I'll be there."

"Good! Make sure you do research on the position and the company before you go in there. I know you're going to ace this interview. I believe in you!"

"I'm sure I will too."

Wednesday, January 25th

Farren takes Latoya shopping for an outfit before her first day at work. Farren purchases a couple of outfits from Looks of Atlanta on Piedmont Rd. Then Latoya convinces Farren that she wants a blonde wig and some blue contacts to somewhat hide her identity. Farren buys it all for her.

Latoya sat in the dressing room with her changing bag. It was just her at the time. Nervous wasn't the word. She was terrified. She stared at herself in the mirror. The wig and contacts had her looking like a totally different person. She felt like a different person too. What was she becoming? She began to second guess herself. Thinking about how she ended up there in the first place. Wondering if she was built for this life. Debating on if she even had the courage to dance naked for money.

"Boo!" a cold hand touched her shoulder. Latoya jumped in fear. She looked back and It was Farren. "Girl, you shaking like a stripper! You ok?! You scared?" asked Farren playfully.

"I'm trying not to be. I just can't calm my nerves. It's just so much on my mind right now," said Latoya.

"Relax. Today is Wednesday. It should be a slow day. Biscuit scheduled you on this day for a reason. Plus, I got something that can calm your nerves," Farren pulled out a bottle of Patron from her purse.

"I'm down with that. Where's the chaser?" said Latoya looking down into Farren's bag.

"Chaser? Baby us dancers don't chase nothing but the paper. We bout to take this to the head. Just me and you," she pulled out two shot glasses and started pouring.

"Wait! I can't go too hard. I have a job interview tomorrow morning at Sephora. I can't get too fucked up."

"Oh. Girl, that's what's up. You bout to have two jobs. Day shift and night shift huh? Good for you. Well we won't go that hard," said Farren as she finished pouring the shots.

They both put there shot glasses in the air.

"This toast is for Latoya to help all of her dreams come true, and for her to have a successful first day as a dancer!"

They tapped glasses and put them in the air then took them to the head.

"Wooo, that's nasty!" Latoya said with a sour face.

"Alright. Now you need to take just two more, you're going to need them."

"Two more?! Did you not hear me just say that I have an interview tomorrow morning? I can't. I'm a light-weight when it comes to drinking. Maybe just one more should be enough."

"Toya, you're about to be dancing asshole naked in front of some total strangers. Fat, ugly, broke, wealthy, it doesn't matter. They're going to be strangers. You can't be sober. Take two more shots to get you right. You will be fine tomorrow morning, I promise," she said as she poured more shots.

"Just one more Farren. I will be fine," said Latoya looking at Farren with a serious face.

"Ok. If you say so. Just one it is. I go on next, and you're after me so we need to hurry up either way," she said handing Latoya her second shot.

Latoya cringed. Then they both tapped their glasses and threw the liquor to the back of their throats. "Uggghhh."

"Good! Aight girl, I'm about to go up, I'll see you later on tonight. Remember, be an entertainer. Have personality. Have fun. You got this." She left and went to the big screen.

Latoya was dressed and ready. The liquor hadn't hit her yet. But she was ready to make some money.

The door to the stage slammed open. It scared the hell out of Latoya. It was Biscuit.

"Toya! What's your stage name? The DJ needs to know."

"Ummm. Stage name?"

"Yes! Stage name! What you want the DJ to call you. You're dancing name."

"I don't know. I didn't think of it yet."

"Well you need to! Give me something now. Quick! Make something up. Just like Farren. Her stage name is Red Kisses. She's light-skinned and she likes to wear red lipstick and she leaves red kiss on a lot of her clients."

"I don't know. My favorite color is black. I'm sweet. Should I be sugar. Black Sugar?"

"Hell No. That's stupid. But we're on the right track. What's some other personality traits of yours?"

"I love looking at myself in the mirror. My friends used to say I was vain."

"That's it! Black Vanity is your stage name. You're welcome," Biscuit leaves and slams the door.

Latoya's heart started beating. She ran back to the liquor bottle and took three more shots.

"We got a new addition to the team! A future star. Introducing for the first time, Black Vanity!" said the DJ.

Latoya walk out on the stage. She couldn't see anything. She felt like a deer face-to-face with an 18-wheeler with its brightest headlights on. At first, she just stood there, posing until the music came on. She was seconds away from running right back into the dressing room and putting on her clothes. But she thought about Tina and Wanda finding her sleeping on a gym floor. She thought about everything that Tina, Wanda, and Grandma Betsy had said about her. Then she closed her eyes. She pictured herself back home dancing in the mirror. When no one was watching. Then she felt the liquor kick in. That's all she needed. The music started. She bent over. And started dancing. Bouncing her body up and down. Twisting. Shaking. Feeling sexy. Moving her body in sync with the beat. Combining the tricks that she knew before with what she had learned from the YouTube videos.

The song went off. She stopped dancing. It happened so fast. Her time was up. She opened her eyes and looked down and saw dollar bills everywhere. The bouncer came with a trash bag and gave it to her. She picked up what was hers.

"I knew she was a star, I knew it. She's going to be special. Black Vanity everyone!" said the DJ.

Latoya went back to the room. Farren ran up to her.

"Girl! Look at you! I'm so proud of you! How do you feel?"

"I feel ok. I can't believe I just did that."

"You did great for your first time! You did way better than I did on my first dance. You just can't be afraid to dance on the poll. I can teach you that though, we can practice together," said Farren.

"Thank you. Because yes, I need it.

"And you danced the whole time with your top and bottoms still on. You never took them off," she said with a chuckle.

"Oh shit. Was I supposed to? I was so caught up in the moment that I forgot to."

"I mean. If the customers are throwing money, which they were, they are expecting you to show them a little something. Ass, titties, something. That's the whole point."

Latoya saw Biscuit from the corner of her eyes approaching her. She became nervous.

"You ok?" Biscuit said.

"Yea, I'm fine. My heart was beating so fast, but I'm fine now. I'm sorry for not getting nake..."

"Good! Well I have a big spender out there waiting for your presence, I need you back out soon. You did a good job," he winked.

"Ok. I'm coming."

"Girl, let's take a couple of more shots, it's time to get this money!" said Farren.

They took more shots. Then Latoya walked out into the showroom and Biscuit directed her to this guy in the back corner in a VIP section. He was dark-skinned with a fresh all white jumpsuit, a mouth full of gold and a hand full of cash.

"Ms. Black Vanity, I've been waiting for you all my life," the guy says.

"Stop lying, you just been waiting for me since 5 minutes ago," she says.

She felt someone slap her butt.

Latoya immediately covered her butt with her hands and looked at the guy. "Are you serious?! What's wrong with you?! Don't put your hands on me! Who do you think I..." Latoya looked up and she saw Biscuit staring right at her with piercing eyes.

"I'm sorry baby, I'm just tryna have some fun. Is that a problem?" the guy said waving around the wad of cash, smiling with his mouth full of gold teeth.

Latoya sighed. "Nah. Just don't be disrespectful with it," she said.

"I got the utmost respect for you, Black Vanity. As a matter of fact, I respect you so much that you're the only chick in this bitch that's going to get all of my money tonight," the guy said holding his cash up to Latoya.

Latoya smiled. "That's what I like to hear," she reached for the wad.

The guy pulled it out of her reach. "Not so fast. First, you're going to have to earn it. So, I'm going to need you to, respectfully, get butt naked and put on a show," said the guy smiling showing off his shiny gold teeth again.

Sho looked over at Discuit. He was still staring directly at her with his arms crossed. She took a deep breath. She closed her eyes. She reached back and unclipped her bra strap. She pulled off the bottom half until she was fully unclothed. Her nipples and pussy felt a sudden breeze but she ignored it. She didn't want to look him in the eye so she started dancing shaking her butt directly in front of him while she looked away. She felt another slap on her butt, but this time, it felt like some dollar bills accompanied the slap. She still cringed a little. "Turn around baby I want to see your pretty face too," Latoya, rolled her eyes but turned around pretty fast. She looked at him and everything was double. "Why you looking at me like that baby. You got something you have to get off your chest," Latoya stumbled to keep her balance and the room started spinning. She felt an immediate rumble in her stomach then orange throw up comes gushing out of mouth like water from a faucet.

The guy jumped up.

"What the fuck!" he screamed. "Ahh hell nah! Not on my all white fit!" the guy looked down at the huge orange wet stain smack dab in the middle of his shirt.

Latoya covered her mouth. "I'm so sorry! I'm so so so sorry! I'll clean it up!"

The guy looked at her with anger and disgust. His fists were balled up.

"Toya, go in the back! I'll take care of it!" said Biscuit walking up and pointing towards the dressing room.

"Biscuit I'm sorry, I didn't know I was that drun..."

"Go in the back!" he pointed to the dressing room with the most serious look on his face.

She went into the back room and sat down. She started weeping with her hands over her face. Farren walked up.

"Girl. What's the problem? Why are you crying?!"

"I'm just a complete failure. I just threw up all over this guy's shirt. I'm a total disaster!"

Farren chuckled. Then rubbed her on the back. "Sometimes you just have to laugh at shit. When you mess up or embarrass yourself, just say to yourself this too shall pass. Girl, it's just a part of the game. You'll get over it. It has happened to the best of us. You had a great first night."

Thirty minutes passed and Biscuit came to the back and sat in the chair next to Latoya. He started laughing.

"You aight?" he said.

"No, I feel terrible. I'm so bad at this. Why are you laughing?"

"Yes, around here, we laugh. We don't take life too seriously. Don't worry. You're good. Shit happens. Stop crying. Here."

Biscuit grabbed her hand and placed a wad of cash in it.

"You're done for the night. I'll see you next Friday," he smiled, then he got up and left.

"See. Through all the bullshit you have to go through, eventually you'll end up with something to show for it," said Farren.

"I guess so," said Latoya as she wiped her face and looked at the money.

Latoya got home then started counting the money that she had made that night. Counting her money was like therapy, the more she counted, the better she felt. The bills were all in ones. It took her two hours to count it, because she counted it twice to make sure it was right. She counted $823. She felt guilty joy that she hadn't felt since she was a 14-year-old. The same feeling she had after she succeeded at stealing money and cocaine from horny, perverted, drug dealers when she was a teenager. But her main goal was to redeem herself from her throw up incident. She had something to prove.

20. Conflict of Interest

January 27th

Ring. Ring. Ring. Ring. Beep. Beep. Beep

Latoya thought those sounds were coming from her dreams. Then she realized it was her phone. She hopped up confused with a slight headache. She looked around and saw neatly stacked money all over her room. She picked up her phone from off her dresser. It was 1:00 p.m. She slept through three alarms and five missed calls, text messages and voicemails all from Lisa. She dreaded calling Lisa back, but she knew that she had to give an explanation.

"What happen Latoya?! Sara said that you didn't show up to the meeting," said Lisa concerned. "I'm so sorry Lisa. I overslept. Is there any way that they can reschedule it?"

"Overslept? Overslept?! This is unacceptable Latoya. Of course, they are not going to reschedule. You had one chance and you blew it. I stuck my neck out for you and this is how you treat me?! You know how bad this looks on me and you?"

"Wooooaaaah. Back up, Lisa. First of all, I appreciate all that you've done for me. I really do. But at this time, it's just not the right fit for me. I have something else in the works right now. Something a little more… lucrative," said Latoya staring at her piles of money.

"What do you mean right fit?! Latoya you said that this would be the perfect company for you. And more lucrative? Please! You tell me what job that pays you more than $48K in salary with no college degree and is a reputable company like Sephora here in Atlanta?"

"Sweetheart. In my line of business, I can make 48K in a month."

"Your line of business? What are you? A stripper?" asked Lisa.

"Maybe so. I respect the naked hustle. I don't have anything against it."

"Well I don't respect the naked hustle. And I do have something against dancing naked for money. And if you want to ruin your career, your reputation, and throw away all of your morals and standards to shake your ass for a couple of bucks, then I can't help you."

"That's fine. I'm too big to fit into your weak-ass, cookie cutter box that you tried to put me in, anyway! I'm going to prove you and whoever else that doesn't believe in me wrong. You fake-ass life coach." Latoya hung up.

21. EntrepreNewHer

"Practice makes perfect," said Farren every time Latoya fell on her butt. "Get up and try it again." Farren watched Latoya closely, analyzing what was wrong with her technique. Latoya told Farren that she wanted to get better at dancing on the actual pole. She said she would teach her and she stuck to her word. So, during off days she would go to Latoya's house and show her moves and also helped her create her own moves. Farren showed Latoya how to slide down it smoothly. She showed her how to twerk from the top of the pole. They practiced doing back flips on the pole. You name it, they practiced it. On their off days they would practice consistently. Latoya was dedicated to being the best entertainer that she could be and Farren was committed to helping her. Farren knew that Latoya was pretty gifted at twerking so occasionally Latoya would be the teacher and she would give Farren pointers.

"People have finally started requesting me. I guess this practice is paying off," said Latoya.

"I told you, be patient, your time is coming. Just keep working. Be the hardest working girl there. When all them other hoes are slacking off, you go harder. Don't ease up at all. Even when niggas ain't throwing money or it's a slow night, you keep dancing like it's potentially a million dollars in there. Because it just might be. It will get to a point where your business is automated. Your clients are going to be there faithfully, just handing over their paychecks to you," said Farren.

"I can't wait."

"After another good session we should reward ourselves by going shopping. What do you think?"

"Let's go!"

"Let's do Phipps Plaza," said Farren.

"Phipps? I can't afford anything in Phipps. I'm not on your level yet," said Latoya.

"Girl, yes you are. And if you ain't, you will be! You have to act like you can afford even if you can't. Come on!"

Phipps Plaza

They both walked into Saks Fifth together.

"See we deserve the best of the best. The best clothes, the best everything. You can't ever let anyone catch you slipping on an outfit, the way that you dress your body shows people how you feel about yourself," said Farren.

While walking through the store, Latoya pointed at some Christian Louboutin that she said looked nice.

"If you like them, try them on," said Farren.

"Ok. Still a steep price range but I'll try them."

She tried them on and she loved how they looked.

"If only if I can afford these," she said as she checked them out and strutted around the store with them.

"What size shoe do you wear? Is that the right size?"

"Yep, they're a size five."

Farren then started looking around. A lady came to her assistance.

"Is there anything that we could help you all with?" said the woman.

"Yes. Can you get those shoes that she's wearing in a size five, please?"

Latoya looked at Farren "You wear size five too?"

"Nope."

"So, what are you doing? I can't afford these right now, Farren."

"I know you can't, and that's why I'm buying them for you."

"Are you serious Farren? Why? You don't have to do this."

"Toya hush. Yes, I do. It's a gift from me to you that's all. For working, grinding to be a better dancer day in and day out. Remember, we deserve the best, and if we're going to be together, then we're going to have to look the part."

Latoya nodded.

The lady came back with the shoes. "So what kind of work do you all do?"

"Ummm. We're entrepreneurs," Latoya said.

"Oh. Entrepreneurs. What industry?"

"We are dancers. We dance for money. Just like my friend said. We're entrepreneurs, since you want to be so nosey," snarled Farren.

"Ok. Just curious," said the lady with a half-smile as she walked away.

Farren looked at Latoya, "That nosey bitch just wants to see how we can afford these shoes. See, don't be afraid to tell people who you are and what you do. Be bold because their story is not your story. Your story is unique to you. It's unique to your circumstances. You don't have anything to be ashamed of. People look at us as if we're less than them. Like we're second class citizens. Because our hustle is different from theirs. Because we collect our coins in a different way. They look at us as if we are at the bottom of the totem pole. But they have it all wrong. Our hustle is authentic. It's pure. It's raw. We don't hide. The naked hustle represents stripping yourself all the way down to your bare body in front everyone and still being confident in knowing who you are."

"You're so right. I need to work on being bold in who I am."

"That's why I bought these for you. To stunt on all those haters that are going to talk shit about you. They need to know that you're the shit no matter what they say and that you appreciate the free PR when they talk about you behind your back."

"I appreciate that, I really do. I'm just glad to have found something that I can finally be good at and enjoy," said Latoya.

"Let's not get it confused. You should be in this to help jumpstart your career. This is not the end goal. The end goal is to get out of the game and create an empire."

"Empire. I like that. What do you have in mind?"

"Anything that you can think of! You just have to dream it up. Clothing line. Beauty products. Apps. Real estate. You name it. That's my goal. To make enough money to get up out of this shit. Not many girls make it out of this lifestyle and are able to make something everlasting. Like a super successful business. Many girls just leave the game, with not much to show for it. Then go live some boring, below average life. Not me. I'm trying to start my own beauty care line. I'm trying to make that shit bigger than L'Oréal. I'm calling it Red Kiss Inc. That's my ultimate dream. That's why I hustle."

"That's so cool! I can see you owning your own beauty line. With your face on all the billboards all around the country."

"Yep. That's my story. That's my ultimate dream and vision for my life. That's why I pursue the naked hustle. And your job is to find out what yours is too."

22. Celebrity Crushed

Latoya was getting dressed at home, preparing to go to work. When she received a call from Lisa. She ignored it and continued getting dressed. Then she received a call again. Annoyed, she picked it up to see what Lisa wanted. Although she really didn't care to ever talk to her again after their last conversation.

"Yes," answered Latoya.

"Hey, Latoya. It's Lisa. You have a second to talk?"

"I have a couple of minutes. What's up?"

"I was just calling to apologize for the way that I handled the whole Sephora situation. I feel like I was a little harsh with my words."

"You don't have to apologize. You spoke your mind. Its ok to feel how you feel about me and my career choices. Because at the end of the day it's MY choice. So, it doesn't bother me at all. I'm going to live my life regardless of how people feel about me."

"But, see I spoke out of anger. It wasn't from my heart. I just felt terrible after it. I'm going to keep praying for you. I respect that your journey may be different from others. I didn't understand that at the time. So, if there's anything that I can do for you, let me know. I owe you. You didn't deserve those words from me. And I just ask for your forgiveness."

"Lisa. I appreciate the gesture. And I do forgive you. But like I said. I'm fine. I don't need any more prayers, favors, none of that. From you, or anyone else right now. You don't owe me anything. I don't want you to feel like you do. But I have to go, I'm already running late for work. Goodbye, Lisa." Latoya hung up the phone. She was on her way out the door to Dreamville. She had a feeling tonight was going to be a great night.

Dreamville 9:00 p.m.

Latoya's shift started at 10 p.m. She had an hour until it was show time. She was in the dressing room hanging out until then. Girls were running around the dressing room in a panic. Like they had lost their minds. Girls putting on extra make-up. They had their best outfits on.

She stopped one of the girls.

"What's going on tonight? Why is everyone panicking?"

"You didn't hear?"

"Hear what?"

"Lil Fresh is going to be here tonight after his concert at Phillips Arena. He's definitely going to blow a check today for sure. He said it at his concert."

"Lil Fresh! Holy shit! Do you know how much I'm in love with him! I've had the biggest crush on him, since 2012. That's my future husband!"

"Not if I get to him first!" said the girl with a smirk as she looked Latoya up and down and scurried away. Her face was as serious as a heartbeat. That's when Latoya realized that there was no way that she would be able to get to him. Not with all the other girls thirsting over him. She knew it would be chaos.

It was 1:10 a.m. No sign of Lil Fresh. They said the concert had ended almost three hours ago. Still no sign of Lil Fresh. The girls were getting restless. The girls started giving half the effort while dancing. They kept looking at the door hoping that Lil Fresh walked in. This was the most girls that Latoya had ever seen at Dreamville. New faces meant more competition. Everyone came to work that day. Either way, Latoya was dancing just as hard as she ever did. She decided that It was going to be a good money-making night for her regardless of a celebrity coming in or not. Latoya kept working while everyone else waited.

At approximately 1:35 a.m., a lot of people started walking in from the front door. At least 30 guys. They were escorted by Biscuit and the security guards straight to the VIP booths.

The DJ then announced. "Oh shit! Guess who just walked in! Lil Fresh and the Rock Solid Music Group! It's about to be a movie! We got some real ballers in the building! It's go time ladies!"

The whole atmosphere in the building changed. All the girls' eyes shifted towards that VIP booth. Even Latoya. She couldn't see him at first. Then she spotted him. And just that quick, there were girls over there in the vicinity, waiting to dance for him. She figured she wasn't quick enough.

Ten minutes had gone by and she didn't see any girls in the booth anymore. She was curious. She asked one of the girls that originally ran over to the booth what happened.

"Girl them niggas ain't throwing no money. They over there acting like divas. And plus, Biscuit over there trying to make sure that girls don't bombard them. So, no girls are allowed over there right now. All that money Lil Fresh supposed to have and he ain't throwing shit," the girl said shaking her head and walking away.

The DJ came on the mic. "Black Vanity, you up next."

It was her turn to get on stage. She was ready. At this point it was just a walk in the park to her now. It was second nature. Latoya got on the stage and she let the music take over her body. She moved to the beat, twerking, thinking about her dreams and nothing else. She projected herself to her bedroom, dancing in the mirror five years ago. Being free from judgement and criticism. She looked over to Lil Fresh, and they locked eyes for a quick second. She had to look away immediately because she almost lost her rhythm. She had to get back into her zone.

After her segment was over, she picked up her money and began to walk down the stairs. Before she could get to the bottom, Biscuit came and grabbed her arm.

"Come with me," he said. She followed him. She followed him right to VIP. The entourage of guys parted like the Red Sea as Biscuit and Toya walked through. They stopped right in front of Lil Fresh.

"At your request, I got her for you. Black Vanity, meet, Lil fresh. Lil Fresh, Vanity," said Biscuit, introducing them.

Lil Fresh nodded at her and then turned to Biscuit. "You always look out for me Biscuit. That's why I come here. You always show love," he gave him a handshake.

"That's what I'm here for. Y'all enjoy," said Biscuit as he walked away and winked at her. She played it off. Like she wasn't really excited to be with him but she was star struck. She had never smelled a cologne as good as his. It was strong and sweet. He had on a pretty basic outfit. A hoodie, with jeans and black and gold Balenciaga shoes. Both his chain and his watch diamonds were glistening and shining like she had never seen before. He looked better in person than he did on television. Low clean haircut. He usually has golds in on TV but he didn't today. He had the prettiest teeth. They were white and straight.

"So, Black Vanity. It's a pleasure to finally meet you. See, everyone told me that there was this dancer here that was new and that was a must see. So, I came here just to see you."

"Oh, so you're trying to make me blush. Please don't do that. I already can't believe you're in front of me right now. I love your music! You're my favorite artist."

"Oh really. I appreciate that," he then reached into his hoodie, pocket and pulled out the biggest stack of money in rubber bands she had ever seen. He had no idea that Latoya would probably dance for him for free if he wanted her to. But a little compensation wouldn't hurt.

"How much do you love my music?"

"I'll just have to show you," she said. She started dancing slowly in front of him.

After dancing for him for a couple songs she didn't realize how much money was on the floor. Piles, on top of piles of money. There was so much money on the floor that she imagined making a snow angel in it. They had ordered bottles on top of bottles. Money was constantly falling from the air. Making it rain was an understatement. It was like a scene from a movie. It was actually fun to her. Bouncing, shaking, jiggling, all for someone that she admired so much that she still had trouble believing that he was in her midst. What a night.

All the girls' eyes kept migrating her way. She could tell that they were envious. At 2:15 a.m., Lil Fresh motioned for her to bend down so he could whisper in her ear.

"I'm about to head out. But check this out, I don't want this night to end. Can you meet me at my place?"

"Ummm. I don't know. What's going to be there?"

He laughed. "What's going to be there? It's my little after party. More fun. More money. More living. More of me."

"I guess I'll slide through. Can I bring one of my girls?"

"Noooo. Just you. What's your number, I'll text you," he pulled out his phone.

"404-555-4203."

"Cool. I'm texting it to you now. I'm out," he said as he stood up from the couch and gave her a kiss on the cheek. His whole entourage started walking towards the door.

The security guards started helping her pick up the money. She then went to the back dressing room. She had made more money in one night, then she had made in a whole month—10K.

While counting money in the back room, Toya could feel the envy in the room. A couple of girls walked by and smacked their teeth. She overheard others talking about how lame Lil Fresh was. Farren eventually walked in and came to her.

"Girl! Look at you! See I told you! You're making me proud! I created a monster. How much do you think you made?"

"At least 10K," Latoya said.

"See. There's nothing like the naked hustle. I didn't get to see Lil Fresh up close. Is he as fine as he is on TV?"

"Yes. He looks scrumptious! He gave me his number too."

"Oh shit! What is he doing afterwards?"

"I don't know. He told me to meet him at his place afterwards. I'm not sure if I want to go."

"Girl. Go! When will you ever get a chance to hang out with someone as famous and rich as him?"

"It's not that. I just don't want to do something I'll regret later you know. I know myself," said Latoya.

"Are you talking about fucking him? You don't have to. Just go and hang out and vibe. If you don't go, give me your phone, I'll go in your place," she grabbed at Toya's phone.

"Ok, ok. I'll go and hang out for awhile," said Toya keeping it way from Farren.

She used the GPS to take her to his place. He was in a loft downtown. It was on the 56th floor. She took the elevator. She didn't know what to think. She was sure Lil Fresh probably invited her over to have sex. She was determined not to have sex.

She knocked on the door. He opened the door. He had changed clothes already. He was in a white robe. It was just him.

"After party? Where is everyone?" Latoya asked looking around the loft.

"I am the after party," he said as he motioned her in.

She looked around at his place. He had some of his albums and singles as plaques. However, the most breathtaking thing about the place was the view of the city. You could see all of downtown. It was as if they were on top of the world.

"This view is amazing," she said walking towards the window.

"You like it? You think you can get used to it?" he asked.

"Of course, I can."

"So, what are you going to do to show me that you deserve a view like this one?"

"Nothing. Hey listen I like you and all, but I'm not here to have sex. Let's be crystal clear."

"Who said anything about sex? I meant, living here."

"Living here?"

"Yes. What part didn't you understand?"

"Ok. I'm not your girlfriend or wife, why would I live here?"

"You're right. You're not. Not yet, at least."

"Why would you want me to be your girlfriend, you don't even know me," said Latoya.

"Exactly, And that's what you're here for. So, I can get to know you better."

"Why would you want a girlfriend? I mean you have all the girls in the world at your fingertips? You have plenty of money, why would you want me as your girlfriend?"

"You think I want a million hoes? Well I don't. I want to share my success with one girl. A girl that I can trust. A girl that I can build with."

"Why consider me though? I mean, you just met me a couple of hours ago. You don't even know me."

"Because there was something special about you. When we made eye contact the first time, I knew you could possibly be Mrs. Henderson in the future."

"Mrs. Henderson? That's your last name?"

"I thought you were one of my biggest fans. Francisco Henderson is my full name."

"You got me. I didn't know."

"Well, if you want to have the key to this place, then you have to earn the key to my heart."

"How do I do that?"

"First, you can start with taking a shot with me,"

"A shot? As long as you don't try to have sex."

"Relax. No one is trying to have sex. I'm just trying to get the after party going."

"Ok. Just one."

He went to turn on some music, then he went to the kitchen and poured up two shots. They took them both.

"Let's play a game called Mercy."

"How do you play?"

"So. The theme of the game is, the first one to say *mercy* loses. We are going to time each other as we perform some type of act on one another. For example, I'm going to suck on your neck, until you *say mercy* and then I'll stop. The longer you hold out without saying it, the better chance you have of winning. We'll time each other. And then you have to do it to me. Whoever says *mercy* in the shortest amount of time loses."

"How many different girls have you played this game with?" she asked.

"Does that matter?"

"Yes. To me it does."

"You're the first girl that I've told about the game."

"I don't believe you."

"Uggghhh. Do you want to play or not?" he said.

"Ok, I'll play."

"Good! Do you want me to go first or you to go first?" he said.

"Uhh. You go first," Latoya responded.

"Ok. Remember, the goal is to go as long as you can without saying *mercy*."

He motioned her closer and then started caressing her neck with his tongue. He was slow and steady. Very patient. She was melting inside. Her panties were becoming moist. He knew it to, and that's why he reached down there and started caressing her pussy too. At that point, she didn't care about the game.

He started taking her clothes off. She helped him. She laid down and he got on top of her. She could not believe what was happening. She was about to have sex with her biggest crush, Lil Fresh the famous rapper. He eased inside her... And to her surprise, his dick was just that: little. However, once he started stroking, she realized that his stroke game compensated for his lack of size. He had really good rhythm. She figured that came with him being an artist. He went up and down, and in circles. They were in motion together, slow, and steady. It was good enough to make her cum all over his sheets. Shortly after, he did the same and they fell asleep.

The next morning, she woke up. She looked to the right of her and saw Lil Fresh in a deep sleep with the sheets halfway on top of him. He was snoring. Loud. Latoya was parched and hungry. She needed something in her stomach ASAP. She hopped up to look in the refrigerator to see if there was something to eat. Nothing. As empty as could be. She figured it wouldn't be a bad idea for her to sneak out to the grocery story to get him some breakfast. There was a

Publix like a minute away. Plus, it would be a good way for her to surprise him with breakfast in bed. He would probably fall in love after that. She left the door unlocked. He wouldn't mind.

At 8:45 a.m., she was on her way back to his condo. She wanted to cook a big breakfast so she had a good amount of groceries. Eggs, bread, cheese, waffles, sausage, grits, orange juice, water, bacon, syrup, fruit to name a few items. She was sure he was used to eating really good so she figured she couldn't slack. Plus, she didn't know exactly what he wanted.

She got to the door with all of her groceries in hand. She tried to twist the door knob. The door was locked. She gently but firmly knocked on the door just loud enough for him to hear it but to not wake the neighbors. *Knock, knock, knock!* Again, no answer. Then she started banging. *Bang! Bang! Bang! Bang!* She rang the doorbell. She stood there for a second… No answer. She pulled out her phone and called him. Three times. No answer. She was concerned. She stayed there for about 10 minutes, groceries in hand, until she finally decided to leave. As she walked away, something told her to look on Instagram. She went to Lil Fresh's page to see a picture of him, fully dressed, driving a Bentley, and telling everyone he was on his way to the airport to head to New York.

23. Guns and Roses

There were always guys that were in love with Black Vanity. These guys just didn't get it. The guys forgot that it was Latoya's job to dance and flirt with them. Of course, Latoya didn't mind them coming back and spending their money on a consistent basis. They are good clients. But sometimes, the men really were in love, and thought they had a chance to date her... especially Edwin.

"Edwin... You know I love you, but you know that I'm not going to give you my number. I have a boyfriend," said Latoya sitting on his lap.

"Farren said you don't have a boyfriend. I asked."

She rolled her eyes. "Farren doesn't know everything about me, you know. I have a personal life, too."

"I understand. But if you really have a boyfriend, why is he letting you do this? If you were my girl, I wouldn't let you do this," said Edwin.

"But Edwin. How? You don't make enough for the both of us, baby. Not with that job that you have working for the city. I'm high maintenance, baby. You don't want me. I require too much. I gotta get my own money anyway. I don't need any man to provide."

"Come on. It's tough for a black man that's been to prison."

"You been to prison, Edwin? For how long?"

"Twenty years."

"Twenty years?!! What'd you do?"

"When I was 18-years old, I killed someone."

"Edwin, I couldn't see you killing someone! You're the nicest person I know."

"I'm like this now. But back when I was young and stupid, I made terrible mistakes."

"Wow. That's insane. How does it feel to have killed someone?"

"I felt numb. Didn't feel anything. But I had to kill him or either he was going to eventually kill me. So, in my head, it had to be done."

"Well, you don't have to worry about killing anyone anymore, ok," said Latoya rubbing his back.

"You never know, If I have to again, I will," said Edwin taking a sip of his Coors Light.

That's when the conversation got awkward and scary. Out of the corner of Latoya's eye, she saw Farren waving for her to come over. Usually when she did that, there was a big spender in the area. She wanted to wrap up her convo with Edwin quick before the other girls eased their way over there. She patted Edwin on the shoulder, "Edwin, I'll be back." She walked Farren's way.

"Hey. Come here let me introduce you to a good friend of mine," said Farren.

"Ok. What's his name?"

"Poison."

"Uh uhh. Poison? What kind of name is Poison?"

Farren laughed. "You ask him. Don't worry, he's a really nice guy. He has a crush on me but I don't give him the time of day."

"Why? Is he ugly?" asked Latoya.

"No. Too much drama, he's a shooter."

"Shooter?"

"Yes. Shooter. Like bang, bang. Big drug dealers hire him to shoot people. He does all of their dirty work."

"Ummm. So, he kills people? Oh, hell no! Why would I want to meet a killer?" asked Latoya stopping in her tracks.

"Girl, come over. I've been knowing Poison for years. He's harmless to us. He's someone that can protect you, not hurt you. Actually, just knowing him will have you pretty much untouchable because every guy is afraid of him. No guy would ever even look at me the wrong way because I'm cool with Poison. But he's probably the sweetest dude you'd ever meet."

Latoya stood there hesitant. Farren grabbed Latoya's arm and they walked over to Poison.

"Poison. This is my friend Toya," said Farren.

"Nice to meet you. Why do they call you Poison?"

"Because when I'm around, usually a situation is about to turn toxic."

Farren nudged him. "Don't scare her! He's just being silly."

"I've just been called that since I was a child," said Poison smiling.

"Ok. Well, nice to meet you," Latoya said walking away.

"I'll see you around," said Poison with a wink.

24. Robbing the Hood

It was a slow day when Farren asked Latoya for a favor. The last couple of weeks had been slow at Dreamville. It was winter so business had slowed down tremendously.

"Toya. You wanna make some money?" asked Farren.

"Of course, I do. My pockets are dry. What's up?"

"It's this dude name Booker that's coming here tonight. He just texted me. He's a super big spender that is a complete wreck. He's always drunk and high and he talks a lot of shit. He always carries lots of cash on him. He's like one of those drug dealers that don't know how to handle money. He's sloppy."

"Ok. Sooo, what does that have to do with me?" asked Latoya.

"He's always telling me that he wants to have a private party. I always tell him no because I know he's an asshole. But now that I have you around I was thinking that maybe we can have a private party for him and take all his money."

"Take his money as in rob him? Hell no. Girl, you are crazy."

"No silly! Just take the money that he's going to offer us. When he's drunk and high, he'll spend whatever on whomever. He really has a lot of money to blow but he's not going to spend it all here. I know he has at least $250,000 probably sitting around his house somewhere."

"So, you want to go to his house, get him super drunk and high to the point where he's incoherent, then get him to spend way more money on us at his house then what he would at the club?"

"Yes."

"No. I can't do that, sorry."

"Ok. I can respect that."

Later on, that night, Latoya walked around Dreamville seeing if anyone was interested in a dance. She saw someone flag her down from the corner of her eye.

She walks over to see a gentleman that was draped with gold chains and smelled like a ton of weed.

"Ayy! You fine as hell. What's your name?" said the guy.

"Black Vanity? What's your name?"

"Everybody calls me Booker…"

Recognizing that this was Farren's guy that she was referring to. She started to kid with him.

"So, you're the guy that everyone is talking about, huh?"

"They talking about me? They should be since I spend so much damn money here," he said looking at his friends sitting next to him.

"Well, I haven't seen any money that you speak of yet... I'm new here," said Latoya flirting.

"And you ain't gone see none of my money if you don't shut the fuck up and start dancing. I didn't call you over here to be flapping your gums, I called you over to shake that ass," he said hitting her on her behind.

Latoya didn't know how to respond. She stood there for a second, and then walked away. She couldn't handle that level of disrespect. While walking away she heard him say, "Ayy Black Vanity I was just playing! Damn, you can't take a joke? Come back!"

Farren was entertaining a guy on the other side of the club when Latoya walked up to her. She whispered in Farren's ear. "About that favor you asked for earlier...count me in."

It was after 4:00 in the morning when Latoya hopped in Farren's car. She buckled up.

"You ready?" said Farren looking at her.

"Yep," she said.

"Ok, this is how it's going to go down. We're going to get him fucked up. And I mean fucked up! But we can't be obvious about it. We have to act like we're kind of drunk too. So, I'm going to be drinking. You too. And then we're going to start dancing and shit.

Play along with him. Get him horny. Then, when he's pissy drunk, we're going to take whatever we can."

"Wait. But isn't he just going to wake up and notice that his shit is gone. And he's going to know that it was us. Am I missing something?"

"By that time, we're going to be gone! And plus, if he ever comes back we'll just say that's how much it cost. He's going to throw mad money since we're making it a private party for him. Ho'o a careless-ass nigga. A sloppy drunk. He doesn't give a shit about money because he gets so much of it. Plus, he's a bit of a duck, he's weak. He's not going to do shit to us, I promise."

"But someone he knows probably will. I don't know Farren. He knows where we work. How much are we trying to take? How much money is not noticeable to him?"

"He'll spend 50K in one weekend on stupid shit. So, we can at least get that out of him tonight if we do it right."

"At least 50K?! No. I can't do that. He'll definitely notice. What if he catches us in the act? Hell no. I'm out! Drop me off here. Let me out," she said while reaching for the car door to get out.

"Wait, Latoya! Just wait. Do you think I would put you in harm's way? Like seriously?! I love my life too. You don't think I thought this through? I have killers on standby just in case shit hits the fan. We're protected. Look, I can't do this by myself. This is going to be the easiest money you would ever make. Trust me. You're not going to leave me hanging are you? I need you on this one. I would do it for you."

Latoya sat there for a minute. A part of her wanted to leave immediately. The other part of her wanted the money and wanted to do Farren a favor.

"Ok."

"Ok. What?" said Farren.

"Ok, I'll do it. But only if you promise me that we will take only cash, and no one gets hurt!"

"I promise. Let's go."

4:36 a.m.

Farren and Latoya got to Booker's condo building. They took the elevator up to the 31st floor. Then arrived at his place 3113. They stood outside of the door. They could hear loud trap music playing inside.

Farren looked at Latoya. "You good?" she asked.

Latoya took a deep breath. "As good as I'm gonna be," she replied. Farren knocked on the door. Latoya's heart started beating. The door opened.

"Finally! Shit! I thought you had forgot about me!" Booker looked at Latoya. "Oh, and you brought me a gift! See, I knew our night wasn't going to end on a bad note!" He said winking. Latoya couldn't help but roll her eyes.

They walked in. His clothes were everywhere. Random boxes. It smelled like they walked into a marijuana farm. She saw mini scales on the counter with mounds of white powder on them. There was stacks of money everywhere. There was a money counter. Other than the junkiness, it was a nice place, for a guy. He had a portrait of Scarface on the wall. The furniture all looked new. A 72-inch television was in the living room.

Booker went to the counter. He put his nose to the counter and sniffed a whole line of cocaine. "Woo! I'm lit! Y'all want some?!" he said looking up with a white tip on his nose.

"Hell no! I'm good on that right now," Latoya said shaking her head.

Farren bumped Latoya with her elbow.

"What's wrong with your friend?! She too bourgeois for me, huh?" Booker said.

"No, she's just quiet and shy. I'll take some. Just get her some liquor, she'll loosen up," said Farren looking at Latoya with an agitated face.

"How bout I pour all of us up. We bout to have a good night," said Booker going to the refrigerator.

"That's cool," said Farren. She then whispered in Latoya's ear, "Don't fuck this up. Just go with the flow."

Booker poured up three snifters of D'Ussé. Then he and Farren went to the kitchen counter and snorted a line together. They then picked the glasses up and started drinking. Farren and Booker gulped their drinks down all at once. Latoya refused at first but they then persuaded her to do the same. She finally gave in and finished the drink.

"Y'all hurry up and go change. I'll be in the room waiting," said Booker.

Latoya and Farren both went to the bathroom.

"Relax girl. I can tell that you're bugging," said Farren as she changed into lingerie.

"I just need to get this shit over with. I'm already regretting it. Not sure why I'm even here," said Latoya just standing there fully clothed.

"You're here for this money! That's why you're here. And It will be over before you know it. He's already fucked up. He's in La La land right now."

"He's not fucked up enough. Neither am I to go through with this shit."

"Ok. We just need to drink more and we'll be good. Hurry up and change so we can drink more. I got you."

Latoya let out a deep sigh, and stripped down to her lingerie as well. They then went back into the kitchen.

"Booker, my friend is sober. We need to make her comfortable. We need to get her more drunk. All of us need to drink more," said Farren.

"All right pour up! As much as you need. And bring me a glass," he yelled from his room.

Farren started pouring. She looked towards Booker's room briefly. Then she dropped a white pill into his drink.

Latoya's eyes widened. Farren looked at Latoya with her finger to her mouth. "Shhhh," she murmured. "Shut up. I got this."

Latoya was a second away from walking out.

"It's going to be fine," Farren said. "Here, just take another shot."

Latoya listened and begrudgingly drank the liquor.

They went to the bedroom. Booker was in bed with just his boxers on. He was laying there with the biggest wad of ones Latoya had ever seen. He could barely hold it with one hand.

Farren handed him his glass. He took a quick sip. Then put it next to him on his night stand.

"What music y'all want to hear? I didn't update my music selection. I have some Old Young Jeezy. That's cool?"

Farren said. "I'll dance to anything. It don't matter to me."

He grabbed the remote to his sound system, then changed the music. Then he looked at Latoya. "It look like you need to drink more. You look scared," he held his glass up for her to come get it.

She shook her head no.

Booker looked at the cup. Then Latoya again. "Come on now. Don't be like that."

Latoya shook her head no. "I already took a shot in the kitchen. I feel good."

Booker looked closely at the cup. "Y'all ain't trying to poison me. Are y'all?" Booker looked at Farren with a side eye. Farren looked at Latoya.

"Of course not! Just drink some Latoya, you're killing the vibe right now," she said.

Latoya walked slowly to the cup with her arms folded. She unfolded her arms and took the smallest sip possible. She barely even swallowed. Kind of let it swoosh around in her mouth.. Then she attempted to give it back.

"No! Drink more of this shit. I have to make sure y'all ain't trying to poison me. I ain't stupid."

Latoya took the glass and drank half. Then she gave it back to him.

"Now, you drink the rest!"

Booker looked at the cup, then looked at Latoya and smiled. "Ahhhh. You're a feisty one aren't you. I like that shit," he then finished the glass.

Farren started dancing. Then Latoya started. To Latoya, it was the most awkward and uncomfortable situation she had ever witnessed. Uncomfortable doesn't even start to describe how she felt. Farren on the other hand, was in a zone. She was dancing like normal. It was as if she had done this before.

After awhile, Latoya settled in. And she was feeling really good. She felt like she could fly. Booker was throwing mad money. There was at least 5K on the ground. Latoya just had to pretend that she was dancing for her future husband in his boxers. But of course, her husband won't have to throw her money. She actually started enjoying it a little.

Whatever drugs she had taken had her feeling like she was superwoman. The problem was that Farren had got way too comfortable. Booker motioned her over to come closer. Now she's giving him a lap dance in his bed. Scrubbing on him.

Latoya is still dancing on the foot of the bed. Somewhat of a sexy slow twerk. Latoya felt like she was dancing for herself because Booker was all over Farren. She feels left out and stupid. She didn't know what to do. She edged a little closer to Farren as she danced on his lap. Then she saw him take Farren's bra off and followed by sucking on her nipples. Latoya started to hear Farren quietly moan. Latoya was shocked. But she guessed it was part of the plan, so she just ignored it.

Then, Farren's dancing motions started to change a little. It looked more like thrusting. Farren and Booker were having sex. She was riding on top of Booker. Latoya could tell because he started moving his hips to hers and she started moaning louder.

Latoya was disgusted. She didn't know that Farren got down like this. It was seamless. She barely even knew Booker. Her perception of Farren changed at that moment. The girl she had looked up to was having sex with a random drug dealer for money. The funny thing was that she couldn't judge because she had done the same. But watching someone else that she looked up to, gave her a different perspective. Especially since she told herself that she would never do it again.

At this point, she felt so out of place. But she started to feel horny and drowsy. Farren and Booker were having sex for at least three minutes. Latoya laid on the bed next to them. She didn't know what else to do. She then felt Booker feeling on her breasts while he had sex with Farren. Latoya didn't even care. She just laid there.

Latoya was dozing off when she heard a loud bang sound coming from the front of the condo. She thought she was dreaming at first. She looked up and saw three bodies in all black run in. They had on ski masks. They had big guns.

"Get the fuck down!" they demanded, pointing their guns.

Latoya dropped to the floor screaming!

"Shut the fuck up bitch! Before we kill you!" one said getting closer and pointing the gun directly to her face.

Latoya shut up quick.

Farren hopped off Booker and wrapped her naked body in the covers.

Slurring his words badly, Booker speaks, "You niggas fucked up booyy...you robbed the wrong nigga.

I'm gone kill you fuckers. Musa's going to kill you and whoever sent you."

Gunshots rang. Latoya and Farren both screamed.

"Shut the fuck up bitches! Get in the fucking closet before we blow your brains out next," they said pointing their guns.

They both got up and ran to the closet. One of the guys had a red bandana wrapped around his neck.

Latoya was whimpering in the dark. Farren hugged her crying. They could hear the guys talking.

"Get all the fucking money. Every fucking dollar. Get the coke. Look for jewelry! Get the safe too! We'll break that shit open later!"

Latoya just knew that she was going to die that night. She just envisioned seeing her sister Leah in heaven.

Farren grabbed her hands. Then she started praying quietly. "God just let us make it out alive, just let us make it out alive. Forgive us for our sins."

The closet door slammed open and one of the men pointed the gun at both Farren and Latoya.

"Please don't shoot!" said Latoya.

"Shut up!" the guy yelled. He turned to the other men. "What about the bitches!?"

"Fuck it. Just leave them," said another.

The guy turned and slammed the closet door back shut, startling Farren and Latoya.

After five minutes, it got really quiet. Latoya was afraid to move.

"You think they gone?" whispered Farren.

"I hope so," Latoya said.

They peaked out the closet. It appeared as if they were gone. They got up. They looked at the bed. Booker was slumped over. The bed was painted with red like something out of a horror movie. His eyes and mouth were wide open.

"They killed Booker! Should we call the police?" yelled Latoya in a panic.

"No! Let's just go! They're going to think we did it! Let's just get out of here!" said Farren.

25. Peace of the Pie

Two weeks later

Latoya was paranoid about Booker. The TV in the dressing room was showing the story on Booker's murder. It was just her and another dancer in the room.

"They're still talking about Booker's murder, huh?" said the dancer.

"Yea. That's a sad story," said Latoya.

"Are you going to the funeral?" asked the girl.

"Oh no. I didn't know him at all," Latoya rebutted.

"Oh really? He was always here. Throwing all his money. Damn Poison, is a rich man right now. Him and whoever else was involved," said the girl.

"Poison? Poison killed Booker?" Latoya was intrigued.

"Yea, girl you didn't know? Well, let's keep that between me and you. I heard that it was Poison and Farren that was in on it. Farren always wanted to rob Booker. Because he was an easy lick. Sloppy. Belligerent. Rich. That's an easy target for her and Poison. I'm sure there were more people involved. But whoever was involved, they got some real money,"

"Oh, really. Well that whole situation is fucked up. Excuse me girl, I need to make a phone call real quick," said Latoya.

Latoya went outside and dialed Farren immediately.

"Sooo. Why didn't you tell me?" said Latoya.

"Tell you what?" said Farren.

"Tell me that everything was planned all along You, Poison, and Booker. You were going to do it your way."

"Toya. I don't know what you're talking about. I am not going to entertain you trying to convict me of something that isn't true."

"Stop the lying Farren. You bought a new car. You haven't been to work in two weeks. Don't fucking lie to me."

"So, you're watching my pockets now?" Farren asked.

"Where's my cut?"

"Toya…"

"I want my cut of the money that was stolen. I was there. My life was put at risk because of you. I want to be compensated for my trouble."

"Or what, Toya? What are you going to do? Go to the police and tell them that you were involved in a murder heist that you want compensation for?"

Toya was silent.

"Exactly. Nothing happened that night. I don't know what you're talking about. All I know is that Booker was killed. I have no clue on who killed him. If anyone asks you, I WAS not there. And it would be in your best interest to say that you were not there either."

"So, this is the real you huh. You're willing to cheat a close friend to get a couple of bucks. Thank you for showing me your true colors."

"It's business Toya. Nothing personal. Once you learn that no one is ever going to give you shit in this life, you'd be better off. Now let's not talk about this ever again."

Livid, Latoya still went back inside to work.

After her shift was over, Latoya was walking to her car when, suddenly, a black Camaro pulled up beside her. The tints were super black, she couldn't see in. She was afraid for her life. The window rolled down slowly. It was Poison with a fitted cap on and you can barely see his eyes.

"Get in," Poison said not looking at her.

"Why. Where are you taking me?" said Latoya full of fear.

Poison looked her dead in the eye and rolled the window down further to show her that he had a Glock 19 in his lap. "I'm not going to ask you twice, Latoya."

Terrified. Latoya proceeded to the passenger's seat. She was shaking in fear.

"What's wrong with you?" Poison said.

"Nothing's wrong."

"Then why are you shaking like that? You are so damn scared. There's nothing to be afraid of when you're with me. When you're with me you should feel the safest. Remember that," said Poison looking at her shivering thighs.

"Ok. Then what do you want from me?"

"I got something for you," said Poison reaching in the back of the car.

He pulls out a duffle bag and sets it on her lap.

"We're doing this out of the kindness of my heart. It's $25K in the bag. Keep your mouth closed. You didn't get this from me. I don't know you, you don't know me. Ok?"

"Ok?"

Poison then reached over Latoya and opened the door. "Goodbye."

26. 21 Questions

Although Booker's murder was still on her mind, It didn't take long for Latoya to go shopping. Two days after she had received Poison's package to be exact. Shopping was a way to take her mind off that situation. It was liberating. She went to Phipps Plaza and got all the clothes that she wanted. Gucci, Prada, and Jeffrey... any brand she wanted, she got. She also redid her whole condo. Well, not her whole condo, really just the new couches for her living room and a new bedroom set.

She had just got home from shopping. There were at least 10 bags full of new merchandise in the living room. She was exhausted so she plopped down on the couch. She knew she had to stay up though because the delivery people were going to drop off her new couch and her new king-sized bed any minute. Forty-five minutes later she heard the doorbell. She ran to open the door.

"Y'all are a little late huh?"

The two gentlemen at the door looked at each other confused.

"Y'all were supposed to be here at 3:05 p.m. and it's 3:45. I may want a discount on the delivery since y'all didn't arrive on time. And where's the couch? Is it in the truck?" she said looking for a truck.

"Latoya, my name Detective Roger Snells from the Fulton County Police Department and we want to ask you a couple of questions. Is that ok?"

Latoya's heart dropped to the floor.

"Oh. I'm sorry, I thought you were someone else. I apologize. What questions are y'all asking about?"

"The death of Brandon Carr, aka Booker," said the investigator.

"I don't know anything about that..." said Latoya.

"Well looks like our visit will be quicker than expected. We just want to know exactly where you were at 4:00 am Sunday December the 21st."

"I don't know. Probably in my bed. Sleeping."

"Well we have some conflicting information. We have some intel stating that you were in Booker's condo during this time, along with another young lady. Minutes before his murder."

"We just need the truth. Please don't fabricate anything with us or else you can be in some big trouble. I don't like wasting my time and I'm sure you don't like wasting yours. So, let's start this again. Where were you on the date of Mr. Carr's death?"

"I was there. With a friend. I'm a dancer. We were supposed to be drinking and dancing for him. That's all."

"Who was your friend?"

"Honestly, aren't I supposed to have a lawyer to help answer these questions. I don't feel comfortable speaking with you about this. Am I under arrest?"

"No, you're not."

"So technically, I can go back in my house without talking to y'all if I don't want to. Correct?"

"Technically, yes."

"So, in that case, I have somewhere to be so I'll be on my way. Thank you, gentlemen."

Latoya closed the door and immediately called Farren.

"Are you with the police?"

"No, I just closed the door on them. They're outside my door," said Latoya.

"You didn't tell them anything did you?"

"No."

"You sure?"

"Yes, Farren."

"Girl this shit is getting crazy. I want to apologize for putting you through this shit. We're innocent but the fact that our names got somehow tied into this shit is crazy. We should be good."

As time went on, the case had been dismissed. Law enforcement could not conjure up enough evidence to indict anyone. No one knew anything. No one said anything. When it comes to drug crimes, everyone is afraid to give up names. Especially when it has something to do with the higher up drug dealers. No one snitched, no one got caught. There were some bigger drug names in play that had the power to keep everyone's mouth sealed.

27. Hot, New, Single

The first time she heard the song, she was at Dreamville working. The DJ shouted her out.

"Not everyone can have a song named after them. Black Vanity you changing the game," said the DJ.

Latoya had no idea what he was talking about. Latoya hated Lil Fresh after that one night, but what she didn't know was that he came out with a new hot single titled Black Vanity Dreams. When she first heard it, she was afraid that he was going to put their sexual encounter out there. But the song was harmless and it basically just mentioned that she was a girl of his fantasy. The song had made her famous.

Latoya started getting booked for club appearances. One night, Latoya was in her VIP section at this club called Prive. She could see everyone looking up at her. They realized that she was the girl on the flier and the girl from Lil Fresh's song. She had on this bomb-ass blue dress. It fit her curves nicely. She was really there just to get her check and to leave. But for some reason the club was poppin this night. She was with three other girls that were associates, not friends. The section next to her was empty for awhile. Next thing you know. A group of three guys came over. All of them were pretty good looking. They looked hood but somehow sophisticated. They dressed nice. All black. Like business people. But they had big chains like drug dealers. So, It was kind of confusing.

After taking another good look at one of the guys, Latoya came to the conclusion that he was fine. Not just good looking fine. His swag was just silent confidence, and he did not have to say a word. He was Puerto Rican-looking, but definitely African American. Good hair. Cute smile. He had a couple of tats on his neck. A gold chain with the label BWS.

A guy with money doesn't excite Latoya anymore because she had money on her own now. But she could tell these guys had some money. She got caught making eye contact with the leader.

As the night went on, this mysterious group of guys ordered bottles back to back to back. Ace of Spades, D'Ussé, you name it, they ordered it. The DJ would shout them out. "I see the BWS boys are in the building, I see you Taq!! The richest niggas in Atlanta."

Next thing you know. She was sitting there minding her own business, and she saw sparkles headed to her section. The girls started dancing. Latoya looked at one of the girls. "Did you order another bottle?"

"Umm. No," she looked to the other girl. "No, I didn't order anything." There was no way that she was going to pay $500 for another bottle. It just wasn't happening.

The bottle service dancers were dancing with the sparkles. She couldn't wait until she stopped so she could ask her why the hell she was bringing another. As soon as she put the sparkle down. Latoya whispered in her ear. "Ummm. I didn't order another bottle."

"Yea, we know. The BWS guys over there ordered for y'all."

"Oh... ok. Ummmm. We don't want it. You can take that back," said Latoya.

One of the girls said, "Wait! Why send it back?!"

"Because we don't know those guys! I'm not about to just drink this shit and then they expect us to do something in return."

"Girl! They bought it for us. We didn't ask for it. Stop thinking so much. If they want to spend money on us let them."

The waitress stood there waiting on Latoya's response. She looked across to the BWS boys' section. They weren't even looking their way. "Ok. We can just keep it I guess."

As the girls opened the bottle and poured it in their glasses, it didn't last longer than five minutes. She sat there wondering why the hell these guys bought it. She decided to go ask herself.

"Excuse me. Which one of you all are responsible for that bottle that was sent over."

They all looked at her like she was crazy. "I'm sorry, we don't know what you're talking about."

Latoya was getting a bit aggravated.

"So, it wasn't y'all that sent the bottle? The waitress said it was y'all."

The leader spoke up. "I thought you were cute and I wanted you to come join us."

"Oh. Well, thank you. But you didn't have to do all that," said Latoya.

"Why didn't I? Did it not work? Are you not here?"

"Yea, but that doesn't matter. What do you want?"

"I want your heart, and I want to be your friend."

"I don't need any more friends, I have too many already, but thanks."

"I agree. That's why you need to get rid of some to make room for me. Just like the ones in your booth that just want to be seen with you and that want to be scavengers. Quality over quantity," he said with a wink. "My name is Taq by the way. What's yours?" he said.

"Latoya. Oh, so you're the guy that the DJ keeps shouting out. And what the hell is BWS?"

"We'll discuss all that later over some dinner. Is that ok with you?"

"Ummm. Maybe."

"Ok. Here," he said as he handed her a phone.

She just sat there with it. Trying to really figure out if she should give her number to him. She never gives her number out to guys anymore. Especially in the club. She would usually lie and say that she has a boyfriend. Or that she's gay. Or some reject of that sort. But this time she just put her number in and gave it to him.

"Looked like you passed the test," he said as he got his phone back.

She rolled her eyes playfully, "What test?"

"Testing to see if you had good taste," he winked.

She laughed. "Whatever," and went back to her section.

It was Sunday morning and she got a text from Taq.

"Good morning gorgeous, do you have a passport?"

How random she thought. Out of all the questions to ask.

"No, I don't. I need to get one though. Why do you ask?" she replied.

"Ok. This week, go apply for your passport. Get your birth certificate and apply."

"Umm. Ok. And why am I going to get a passport?"

"Because next month, you and I are going to Colombia. I need you to be ready."

"That's funny. First off, I don't know you like that. I mean we just met this weekend. Why would I just up and plan a trip with you? We haven't went on a date or anything."

"Our first date will be to the post office to get your passport. Can you be ready at 1:00 p.m. on Friday?"

She laughed out loud, then texted back. "What is wrong with you! You are crazy. You don't even know me."

"I'm crazy enough to take a chance with you and to get to know you. Yes, I am. Friday at 1:00 p.m.? We'll get lunch afterwards."

She was baffled. She just agreed. "Ok. I'll be ready at 1:00 p.m."

28. Mr. Big Shot

He was punctual. At 1:00 p.m. he was in her driveway... with a Lamborghini. A yellow Lamborghini at that. He hopped out wearing a very nice outfit, it was all white. It was some designer's clothes that she didn't recognize.

"This is a nice place," he said looking around at the condominiums.

"Ummm. Yea, but not as nice as your car.... Who the hell are you?"

He smiled, "Maybe you can find out for yourself in due time."

"Ok. Whatever... Taq!"

They went to the post office with all of her documents and applied for a passport. He paid the $160 fee for her. Afterwards, they left and went to eat lunch at STK. They valeted the car and walked in.

"Mr. Taq!" Yelled the host standing by the front door. "How are you?!"

"I'm well. Thank you! This is my girlfriend, Latoya,"

Latoya looked at Taq with a side eye. "Umm. Don't lie. Yes, my name is Latoya. I'm just a friend of Taq's. I am not his girlfriend."

Taq smiled, "I'm sorry, not my girlfriend yet. Excuse my ambition, I like to speak things into existence."

The host smiled. "Well greetings, Latoya! It's a pleasure to meet you. Welcome to STK! We're going to go ahead and get you all seated. Come right this way."

They followed the host to a booth in the back and they were seated.

"You must come here often. That host was overly excited to see you," said Latoya.

"Yea. I'm a longtime customer here."

Moments later, a 50-year-old looking handsome white man with a black suit walked up.

"Taq. Good to see you again," he reached his hand out.

"Mark. Good seeing you, man," said Taq shaking his hand back.

"Latoya, I'm the restaurant manager here. Taq knows me very well. I want to make sure that you all have a wonderful experience with us. If there's ANYTHING. I mean ANYTHING, I can do for you all, please let me know."

"Thank you. You know I will, Mark," said Taq.

Mark then walked away.

"Ok. Seriously, who the hell are you?" Latoya asked again.

"Have you drawn any conclusions yet? I don't want to tell you, I'd rather you use your own judgement based on your observation," said Taq with a grin.

"Ummm. Let's see. It seems like you are pretty successful, that's for sure. Pretty successful at something."

Taq nodded. "Yes, I would have to agree."

"I'm a little afraid to ask, but... what do you do?"

Taq looked at Latoya and smiled. "Whatever it takes."

"Well. I like that answer. Because that's what I do as well. Whatever it takes."

"Welp. It looks like we're going to get along just fine then," said Taq.

29. Stupid Cupid

Dreamville 12:30 a.m.

It was a slow night so, unfortunately, she had to go with the guaranteed money. Edwin. Latoya gave him a half-ass dance because she knew he would pay her either way. He was just happy that she would even talk to him.

"When are you going to stop playing with me Black Vanity," said Edwin looking up at her from his chair.

"What are you talking about? How am I playing with you?"

"I called you the other night, but you didn't answer. And I texted you."

Latoya stopped dancing and turned to him. "Wait a minute. You were that random 678 number that called me last week? I don't answer unsaved numbers. How did you get my number?"

"Farren gave it to me. She said that you wouldn't mind."

"Ugh. I'm going to kill her! What else did she give you! My address?!"

"Yea. I had to beg for that though."

She looked him square in the eye, "Listen Edwin. I want to make this very clear. If you ever show up to my house, I will call the police on you. And I will do whatever I have to do to make sure you go to jail. You don't want that, do you?"

"Damn. It's like that?!"

"Yes! And I'm going to change my number too. UGH!"

Latoya stopped dancing with him and started looking for Farren. Ever since the Booker situation she had kept her distance from Farren. And she really hadn't talked to her at all since then. Just pretty much hi and bye. Latoya knew that Farren was trying to play petty games by giving her number to Edwin. Latoya was ready to curse her out. She went to the dressing room and busted open the doors and saw Farren talking to another chick.

"Well, well, well, look who we have here. My little student has turned into a superstar. She got a song named after her and now she doesn't know how to act. Busting through doors like she owns the place," said Farren.

"Ummm. Farren. What the hell is wrong with you?" Latoya said.

The other chick looked at her "Ooop. I think that's my cue to leave," she left.

Farren looked confused, "What's the problem, what happened!?"

"You gave Edwin my address and phone number and shit! Have you lost your damn mind?!"

"Ohh! Shit. Girl, you scared me. I thought something was seriously wrong," she began to laugh. "I'm sorry. Edwin just really, really likes you. I figured one day you'll give him a chance," Farren shrugged.

"That's not funny. And. No! Never. Stop boosting his head up. It will never happen. Stop trying to be cupid. I already have a man."

"Oh shit. You got a man? Who is he? Lot me guess, it's Lil Fresh, that's why he named that song after you?" asked Farren.

"No. Hell no. You don't know him. Well, we're not official yet but we probably will be soon. His name is Taq."

"Taharq Taylor?!"

"Taharq? No his name is Taq. Who the hell is Taharq? I think you're talking about someone else."

"There's only one Taq. Is he tall and Puerto Rican-looking? Rich guy?"

"Maybe. Why?"

"Ahh shit. You have to be kidding me. Taharq is Taq. Taq is his street name. Everyone calls him Taq but it's short for Taharq. I heard that he was messing with someone new that worked here, I didn't know it was you!"

"Why does that matter?"

"You should delete his number right now. Where's your phone?" Farren reached out for Latoya's phone.

Latoya refused. "No Farren. What's wrong with Taq?"

Farren looked at Latoya like she was crazy. "You must not know who Taq is. Taq is the biggest name in the dope game. Like Big Meech type of big. He's rich as fuck. He's very powerful. But he's very dangerous. You're not built for that type of life. Don't let all of the cars, real estate, and boats fool you. All of his businesses are a cover up. Plus, he's a no good dog just like any other nigga out here. He ain't serious about wifing you girl."

"And how do you know all of this, Farren? Let me guess, you heard it from someone," said Latoya with her hand on her hip.

"I just know, Latoya. Believe me. I suggest you stay away from him. It's ok to know him, just keep your distance," said Farren.

"Thanks for the advice. But I'm a grown-ass woman, and I made a grown-ass decision to talk to Taq. Let me deal with the consequences."

"Ok. Do you. Just remember, you've been warned," said Farren.

Latoya didn't trust Farren anymore, but what Farren explained about Taq being a big time drug dealer in the streets made too much sense. Especially since he didn't reveal exactly what he did when Latoya had asked. Latoya still could not understand how Farren was so against Taq. Especially since the guys that Farren previously had relations with were mostly dope dealers. Dangerous? They were all dangerous.

Probably more dangerous than Taq because they were lower level dope dealers. Latoya was more skeptical about taking Taq serious now, even though she admired him. But there was no way she was going to renege on a free trip out of the country. She still needed a vacation.

30. Baecation

Cartagena, Colombia

"Why are you doing all of this?" They sat on the beach and had the locals feeding them native cuisine. Treating them like royally.

"Doing, what?" Taharq said while eating his fish.

"Doing all of this? Flying me out and shit. I mean. You probably do this with all of your groupies and hoes."

"Which one are you? A ho or a groupie?"

"Ugh! Neither!"

"Ok then. I won't fly a ho or a groupie out. I never did. I never will,"

"So why me then? Why fly me out if I know you got all these girls chasing you?"

"What makes you think that I have hoes chasing me?"

"Come on Taq. You're good looking. You got plenty of money. Nice-ass cars. These hoes all over you. Let's not play dumb. Why me though?"

"You'd be surprised. I know what I'm looking for."

"And that is…"

"I'm not looking for any hoes, I'm looking for a queen."

Latoya rolled her eyes. "Here we go."

"I'm serious. Trust me, I have had my share of hoes and groupies. They were all expensive. They wanted me for my name, my money, and this lifestyle. But see you're different. You'd be a bonus and not a burden. You don't need me, you've got your own and that's what I like about you. I'm looking for someone that's actually worthy of my time. Someone that I can build a dynasty with. Someone that I can trust with my life."

"You think I can be that?" asked Latoya.

"I don't know. Do you think you can be that? Trustworthy? Loyal?"

"For the right man, yes."

"Who's the right man for you?"

"Hmmm. Let me think. Someone that I can trust. Someone that is faithful. Someone that I can build with too. Someone that is about their business."

"Sounds really familiar. Can I put my application in? I think I'd be a good candidate," said Taq.

"What makes you think that you're a good enough candidate?" asked Latoya.

"Because you're interviewing me right now. So, I must be doing something right."

Toya was silent for a second.

"What's wrong? Say something," asked Taq.

"To be completely honest with you. I heard something about you that was very disturbing, and it made me question if I could ever be with you."

"What is that?"

"I heard that you're a drug dealer. Is that true?"

"Ummmm. I'm an entrepreneur."

"You lied to me. You didn't tell me that you were a drug dealer. That's unacceptable."

"I told you I would do whatever it takes. By any means necessary to live my dreams. I have a lot of different businesses."

"Well, I don't appreciate the fact that you lied to me. Plus, I told myself that I would never date a drug dealer a long time ago. And I don't know if I can break that promise. So, I really appreciate all of this hospitality but I don't think we can become anything more than just friends."

Taq was silent. He stared at the ocean and watched the waves splash onto the shore. Then he got up and started walking towards the resort.

"Wait where are you going?!" yelled Latoya.

Taq said nothing and continued walking all the way back until he was back in the suite. Latoya followed him.

"Are you going to speak to me? I'm sorry if I made you mad. Say what's on your mind?"

After about ten minutes of silence, Taq finally spoke.

"I didn't tell you that I was drug dealer because I was afraid that you wouldn't think I was worthy of being your man. I didn't think you would accept me. And I was right."

"Worthy? Me? Ha ha. Hello! I'm a stripper in case you didn't know. There's nothing you should feel like you should hide from me. I keep it real. But I haven't always kept it real. I feel you on the fear of not being accepted because I used to tell lies so that people would like me or so that I could fit in. But I grew out of that though. And, don't get me wrong, I don't knock anyone's hustle. But I just can't date a drug dealer based on an experience with a past relationship that has screwed me up for life. So, it's personal, doesn't have much to do with you."

"Maybe if you knew my life story, then I would be the exception?"

"Tell me your story. Who the hell is Taharq Taylor? We're on vacation and I have nothing but time," said Latoya hopping on the bed and folding her legs Indian style ready to listen.

"Well to start, both of my parents died in a car accident when I was 5-years old. So, I became an orphan. My dad was black and my mom was black and white. So, I was a skinny mixed kid at this all black orphanage. All the girls liked me but the guys hated me because I was different. They bullied me. Every single day I was getting into fights with the other older guys. I stayed with a black eye. That's where I learned how to fight. Nobody wanted to adopt me and I hated the orphanage, so I ran away. I was on the streets at the age of 11. I was homeless. I was starving. For me to survive, I would just steal things and sell them for money."

"OMG. What would you steal?"

"Everything. Anything. Cars, computers, clothes. Anything that seemed reachable, I would get my hands on it. I had so much respect in the streets because I had a lot of money for an 11-year-old kid and I would beat up any and everybody that looked at me wrong. All the kids were afraid of me and they looked up to me. Even older kids that were 16 and 17 looked up to me or respected me. It got to the point where kids, older and younger started working for me. I would tell them to steal. I would show them how. Give them the keys to the game, then have them working for me. They would bring me a percentage of everything that they stole. They were loyal. Guess what our gang was called. You're going to laugh."

"What were y'all called?"

"Nacho Gang. I made it up because we really believed that anything we saw was NOT YOURS and it would eventually be ours. And we were all about our cheese. I had like 10 kids working for me when I was 14."

"So, how did you get in the drug game?"

"Well there was this big drug dealer that we stole from. On accident. We didn't know he was in the drug game. We stole a television from his house. The guy caught one of my kids and asked him who he was working for. He was going to kill him. The kid told him who I was. The guy called me to show up so he wouldn't kill him. He didn't know I was 14. Come to find out, he was Musa, one of the biggest drug dealers in Atlanta. When he met me, he was so impressed that he took me in. It was like he bought my little business. Nacho Gang now had an investor. It was like hitting the lotto.

"So, y'all worked for him?"

"Yes. We worked for Musa, but he adopted me too. He became my father. I was the only one from the Nacho Gang that actually lived with him. We had unlimited resources. I probably was worth half a million dollars at the age of 16."

"Damn..."

"But the real money came from the knowledge that I acquired from Musa. He taught me about business, he taught me about life. He taught me everything, really."

"What was the biggest lesson that he taught you?"

"The law of polarity. Without hot, there is no cold, without darkness, there is no light. Without, up, there is no down. So, I'm aware that life is always about cycles and seasons. You just have to be ready for both sides of the spectrum."

"That's deep."

"He also taught me that if I wanted to last in this drug game, I would have to think smart and not be like every other dealer. I would have to invest and think like a businessman. He told me that I needed multiple streams of income and to own real estate and invest in companies to separate myself from the pack."

"So, where is your father Musa now?"

"He's dead to me."

"He died. How did he die?"

"He's not actually dead. I just don't like talking about him. Let's just say the student became the master. And he'll never be able to accept that. He wanted me to continue to be his servant working under him while he continued profiting off my talents. When I told him that I wanted to branch out and start my own organization, he downplayed it and belittled my ambitions. He said that I would never last. All I wanted was his support. But he denied me. So, I left him behind and started my own organization from scratch. I knew that I was smarter than him. Now, I have more money than him, guaranteed. My organization is thriving. I'm expanding my operations. And he's jealous of my success. My idol became my rival."

"Do y'all ever talk?"

"I haven't spoken with him since I left and I'll probably never speak to him or see him again."

"Why?!"

"Because our egos are too big."

"Do you still love him?"

"I loved him at one point. He was my father and mother. He was my everything. He was like a God to me back then."

"I think y'all should meet. I mean. Maybe he's changed. You ever heard of forgiveness. It's for your sake, not his. Grudges are never good."

"Trust me, he doesn't want to see me. And I for damn sure don't want to see him. Maybe one day we'll meet again. But let's talk about something else, enough about him."

"Ok. What motivates you now? I mean you have pretty much everything you want. What keeps you going?"

"First off, to prove everybody that doubted me and didn't believe in me wrong. Also, when I was hustling to survive, money motivated me. But once I started to expand my mind, I read a book and learned about the Black Wall Street and that sparked a new kind of motivation for me and changed my life forever. Do you know about Tulsa, Oklahoma in 1921?"

"Not exactly."

"Oh shit. Well, let me give you a quick history lesson. See, I never went to school, but I know they didn't teach y'all this. My father taught me this. In Tulsa, Oklahoma, there were striving black communities that existed. Black doctors, black lawyers, black-owned businesses. Black everything, a whole thriving black community similar to the Jews.

But the government and the KKK burnt that shit down because they were hating on us."

"OMG! Are you serious?"

"Yes. That is the shit that motivates me! That's why I named my organization after it BWS, aka Black Wall Street Mafia. This drug dealing shit is only my way out. I'm cleaning up my money as we speak. I own multiple real estate investment proportioo. I have a dry cleaning business. I have a car wash. I got a barbershop. I'm trying to leave this game. But I have to become 100 percent legit, you know."

"You can do it! You're on your way. Shit, I want to stop this dancing one day too. I can't dance forever. I need an exit strategy.

"That's why I need someone like you to help me! To motivate me. To keep me grounded. We're in the same boat. We both have big dreams. We both like to handle our business. I need a ride or die chick! That's not in it for just the money. That's in it for the journey. You're like my second self. You understand what I'm saying?"

"So, you're considering me to be all of this?"

"Toya. I have eyes everywhere. You may not have seen me, but I've been watching you for the longest. I know you are the shit. This Black Vanity character is nothing more than, little ole Latoya Robertson trying to create a better life for herself. There's no other person on planet Earth that I believe can represent me, as well as my organization, better than you can right now."

"Ok. So, what are you waiting on?"

"I'm waiting on you to accept it."

"Accept what?"

"Accept the role of being the first lady of BWS."

"Oh, first lady? I don't know about all that."

"What are you afraid of?" asked Taq.

"I'm not afraid of anything. I just don't know what I'm signing up for. What does it mean?"

"That means I'm the president and you'd be my right-hand woman that's willing to hold me and my organization down."

Latoya was hesitant at first. She said nothing. She thought it was kind of corny but cute at the same time. First lady? She looked into Taq's eyes and saw that he was as serious as a heart attack. His eyes were yearning for some type of commitment from Latoya. Latoya felt pressured. She decided to play along. What did she have to lose? It sounded fun. She had never been the first lady of anything.

"So, what do I have to do to accept this first lady role?"

"Just give me a kiss," he said smiling.

She smiled and gave him a kiss. It was passionate. Real. It was like a signature on a dotted line. One of his hands softly held her neck and one of his hands firmly gripped her butt. For some reason, she had never been this turned on before. They locked eyes. Just to confirm that they were both serious about what was about to happen. Their lips touched again. And again. Then their tongues met for the first time. He kisses her then backs her up against the wall.

She had on a dress, so it was easy to slide off her panties. As soon as they were off. He lifts her dress up, kneels down, and lifts one of her legs up and puts it on his shoulder. He slowly starts to caress her pussy lips with his tongue. It was warm. He definitely knew what he was doing.

Then he starts massaging his fingers on her clit along with his tongue. She put her hand on his head. He then puts her other leg over his shoulder and lifts her up against the wall while on his feet. Then his tongue starts going crazy in her vagina. His tongue did tricks as if it was an acrobat in a circus. He made smacking and slurping sounds. Her toes curled, knees locked, and her body shivered as a rush of euphoria ran through her.

She had an orgasm and he knew it. She had to return the favor. He let her down and immediately unzipped his pants. She could feel his dick. It was as hard as a college engineering class. She pulled his dick out and it was huge. She looked up at him. He smiled and shrugged. She then licked it like her favorite popsicle. She massaged it with her tongue. She kissed it. Then spit on it. Then she put it in her mouth.

She used both hands. One grabbing on his nuts and the other massaging his dick as it went in and out her mouth. Her goal was to please him, just as he pleased her. His moaning turned her on.

"How do you want it?" she said looking up at him.

"Shhhh. Take your dress off and lay down on your back," he said. Latoya listened and got naked.

He got on top of her and their tongues met again. He had taken off everything but his gold chains. His chains rested on her breast and for some reason it turned her on even more. He eased inside of her. Her pussy was so wet that it was like fucking honey. He started thrusting inside of her. She was having orgasm after orgasm. At this point she just wanted him to do the same because she had already been overly satisfied.

They changed positions and she got on all fours. He went inside again, this time, he started hitting her from the back. One hand pulling her hair, the other controlling her waist, he started pounding her. She could feel him in her stomach. It was as if he had touched her soul.

"Taq!" she yelled. "I'm coming!"

He immediately pulled out and she felt him burst all over her butt.

"Woooo. Me too," he said flopping on his back next to her in the bed.

She laid there on her stomach. He got up and went to the bathroom and grabbed a towel. He wiped her off. He laid back next to her. "You good?" he asked.

"Yea. Are you good?" she rebutted.

"Better than ever now that I got you." He smiled.

"Oh really?" she said turning to him on her side and smiling.

"Yep. Honestly though, are you ready for this life? Do you know what you just signed up for?"

"Umm. To be your girl? Well at least I think that's what I signed up for."

"Latoya, I'm not a regular guy. I want to mentally prepare you for this life. I'm a very powerful person. Probably more powerful than you could imagine. So, when people find out about us, they're going to be jealous."

"I mean that's obvious. That's in any relationship."

"No. You don't understand. You're like Meghan Markle. You just walked into royalty. You have a throne now. I'm the King, and I just crowned you as my Queen. Hoes are going to hate you. They are going to try to size you up. They are going to discourage you from being with me. They are going to talk shit about me. They are going to try to sabotage us. You're going to be a target. Hoes and niggas are going to hate on you... But you have to make a promise to me."

"I'm listening. Go ahead."

"Promise me that no matter what, we will stay down for each other. We will ride together and die together. No matter the situation. No matter the storm. We got each other's back."

"I promise, as long as you have my back," she smiled.

"Of course. Pinky promise?" he said holding his pinky out and smiling.

"Yep."

They locked pinkies. Then kissed.

Back to the States, Atlanta, Georgia

Taq and Latoya enjoyed first-class seats to and from Cartagena, Colombia. As soon as the plane's wheels hit the ground and they landed at Hartsfield Jackson Airport, Taq started making recommendations for Latoya, his new first lady of BWS. He was determined to move her in with him as soon as possible.

"Call a moving company. Move your stuff to my address. I'm sending you my address right now."

"Wait. I'm moving in already? I'm going to just break my lease?"

"Fuck that lease. I'll buy the shit. Yes, move in, what are you waiting for, if you're serious then you'll move in."

"Ok. Let me start googling companies then."

The next day, Latoya was relocating. She found a company called Synergy Moving to help her move. It took Synergy Moving a full day to pack all of Latoya's stuff. She didn't realize how much junk she had bought until she had to move. Latoya rode in the truck with the movers as they went down to south Atlanta where the GPS took them. It was a 45-minute ride. Once she finally saw Taharq's place, she realized that he was right. He was not a regular person by far. The estate was so big she could not see the mansion from the front gate. The moving company workers kept looking at Latoya in disbelief, trying to figure out who she really was, and how she had gone from a condo to a multi-million-dollar estate. Latoya was in just as much of a shock as they were. The moving truck pulled up to the gate entry, then they pressed a button.

"Yes," someone answered from the speaker.

"This is Latoya."

The gates slowly opened. They drove in and they finally could see the mansion. Latoya was certain her life had just changed.

They pulled up to the place, there was a chunky black guy outside wearing a plain white T-shirt and khaki pants smoking a blunt. She remembered him from the club when she first met Taq. It smelled like it was some strong weed that he was smoking.

He walked up to the moving truck.

"Latoya?" he asked.

"Yes?"

"I'm Pat. Nice to meet you. I'm the general manager for BWS. I handle all of Taq's affairs. I'm here to help you move in."

"Ok. Nice to meet you. Where is Taq?"

"Taq is out handling business. He'll show up later on. Go ahead and park in the front then y'all can start unloading."

The men parked and started unloading. They began taking her stuff in and she was able to get a good look around the place. She saw a lot of artwork. Pictures of Scarface. The Godfather. The Goodfellas. Big Meech. Malcolm X. And Barack Obama. There were old vintage pictures of Tulsa's Black Wall Street. The living room was huge. Huge chandelier. Marble floors. Fancy-looking couches.

"Follow me. I'll show you where your room is," said Pat.

He took her down a long hallway. Then made a left.

"This is your spot. It's pretty much already decorated. But it's up to you to fix this shit up however you want to."

"Ok. Thanks Pat. This is super nice. Question. How many rooms does this place have?"

"It's like 10."

"How many people stay here?"

"Just you and Taq. I'll occasionally stay here when I have meetings."

"Meetings? With whom?"

"With some of the other leaders. Listen Latoya. You have to understand. This is a huge organization with a lot of moving parts. You're dealing with the leader of a multi-million-dollar organization. The less you know. The better. Believe me. As a matter of fact, no one should even know this address without permission from Taq or myself. No visitors. All you need to know is that I'm responsible for Taq's affairs, if there's anything that you may need I'll be able to help. Things that you don't need to bother Taq about, just let me know. Comprender?"

"Understood."

"Also. There's another person that I'll introduce you to. He's new to the organization. Ay Poison, come meet Black Vanity... I mean the new Mrs. BWS!" Pat yelled.

"Wait. Poison? I think I know him?" The name made her cringe. Latoya was confused.

"How do you know Poison?" Pat turned to her like he was surprised.

"Well, I just know him from work. Through a mutual friend. So, he's part of the organization too? Isn't he dangerous?" Latoya was concerned but was afraid to ask too many questions.

"He just joined us recently. And dangerous? Ummm. When we need him to be. Just know that

Poison is responsible for security for us. You are very safe around him. Trust me."

Poison came from downstairs. "Nice to meet you, again, Latoya."

"Likewise," said Latoya.

Pat's phone started ringing. "Hold on. Taq is calling me. Yes boss. Yes, she's here. Ok. Ok. Will do." He hangs up.

"Taq is here. Come outside with me." Pat walked outside.

Poison grabbed Latoya's wrist and stopped her in her tracks as she started to follow Pat. With a low voice he spoke,

"Remember. That night never happened. Ok?" insisted Poison.

Latoya nodded in agreement and looked down at her wrist waiting for him to let go.

He smirked then released her wrist.

She continued outside, and to her surprise she sees Taq standing beside a pink Lamborghini.

"Toy, I got you a toy," he said.

"You can't be serious! What the fuck! This isn't mine?!"

"Come play with it. Because it's yours." He winked as he stepped aside and pointed for her to get in.

She ran down to him and gave him the biggest hug and kiss. Then he slipped her the keys. The interior was pink and black. It had BV on the head rest. She put the key in the ignition and cranked it up.

"I'm about to take it for a little spin! Baby you gone come with me?!"

"Nah you go ahead. You need to enjoy it by yourself."

She swerved off into the road. The engine felt so strong. It was powerful. It was fast. She felt like she was in a Fast and Furious movie, all she needed was Tyrese and Vin Diesel. Now, she could see why people loved luxury cars. There's no way that she could go back to a regular car after this. She got to the road in front of the property and there was no traffic so she decided to put her foot on the gas. She got up to 100 mph then she slowed down. Scared to do too much, she was on the road for ten minutes then she went back to the property.

"Did you like it?" asked Taq.

"I love it, baby! Thank you so much!" she said giving him another hug as she walked in the house.

"Good. I have one more thing for you. Follow me."

She followed him to his room, which was enormous. His bed was the size of two king beds. He had a 72-inch TV on his wall. He went to the dresser next to his bed. He pulled out a black cloth. Opened it. It was a huge gold necklace laced with diamonds and it read Mrs. BWS. It was so shiny; the diamonds were dancing like Chris Brown in a music video.

"So, the car is a gift, but this is a symbol of my love for you. Now, I love this organization that I built. More than anything. For me to name you the first lady of BWS is a big fucking deal. I dreamed of having a woman represent my shit, but this by far exceeds my dream," said Taq looking at the chain.

"You are just... I don't even know what to say. How much did this cost?" asked Latoya.

"More than you can imagine. Put it on!" Taq held it to Latoya.

Latoya put it on and looked in the mirror.

"That shit look good on you too. But remember, this isn't some shit you can wear out on the regular. Better yet. NEVER wear it out unless you are with me or Poison. People will be hating and shit and they'll try to rob you just because."

"Ok. So, when will I be able to wear it?" She said looking in the mirror.

"Well first, you have to wear it when you're not wearing anything else," he said as he approached her and started to unzip her jeans. After moving all day, Latoya was tired and not really in the mood for sex, but she figured that since Taq had just bought her $200,000 car and moved her into his luxurious mansion that she would have to probably bite the bullet.

Their lips met again viciously like they had missed each other. He ripped off her shirt and bra and they started towards the bed. She assisted him in pulling off her jeans and then her panties. She took off his shirt and unbuckled his pants. She got him naked, got on her knees and went straight to giving him head. He deserved it. She grabbed his dick and licked it like an ice cream cone. Then she made sure her mouth was as wet as can be. Her mouth was so wet her hands started slipping off of his dick. She played with the head using her tongue. He started moaning and that turned her on.

After head, he told her to turn around and to get on all fours on the bed. He comes up from behind her and lifts her waist up until she's doing a handstand. Ass in the air, as she held her balance upside down, and he holds her waist, he starts licking her clit. She was in a twilight zone. She never got her vagina ate upside down before. It took her two minutes to have an orgasm. He then lays her down on her back. And starts fucking the shit out of her like he was mad at her. After ten minutes of him on top, he had an orgasm and he came all over her stomach.

"Don't nut on the chain!" she said trying to move the chain from her stomach.

"Damn! Too late!" he said as he tried to aim somewhere else at the last minute.

"Ahh shit. Well that was smart of us," Latoya said shaking her head.

He laughed. "It's cool. I got some jewelry cleaner that can get it all off. We're going to need it for tonight. So, wash up. Get dressed. Tonight, we're going out to celebrate."

Latoya went to her room to start getting dressed. Her bags weren't even unpacked. She sorted through her luggage to pick out what she was wearing for that night. She decided to put on her black dress with Christian Louboutin heels along with the BWS chain. She looked at herself in the mirror on the bedroom wall. She never looked as good or felt as good as she did tonight. After an hour and thirty minutes of getting dressed and doing her makeup. She walked out of the room. Taq, Pat, and Poison were sitting in the living room dressed up and ready to go.

"You look stunning baby!" said Taq.

"Thank you!"

"And have you met Poison yet?"

"Yes, I've met him," said Latoya.

"Good. Well, he's security for us now. He's here to protect you, ok?"

"Ok."

"Ay Pat take a picture of me and the first lady. We have to let everybody know who the queen of this shit is."

They posed together and took the pic.

"This shit bout to break Instagram, watch," said Taq.

And it did. Before Taq posted that picture and tagged her in it, she had 25K followers on Instagram. Shortly after, she had 32K followers. Apparently, this was a big deal.

31. Idols become Rivals

Taq, Pat, Poison, and Latoya were in the car on the way to a party in the city to celebrate. They were in a Mercedes truck. Taq and Latoya were in the back seat, while Pat and Poison were in the front. Moments after Latoya made her debut on Taq's Instagram page, Latoya got a call from Farren. Latoya ignored the call on purpose. Farren calls again. Latoya ignores it again but this time she texts Farren, "Hey What's up?" just to see what she wanted.

"Girl, what are you doing?!" said Farren.

"What do you mean what am I doing?" she replied.

"This shit with Taq?! All up on Instagram and shit flexing. I told you this nigga was no good. You just never listen huh!?"

"Farren. I don't see why it's such a big deal. Do you and Taq have history or something. Let me know now."

"No, we don't. I'm just trying to protect you. He's a dangerous guy, you could get your heart broken, and I don't want you to get hurt."

"I'm a big girl Farren. I don't need you trying to tell me what to do and what not to do with my love life. Let me develop my own opinion about Taq and not just listen to yours," Latoya then turned off her phone so that she could enjoy the night.

They arrived at the venue and parked right in front in VIP. One thing about Taq, he made sure that he didn't look like a drug dealer. He had on a grey blazer button down with some hard-bottomed shoes.

They all showed up to the club together around 1:30 a.m. They walked right up to the VIP line. When the security guards saw Taq, they moved everybody out of the way as he walked up. Everyone sized Latoya up. Guys and girls.

When they walked in, it was like walking in with a celebrity. The DJ started calling them out.

"Looks like some real money just walked in. BWS is in the building. What's up Taq! Shout out to the first lady of BWS, Black Vanity, I see you."

Once they got in the VIP section. People in other sections started slowly coming and speaking to Taq. Out of respect. He introduced Latoya to every single one of them as Mrs. BWS."

"You're too popular for me," Latoya said.

"Oh really? Is this too much for you?!"

"No. It's fine."

"Tell me what's on your mind? Be honest," asked Taq.

"Just thinking."

"Thinking about what?"

"Thinking about just how successful you are at such a young age. You're 32 and you're wealthy. You should be on the Atlanta Under 40 list. Or maybe even the Forbes Under 40 list."

"Come on, baby. Who wants to put a drug dealer on a prominent list like that? You'd have the Feds all over me then."

"Don't look at it like that. You said that you wanted a way out, right? Then maybe you should try to rebrand yourself, change up your image and promote entrepreneurship in the community. Educate the youth. Talk about the businesses that you have, and maybe you can invest in other people's businesses. The possibilities are endless."

Taq nodded. "I'll think about that. See that's why I need someone like you. To bring me fresh ideas and a new perspective."

Taq's Estate

After partying hard. The club closed and they were walking in the door around 4:30 a.m.

"So, which room am I sleeping in?" said Latoya walking down the hallway.

"Is that even a question?" asked Taq.

"Yes. That's a legitimate question. I have my own room so I'm not sure if I get to sleep with you."

"Yes. You have your own room in case you get tired of me for a night that's all."

"Ok. Just making sure," said Latoya.

They opened Taq's bedroom door. They both froze and stopped dead in their footsteps. What they saw startled them and almost gave them a heart attack.

"What the fuck are you doing here?!" said Taq.

Pat and Poison ran to the room to see what all the commotion was about. Poison pulled his gun out from his waist.

They found Farren lying comfortably on his bed with nothing but red lingerie on.

"Taq you gone tell her the truth?!" asked Farren.

"Red. What are you talking about how did you get in here?!"

"You're in love with me! You know you are! And you just up and find someone to replace me?! And out of all people, Black Vanity? A chick that I molded and taught the game!"

"Replace you?! Farren you just did work for me. We never did anything together?! We never fucked. None of that."

"But you took me out on dates! Did you tell her that?!" said Farren.

"Twice and that's it! And they were for business purposes only! Pat and Poison, please get her out of here!"

"No don't you do this shit to me Taq! You know I was supposed to be Mrs. BWS! You told me you were looking for a queen. You said it!"

Both Pat and Poison came and grabbed Farren.

"Poison don't touch me! We go way back! I'm the one who introduced you to Taq! If it wasn't for me, you would've still been killing for ponnioe. Got your hands off me!" she said struggling as they carried her out.

"What the fuck was that all about?!" Latoya asked.

"It's exactly what it sounded like. She thought she was going to have your spot but she didn't."

"Ok, how does she work for you?" asked Latoya.

"Her and Poison did a job for me recently, that's it."

"Oh my God. It all makes sense now! So, you killed Booker?"

"Absolutely not."

"Why lie to me?! I was there. You orchestrated that whole thing?! You almost had me killed!"

Taq turned to her and looked her square in the eye. "I swear to God on my parents' graves I didn't know who you were at the time. I'm sorry. Farren just insisted that someone join her and she picked you. If it was up to me, she would've done it all alone."

"But why?! Why did you have to kill him?!"

Taq grabbed Latoya by the shoulders held her firmly. "Latoya, listen to me! And I need you to internalize what I'm about to stay. If you're going to be with me and we're going to make this relationship work, you're going to have to understand that we NEVER speak like that around here, ok. Don't ever question my business dealings. Ever! That was a business transaction that went south! That's all! I don't know anything more than that. And you better not speak of that ever again around me or anyone else; do you understand?" said Taq with his towering voice and his eyes piercing directly through Latoya forehead.

"Understood."

Business is Booming

After that crazy first night of Latoya moving in with Taq, everything eventually simmered down. Life was smooth sailing for Latoya. She didn't have to dance anymore. BWS was paying her 10K a month from the business account. Taq paid her that specifically so that she didn't have to dance. He respected the naked hustle, but not for Mrs. BWS. He wanted her to make money in other ways. And she did. Her new found notoriety started paying off. Her club appearance bookings started shooting up now that she had a song named after her and she was the first lady of a mysterious mafia group. People were DMing her left and right to show up and party with them. A thousand here, a thousand there. How can you beat that? Being the first lady of BWS had its benefits. Her brand was growing. Her social media followers were growing. Her bank account was growing. People loved the pink Lamborghini too. It was her trademark.

Club appearances were the easiest money maker for her. She just shows up. Partys. Gets paid then leaves. This night she was at Opium Nightclub. It was a big night with lots of celebrities. She brought the pink Lambo out tonight, of course. Parked it right in the front of the club. It was a super long line. As her and friends walk up to the VIP, in her peripheral, she saw a familiar face. Wanda. She was standing in line by herself. They made eye contact and she walked right past her.

"Wait y'all, before I go in. I see an old friend of mine."

"Old friend?" they asked.

"Yea, old friend. I feel bad just walking by her. Should I bring her with us?"

"Shit. You're one of the hosts. The club is paying you to get in not me," said one of the girls.

"Yea you're right. I'm going to get her."

She walked back to the back of the line. And waved towards Wanda.

"Wanda. Come with me."

"You sure? I don't mind paying," said Wanda surprised.

"Just come. It will take you forever to get in. Just come, I got you."

She got out of line and followed Latoya.

The club was crazy. Latoya could feel that Wanda felt awkward around her and her new friends. But she didn't care. The bottles and sparkles started coming in. Latoya made sure that Wanda drank up and enjoyed herself. Once the liquor started flowing, Wanda started to speak her truth.

"Toy, I just wanted to let you know that I'm sorry for not talking to you after what happened. And I forgive you," said Wanda with a slur.

"No need for apologies, girl. You did nothing wrong."

"Yes, I did. I never gave you the opportunity to explain what happened. I just turned my back on you and sided with Tina," said Wanda.

"It's ok. I apologize for it as well. I moved on from it. I'm stronger from it."

"And I'm sorry for not being a skinny bad bitch like your new friends that are here with you. Y'all are some dime pieces and my fat ass is bringing y'all average down. They probably hate that I'm here. They've been looking at me sideways ever since I joined y'all. If they say something slick I might have to punch one of them in the throat."

"Girl, you are good. These girls ain't my real friends. They are just here for eye candy. And if they say something slick to you, don't worry, I'll punch them in the throat for you."

"That's good to know. That's why I love you! So, I have a question for you, since they aren't your real friends. Can you and I be friends again? Because Tina and I fell out and I'm friendless at this point. I mean who goes to the club by themselves, a lonely bitch like me."

Latoya looked at Wanda. "Anybody that I consider punching someone in the throat for has to be my friend."

Wanda smiled and they both hugged.

Waffle House 4:00 a.m.

Wanda and Latoya met up at the Waffle House after the club. The other girls went their separate ways.

"Girl! Tonight was epic! It felt like the old days! I haven't had this much fun in a long time!" said Wanda.

"Me neither. I'm so happy to see you."

"No, I'm happy to see you! I thought that you would never talk to me again! I thought you were too big for little ole me now!"

"Never that. Question, in the club you mentioned that you were friendless? What happened between you and Tina?" asked Latoya.

"Actually, Tina and I don't speak anymore," said Wanda.

"Why?"

"Well, after she moved out of Marvin's place, Tina and I moved into an apartment together. We just agreed to split rent until she got her own place or found a new man. But it didn't work out at all. At first, everything was ok, but then she started getting upset with me about every little thing. She would talk about how the apartment was dirty and how she wasn't used to dishes staying in the sink. I put up with it as long as I could, until I overheard her on the phone, saying how she felt like she was living in a pig's pen and called me a slob of a roommate. After that, we had an argument and I just packed up my shit and left. Her and I haven't talked since."

"That sounds like Tina. She definitely has OCD," said Latoya.

"Well what about you? You big time now! What do you do?"

"You know what I do Wanda. Don't act stupid."

"A dancer, right?"

"Yep. I WAS a dancer. But I'm not anymore. And if you want to judge me about it and try to give me a sermon on it I don't know if we can go back to being friends."

"Girl. Judge you? If I could've lost about 75 pounds I probably would've been dancing right alongside you!"

Latoya laughed.

"You got you a boo yet?" Wanda continued.

"Well. I do have a new boo. His name is Taq. We've been together for a couple of months now."

"Oh shit! What's the tea on him?!"

"Well. Just know that he's fine as fuck. He loves me. He's willing to do anything for me, and he takes good care of me. That's all that matters," said Latoya eating her food.

"Amen to that. He must be a little hood, huh. Toy, I know you like them hood," said Wanda giving her a shrug.

"You know I do. But other than that, all is well with me. When I was living with Tina, I was at rock bottom, lost, fighting to find my path in this life. Broke as fuck. But things worked out. My path may not be the traditional path that someone would take, but at the end of the day, I'm still proud of me for making something out of nothing."

"And I'm proud of you too. Give me a hug!" said Wanda.

32. Surprise Party

One year later

She had a feeling he would forget. Just like any man. Taq is no different. It was their one-year anniversary and she hadn't heard from Taq all day. She was sitting at home angry, contemplating on what verbiage she should use when she viciously, but respectfully curses him out whenever she sees him. She finally received a text from him at 9:30 p.m.

"What are you doing?"

"I'm home about to go to sleep. Why?" she said.

"Did you eat yet?"

"Nope."

"Good. Put your best dress on in your closet and be outside in 30 minutes."

She almost pissed on herself she was so excited. She hopped up, took a shower and did exactly what he said. However, it took her longer than 30 minutes, more like 45 minutes. She got outside and there was a butler standing outside a Mercedes truck. He appeared to be a chauffeur.

"Toya, pleased to meet you, I'm Devon," he opened the door for her and she hopped in.

"Where are we going?" she said.

"You shall see," Devon winked.

They pulled up to Pappadeaux. Latoya's favorite restaurant. The parking lot was empty. Devon walked her to the front door where she saw Taq waiting.

"You remembered!" she said walking up to him.

"How could I forget?" He gave her a hug and kiss.

"Why is the parking lot empty? This place is always packed." she said looking around.

"Because we bought it out for tonight. This is just for me and you. The waiters are ready to serve us,"

"You are too much! This is crazy!"

"Crazy for you, my love!"

They entered the restaurant. There was a small band playing soft, slow music for them. The host had them seated.

"Taq, I can't believe you did all this for me. You probably did some similar shit with some of your hoes back in the day. Don't lie to me."

"Girl you are the best thing that ever happened to me. Why would I do such a thing. No one else deserves shit like this. You know how much all this shit cost?"

"No. I don't wanna know, because I know this is cutting into our profits. I just want to enjoy it. Pat will probably freak out when he looks at the numbers and finds out what you spent here."

"First off, No he's not. Business is booming. We're making more money than we ever have. Secondly, Pat knows that my woman gets whatever she deserves. Thirdly, I know the owner so we worked out a pretty good deal."

The waiter brought out crab cakes.

"Here's your appetizer. Hope you enjoy," said the waiter.

"Grab your silverware. Let's dig in," said Taq.

She grabbed and unwrapped her silverware. She almost fell out of her chair when she saw what accompanied her fork. The biggest diamond ring that she had ever seen in her life. It shined so bright, it felt like the sun was in her eyes for a second.

A videographer came out and started filming. All the employees gathered around. The band began singing *Let's Get Married* by Jagged Edge. Taq got on one knee.

"Latoya Robertson, you're the best thing that ever happened to me. You are my world, and now I can't imagine living this life without you. Will you marry me?"

Her life flashed before her eyes. There was fear that came across her heart but also, faith. She chose faith.

"Yes!" she said with a tear. He slid the ring on. The videographer filmed them hugging and kissing!

"I'm getting married y'all!" She said to the camera holding up her ring.

A waiter walked up to the table. "Congratulations to you both," the waiter said.

"Thank you!" they said.

"This is a really beautiful moment and I really hate to spoil it but, Taharq Taylor. You are under arrest. You have the right to remain silent. Anything you say can and will be used against you in a court of law. You have the right to an attorney. If you cannot afford an attorney, one will be appointed for you!" The waiter was pointing the gun at Taq and pulled out his badge.

The band stopped abruptly. All of the employees pulled out their badges. And held their guns out. "Hands in the air!" they shouted.

Taq put his hands in the air. He shook his head. "Y'all have fucked up big time," he said.

"What the fuck is going on Taq?!" asked Latoya.

"Calm down. Keep your mouth shut. Everything will be fine. Tell Pat to call my lawyer. I'll call you as soon as I can."

They put him in handcuffs and walked towards the exit.

"Latoya Robertson, can you come with me please?" some officer said.

"Where are y'all taking me?"

"Don't worry. Today, we're taking you home...for now. Come," the officers said as they escorted her into the cop car. It was a silent ride home until she got to Pat.

"Pat?! What the hell is going on?! Why did they arrest him?"

Pat paced back and forth. "Don't worry about it, Toy."

"No! Pat. Don't do that! If you respect me, then you'll let me know the truth. This is my fiancé that we're talking about now. Stop hiding shit from me. You always do that."

"I don't want to tell you because you're going to panic."

"Fuck panicking! I'm panicking because you're not letting me know shit!"

"They are trying to indict him for drug trafficking."

"Ugh! Trafficking?! This can't be life," said Latoya plopping on the couch as if she was about to faint.

"He's going to be fine. They have nothing on him. Plus, we have the best lawyer in the land. He'll be out in no time," said Pat with confidence.

"You sure?"

"Positive. We've been through this before. Everything will be fine."

"Well, how long will he be locked up?"

"Not long. I'll keep you updated on everything. Just lay low for a while. Always let Poison and I know when you come and go. People may try to make a move against us since Taq is locked up. We have to be smart."

33. Touchdown in the DMs

6 months later

It had been six months since Taq had been arrested. Pat and Taq were becoming less and less confident on when they believed Taq would get let out. Latoya was becoming impatient.

She never checked her DMs on Instagram. But since Taq had been locked up she was lonely and bored. She had time on her hands. So, one day, she looked through all of her direct messages. Most of the messages came from guys who looked either thirsty, broke, lame or all of the above. But there was this one direct message from a guy named Manny Davis. It was about a week old. The message read. "Just wanted to let you know that you're gorgeous," Latoya saw the little blue check mark showing that he was verified so she was guessing he had to be a somebody.

She started looking through his pictures and then she realized that he was fine. Very muscular. Six pack, big chest. Big arms. In a lot of pictures, he was working out so he had his shirt off. He had a nice smile. Was dark-skinned with a lot of tattoos. She could tell that he was a football player for someone, but she didn't watch sports so she had no clue of who he really was and who he played for. She would never do this if Taq was out of prison, Taq would kill her. But she decided to respond to his message.

She simply responded "Hey." Then she went and liked two of his pictures just to show him that she was interested. He responded back, and the conversation eventually led to them exchanging phone numbers.

Manny was a football player at the University of Michigan. Apparently, he was a damn good one too. He was an all-star running back that everyone knew. Manny's schedule was super busy but periodically he and Latoya would text each other and facetime each other here and there. Maybe twice a week, for a couple of minutes. Not as much as she spoke with Taq though. She spoke with Taq every day, multiple times a day. She would never talk to Manny one day without speaking to Taq in that same day out of respect.

Two weeks after they exchanged numbers, Manny tells Latoya that he wants to fly her out to Detroit to celebrate the fact that he was entering into the NFL draft. A draft party it was. He said that he was planning on getting drafted in the 2nd round and he wanted all of the people that he cared about there. At first, she was super skeptical, but she was so bored with herself and lonely that she needed to get up and do something. She was still doing club appearances but she had nothing to do during the day except for work out and go shopping. And if she was going to do any dirt, it damn sure was not going to be in Atlanta.

The city is too small so she needed to be as far away as possible. Detroit was perfect.

She arrived at Detroit Metropolitan Airport at approximately 10:00 p.m. He had a driver waiting for her at the curbside with a huge sign that read Latoya Robertson. The driver then took her to the Ritz-Carlton. Manny texted her and told her that he had a suite and that she needed to check in at the front counter. She did just that. She went up to the 27th floor, room 2790. She could hear the music from outside. She knocked twice. He opened the door. He had on an all-white suit along with a big white smile. Latoya was pleased that he was finer in person than he was on Instagram.

"You made it!" he yelled.

"I made it," she responded.

"Here, let me grab your stuff. Come in, everyone here is like family don't be shy." He reached for her bags and motioned her in. There was about five guys there drinking and talking loud.

"Hey y'all. I want to introduce y'all to my friend, Latoya. She came all the way from Atlanta to see me and to celebrate with me!" He carried her stuff into his main room. She could feel the guys' eyes penetrating her as she followed Manny into his room. He closed the door behind them.

"Damn! Finally! You know how long I've been trying to shoot my shot with you to get you to notice me?! For a damn long time!"

"I know. I noticed you, but I was just so busy and tied up with the shit that I had going on that I didn't need to respond. It would've just confused things."

"And you probably got so many DMs unread that you skipped over mine, huh?"

"Ha ha. I do have a lot of DMs. But I didn't skip over yours. I was just in a relationship at the time."

"And you're single now?"

"Ummm. I'm just living life right now. I'd rather not talk about it. Enough about me, let's just talk about you! You're the man of the hour. So, who did you end up getting drafted to?!" asked Latoya.

"You didn't hear about it?! I was drafted by the Buffalo Bills!"

"Congrats! That's great!"

"Yes. It's always been my dream to play in the NFL since I played in pee wee league. And now I'm here! Dreams do come true!"

"They sure do! And you deserve to celebrate."

"You God-damn right I'm about to celebrate. And you're going to celebrate with me! I just became a multi-millionaire! So, get dressed! Now what type of liquor do you drink?! You name, we got it!"

"Do you have Patron?!"

"Say no more. Of course, we do!"

Latoya had the room and bathroom to herself as she got dressed. Afterwards she joined everyone in the common area and took multiple shots with everyone.

Club Ecstasy

Everyone was hyped. VIP was popping. They had multiple VIP sections. Latoya and Manny had their own VIP section and his friends were in the VIP next to them. Random people kept coming and introducing themselves to Manny and congratulating him. Latoya was super drunk. She was finally comfortable.

As the night went on, Latoya and Manny's vibe grew stronger. Around like 1:00 a.m. two new girls joined Latoya and Manny in the booth. They spoke to Manny and gave him a hug. They didn't acknowledge Latoya at all. Manny acknowledged them and then started pouring them drinks. Latoya kept making eye contact with one of the chicks. The girl was sizing Latoya up the whole time. She was also being overzealous, shaking her ass, talking loud, and being super dramatic.

The chicks got up and told Manny that they would be back and left the booth.

Manny turned to Latoya, "You ready to leave?" he asked.

"It's up to you. You're the man of the hour," Latoya shrugged.

"Let's go." Manny grabbed her hand and headed towards the door.

Latoya wasn't planning on having sex with Manny. BUT. SHE. WAS. HORNY. And she hadn't had sex in a long time. Manny was innocent to her. No one would know. And he was a college kid that just graduated and was just looking to have fun.

The Uber dropped Manny and Latoya off at the Ritz. They were both sloppy drunk. His phone was blowing up.

"You have the hotline I see," said Latoya

"Yea. I need to change my number now. It's just everyone sending me congratulations texts and trying to join on the Manny Davis bandwagon now, that's all. I'm about to turn it off."

He slapped Latoya ass as he walked in the room.

"Mmmmm Hmmm. Look at all that cake back there," Manny said.

Latoya turned around and faced Manny while pointing her finger directly in his face, "Hey, what you're not going to do is disrespect me. We can have fun but keep your hands to yourself."

"I'm sorry. I'm just super excited that you actually came to see me. Plus, I get touchy feely when I'm drunk."

"Plus, it's not your birthday so you can't get this cake," said Latoya playfully.

"Girl, every day is my birthday," he grabbed her by the waist and pulled her close.

They locked lips. Feeling on his big arms turned her on. He began to take her dress off. They were both naked, in seconds. His body was amazing. Big chest, six pack, strong shoulders. He looked like he lived in the gym.

He was aggressive, just as a football player would be. He threw her on the bed.

"Get on all fours. It's time to eat some birthday cake."

She listened and shifted.

He grabbed the inside of her waist, slightly lifting her up.

His tongue did a nose dive in her vagina. Then he started doing backflips with his tongue inside her. His saliva and the fluid dripped down her leg like a faucet that hadn't been completely turned off. She loved the feeling.

Then he turned her around and got on top of her. She felt like he shoved a bat in her stomach. He started punishing her vagina. It was painful pleasure because Latoya hadn't had sex in awhile. She screamed but she couldn't help it. He voraciously stroked for about five minutes until they both had an orgasm and fell asleep.

Knock. Knock. Knock. Knock.

She woke up and looked at her phone. It was 8:30 a.m. and someone was banging on the door.

Room service, she thought. Latoya got up and went to the door.

"We're fine. We don't need any room service right now. Please do not disturb," said Latoya in a drowsy voice.

"This ain't no fucking room service! Where is Manny?!" a girl said.

Caught by surprise, Latoya rubbed the morning crust out of her eyes and looked into the peephole. It was the girl from the club that was in their VIP booth. With a little baby boy in her hands.

She went to the bed to wake up Manny. He was snoring. She tapped him on the shoulder.

"Hey. Manny, wake up. There's someone at the door. The chick that was at the club. She's looking for you. She sounds upset."

"Let her in," he mumbled still half sleep.

"What?! So, she can come in here and raise hell? Who is she? Manny is there something you need to tell me now?"

"Just let her in. That's just my baby mama. She ain't gone do shit," he said still not moving.

"That's not the point Manny! I didn't know you had a chick! Nor did I know you had a child. If I would've known that, last night wouldn't have happened."

"Well, you didn't ask. And besides, she's not my girl. We just have a kid together that's all. Let her in."

"No, you let her in," Latoya said folding her arms.

"Ughhhh." He hopped up. Butt naked. He looked around the room for his shorts. He slipped on his shorts and shirt and sluggishly walked to the door.

Latoya gathered her panties and bra, and hurried to the bathroom. Closed the door and locked it. She didn't want any problems. She sat on the floor and held her ear to the door.

Manny opened the hotel door but blocked the entrance with his body. "What do you want, Dominique?!" said Manny.

"So, you can't answer the phone?" said Dominique.

"I was sleeping."

"No, you weren't. You were fucking that stripper bitch. You don't have to lie," said Dominique.

"Why you talking so loud?! Lower your voice."

"No! I want that stripper bitch to hear me. I know she's hiding in the bathroom," said Dominique trying to look around Manny and into the room.

"Why you come in here with all that Dominique? That stripper bitch has a name. Don't be disrespectful. Watch your mouth around my son. And why would you bring him here. You and I are done.

So, there's no reason for you to be here right now. Stay out of my business."

"You're right. I brought your son to remind you that you had one and that you need to act like it. I'm just trying to look out for you. Remember I was here before all of this fame and glory. You want to fuck all these hoes since you got drafted to the NFL like you're untouchable. You're not thinking about the fact that you're a brand now and that you need to be careful. You might mess around and catch an STD or get a chick knocked up. These chicks just want your money, they don't want your stupid ass. I hope your dumb ass wrapped it up."

"Get out of here with that shit before I call security on your ass. I'm a grown-ass man. I can handle my own. I'll come get my son later on. Bye!"

Manny slammed the door.

Latoya heard footsteps to the bathroom.

"She's gone. You can come out now."

Latoya opened the bathroom door.

"I'm sorry about that. She's just jealous. She wants me to be with her so bad. Every single time she sees me with another chick she gets jealous and insecure."

Latoya started looking for all of her belongings around the room.

"I have to go."

"Go. Go where? Your flight doesn't leave until tomorrow."

"Go home. Back to Atlanta. This was a mistake. I made a huge mistake."

"Look. I know I should've told you about my baby mama. I'll admit I should've said something. Let's go get breakfast somewhere. Let me make it up to you."

"No. Stop it. I'm going home. It has nothing to do with you. The only reason I came up here was because I was bored and horny and you were cute. I have a man. He's just locked up. If he found out what I did, he would probably kill me and you."

"Oh shit. Damn. It's like that?"

Latoya looked up at Manny, "Yes. It's like that. And tell your paranoid-ass baby mama that I don't want your money I have my own. Between me and my man, we probably have enough money to be part owner of a NFL team. I'm good."

Latoya bought the next one-way flight back to Atlanta that afternoon. She couldn't wait until the next day.

34. Connect. Calls. Collects.

Hartsfield Jackson Airport

Latoya landed in Atlanta, and as soon as her phone was taken off airplane mode, she had three missed calls from Pat and two missed calls from an unidentified number. And two text messages from Poison and Pat asking for her whereabouts. She was terrified. She just knew that they had somehow found out about Manny. She thought of every excuse in the world. She made up different lies in her head. She was trembling while getting off the plane. She knew she had to respond immediately. So, she called Pat.

"Where the hell were you? We've been blowing your phone up all day!" exclaimed Pat.

"Relax. Sheesh. I was on a flight. Is everything ok?"

"Flight where? You didn't tell anyone you were flying out!"

"Detroit. And since when did I have to tell everyone of my whereabouts?"

"Since you became the first lady of BWS! And either Taq, myself, or Poison need to know your whereabouts. You need protection at all times. You have to treat your position like the first lady of the

United States! You don't know how many haters have their eyes on you and are ready to strike at any time. Especially since Taq is locked up. And what the hell were you doing in Detroit?"

"I got booked for a club appearance up there. Damn! I understand y'all want to protect me but I don't like to live in fear. You don't have to have security up my ass 24/7. That's annoying. I'll talk to Taq about it. But yes, I'll do a better job of communicating next time," Latoya was relieved that they knew nothing about Manny.

"Good, Taq wants you to call him. Long story short, our production has to halt. The whole business is going to have to stop until Taq gets out. We may have to move some money around again so your monthly income is going to have to stop temporarily. All of ours will. We just have to be patient until things settle down. I'm sure you've been saving your money so you should be good for awhile."

"Huh. Saving? To be completely honest. No, I haven't. I was getting so much money, I thought It would never stop. I don't have much saved at all."

"What?! You can't be serious right now! Taq never spoke to you about this?! Rule number one, with BWS, save as much as you can! Because you never know when your income stream will dry up. You have to be ready for the rainy days. It's not how much you make, it's how much you keep! There's a reason why we're called the Black Wall Street Mafia. We're not like any other drug organization, don't let the luxurious lifestyle fool you, we make very wise financial decisions. We've got tons of money stashed away and that's why we can live the way we do."

"I know. I know. He did tell me but it went in one ear and out the other. So, what am I supposed to do now? I'm not going back to stripping. I ain't going back to being broke."

"Come on. By now you know what you have to do Mrs. BWS, whatever it takes. That's our motto and it will never change."

Latoya's phone was ringing. It was Taq.

"Hello," she answered.

"Where were you?" asked Taq.

"I had a club appearance in Detroit, so I flew up there really quick," Latoya lied.

"Ok. You have to let us know where you're at. It can get dangerous since I'm in here."

"I know. I'll keep y'all updated. I'm sorry, it won't happen again. I miss you so much!"

"Baby, remember I said that in order for us to make our relationship last, we have to stick together and hold each other down no matter what?" said Taq.

"Yes, of course."

"Well, I need for you to stick to your word and show me that you were serious. Follow my lead."

"I promised you that I will and I'm sticking to it. But it's tough. I'm trying though. What else do you need from me?"

"I just need you to understand that business is going to have to halt until I can get back in the streets. So that means that money is tight."

"Pat told me. I'm not going back to dancing that's for sure. I haven't danced in over a year!"

"I'd rather you not dance but do whatever you have to do. Innovate, think outside the box, you're a smart girl. Just be the queen that I believe you are and hold down the throne until I get home."

"I got you. Whatever it takes. Any idea on when you're coming home though?"

"I'm not sure how long. I can't tell you the time. But everything is under control. We just have to make sacrifices that's all, to get where we want to be."

"Shit baby! I got you but damn I miss you! I'll stay strong though."

"I'll be out before you know it. And I promise you, that I am not going back to jail, this is it! I've been in this place too many times! I am done!"

"Pinky promise!?"

"Pinky promise!"

Latoya had full faith in Taq. He's the smartest person that she'd ever met. She knew he'd finesse his way out of prison soon. And that's exactly why she was determined to stick by him.

35. Ebony Envy

Latoya made a phone call to Dreamville. Biscuits mom, Rosie, answered. "Hey Rosie! Can you put me on the schedule, I'm coming to work tonight?"

"Black Vanity? Is this you?"

"Yes, it's me."

"Girl, I thought you would never see this place again. What brought you back?"

"You know how things get sometimes. Money gets tight, and you have to go back to the drawing board. Just for a little while."

"I understand. But listen up, between me and you. Be careful, around here," said Rosie almost at a whisper.

"What do you mean Rosie?"

"Just be careful. Jealousy is a strong emotion. Word around town is that you stole Farren's man."

"Are you serious?"

"That's what people are saying. But let's face it, you came here and stole the show, created a name for yourself and became more successful than everybody else. That's the real reason why they're jealous."

"They can be jealous all they want. I'm just coming to get my money and leave anyway. I don't have to speak to anyone."

"If you say so. I'll put you on the schedule," said Rosie.

That was the plan. To get her money and go. She pulled up to Dreamville and was shocked. She saw fliers everywhere with her name and picture saying that she would be returning that night. It made her happy because that meant she would be able to make some money. She had almost forgotten that she was so popular. She got to the dressing room and saw some new faces but most were girls that were there before. It seemed like all the girls couldn't believe she was there. She was famous in their eyes.

Although the hype was real, the night was rough. Latoya felt like it was her first night dancing. She felt uncomfortable being naked since she hadn't danced in over a year. She was timid. She was rusty. She felt people noticing her struggle. She barely got naked, she barely danced, and when she did, the money that was thrown was pennies compared to what she was used to. She hated it. She was ready to leave so that she could go home and cry herself to sleep.

After work, she was getting dressed to head out. Farren, India, and one other girl walked in.

"We haven't seen you at work in awhile. Money must've dried out since Taq been locked up," said Farren.

"Money is never dry. I just came to get extra spending money that's all. You can never have enough money. And I have my own money," said Latoya.

"Really? I taught you everything you know girl. You can't fool me. You bought that pink Lambo with your own money too, huh?" she said.

"That's none of your business. Maybe, maybe not."

"You must have some good cooch for Taq to buy you that shit," said India one of the other girls.

"Watch your mouth. That's my man you talking about. My man can buy me whatever he wants. Y'all just mad cuz he didn't want y'all broke-ass hoes. And he never will."

"Baby girl, don't get your panties all in a bunch, Taq is community dick. You ain't the first one to smash, him and you definitely won't be the last," said India.

"All I know is he ain't going to want to fuck you." said Latoya.

Annoyed by the back and forth, Latoya ended the conversation and began walking to her car. She was right up to it. Suddenly she heard footsteps, then she felt a sharp pain upside her head. She went flying to the ground. "Talk slick now bitch!" said Farren. She felt multiple kicks and punches as she fell to the ground. Blows to her head and her ribs mostly. She had a flashback, back to that one time she got jumped in the bathroom when she was in grade school.

"I'm about to stab this bitch!" One of the girls pulled a knife out of purse and tried to stab her, but Latoya saw it and caught her arm midway, holding it with all her might.

Skiiiiirrrrrtttttttt! The screeching sound of tires scrubbing the ground of the graveled parking lot interrupted the scuffle. The smell of rubber burned from the tires of a car that swerve up so close that Latoya thought she was going to be ran over. She couldn't see but it startled the girls. The car door swings open.

"Back the fuck up, Farren. Get off her!" yells Poison as he jumps out the car with a pistol pointed at the girls.

The girls all put their hands up and backed up.

"Oh shit. So, you gone shoot me now, Poison? After all of what we've been through. You took my 25K and gave it to her, now you want to save her?"

"That's the first lady of BWS. You know Taq is going to fuck you up once he hears about this," said Poison.

"Taq isn't going to do shit from behind bars until his name is clean. Plus, Taq knows who the real queen is. I taught this bitch everything that she knows. She's just a fake, wanna be me."

"Get in your car, Toy. I'm going to follow you to make sure you get home safe," said Poison with his gun and eyes still pointed at the girls.

"And Latoya, this ain't over. Next time Poison won't be here to save you. I'll see you again. Your face is dead in these streets," said Farren.

Latoya managed to get up and head to her car. She closed the door. The girls looked at her in anger, upset that they didn't get her like they wanted too.

36. Kiss of Death

Taq's Estate

Latoya was crying in the bathroom and looking in the mirror. She had a cut on her eyebrow and it was swollen. Poison came in with a rag, some ice, and some peroxide.

"Stop crying. Everything will be alright," Poison said.

"How did you know I was there?"

"It's not hard to find you."

"Damn. You just be following me around without me knowing. That's borderline stalking. I don't know how I feel about that."

"My job is to protect you, Toy. No matter what. I would do whatever it takes."

"Well sometimes I need my space. I'm a grown woman, I can hold my own."

"Just like tonight, right? When Farren and her crew almost sliced you up and kicked your face in?"

"Shut up. Put this peroxide on my eye," Latoya motioned him over.

Poison came close and used a Q-tip to put the peroxide on the cut above her eye. It burned slightly. All of a sudden, he grabbed her face with both hands and kissed her on the lips. She pushed him off immediately.

"What the fuck is wrong with you?! Have you lost your mind?!" said Latoya wiping her mouth.

"I'm sorry! My bad! I got carried away!" said Poison, embarrassed.

"Are you trying to die?!"

"Listen Toy! I'm sorry! I have a confession. Since I first laid eyes on you, when Farren introduced me to you that one time at Dreamville, I'd been obsessed with you. I've been wanting to do that for the longest. I've been in love with you."

"So what? You know better! Why in the hell would you disrespect Taq like that?!"

"And I would ask you the same question about your dick trip to Detroit. Why would you disrespect Taq like that?"

Latoya was shocked. "What are you talking about?"

"Come on Latoya. Don't play dumb. Remember, I am your guardian. I get paid to protect you and know where you are at all times. I know everything. I know what happened between you and Manny Davis."

"Are you trying to blackmail me?"

"Why would I do that? I'll admit that I was jealous. But, I respect you as a woman. You made the decision. Only I know, Pat knows nothing. If Pat knew he would definitely tell Taq. He has more loyalty to Taq then he does to you."

"Ok. I understand that. And I appreciate you keeping that to yourself. So, is that why you tried to kiss me? Because I cheated on Taq?"

"That's the only reason why I tried to kiss you. I could see that you were lonely and you needed someone. I could sense you hurting inside. Because, in all honesty, I'm the opposite to Pat. I have more loyalty to you then I do Taq. Plus, who knows when he will ever get out of prison. He's could get 20 – life. I respect Taq. I love Taq. That's my boss, I'd kill for him. I have killed for him. But I'd die for you. I'm in love with you Latoya."

Latoya put her hand on Poison's shoulder and looked him in the eye. "Poison, I appreciate everything you have done for me. I love you as a friend, however we cannot be lovers. I am in love with Taq. I love my life, and I know you love your life as well. How about we forget this ever happened. You keep your little secret about my trip to Detroit and I'll keep our little baby kiss to myself. I won't tell Taq. Plus, I'll find you a woman 10-times better than me. Deal?"

He smiled. "Deal, only if you give me a kiss back,"

"Ugh," said Latoya smacking her teeth. She grabbed Poison's face and gave him a peck on the lips. "Happy now?" she said

Poison smiled.

37. Favor for a Felon

Taq's Estate

Latoya was chilling on the couch watching TV when she got a call from Grandma Betsy. She hadn't talked to her in a while. She hoped that Grandma Betsy had not found out about her dancing career.

"Hey Grandma! I haven't heard from you in a minute. What's up?"

"Hey Latoya. All is well. I'm sure you've heard the news."

"What news?"

"Well if you'd answer your phone, you would know."

"I answer my phone for everyone but... oh," she said.

"Yea, Oh is right. Your mother, has been calling for years from prison and you haven't answered."

"Grandma, there's nothing for us to talk about."

"There's plenty of things for you to talk about. She's your mom. She's your blood. Sometimes you have to forgive, just like Christ forgave us for our sins."

"I understand all that Grandma, next time I'll answer."

"There won't be a next time, because she's getting out of prison tomorrow and I want her to come live with you."

Latoya was just about to take a sip of water then she spat it right out in shock.

"Grandma, you know that can't happen. I haven't talked to my mother in years. And there's no way that I can look her in her eyes after what happened with Leah."

"That's exactly why I think it's a good idea. Let me tell you a little secret. Do you know why I've invested so much time in raising you?"

"Because you love me?"

"Yes, but also because I failed miserably at raising your mother. I let the streets raise your mother why I chased your grandad around town trying to get him to commit to me. I hated your granddad so much for leaving me for another woman. So, I took my frustration out on our child. Your mother, Martha. Just because she was the only thing that reminded me of him. I neglected her and she turned to the streets. And she knew it."

"Wow, Granny. Everything makes so much sense now. And that's why you invested so much in me. But what doesn't make sense is the fact that you want her to stay with me."

"I want her to stay with you because your mother and I have resolved our tension. She forgave me. Now it's you and your mother's turn to resolve this tension. Plus, she specifically asked me to ask you if she could stay with you. She still loves you and she says that she's proud of you. It would mean the world to me if you gave her a chance. Just a place to stay until she gets on her feet."

Latoya sighed.

Latoya arranged a driver to go pick her mother up. She waited anxiously for her at home. She wondered how awkward the interaction would be. She paced around the house, knowing the woman that she once hated would soon be in her presence for the first time in over 10 years. Then, the front gate alarm rang. She was there.

Latoya stood on the front steps watching the car drive through the estate and down the swervy, long, narrow roadway approaching the mansion. Her heart pumped, she didn't know what to expect.

The car stopped. Latoya approached the car. Martha got out of the car with an envelope and tote bag. She reminded Latoya of an older version of herself. But skinnier. Martha was still pretty at the age of 48. She had healthy hair down to her shoulders. And a nice coke bottle shape. She had on shades. She looked at Latoya and smiled.

"Come give your mama a hug, little girl, don't be like that!" said Martha.

Latoya smiled and approached her.

They hugged each other hard.

"Baby girl, I missed you. And I want to thank you for letting me stay here with you."

"Mama. I missed you too. You look amazing by the way."

"Well you know where you get your good looks from?" she said jokingly.

"I sure do. Come on in," said Latoya.

"Latoya. Baby, this is beautiful! I didn't know you were living like this!" she said.

"Thanks, Ma. I wish I could claim it and say that it's all mine. But it's not. It's all Taq's he bought this. I didn't."

"So, who is Taq? Where is he?"

"That's my fiancé. Honestly, he's where you just came from. He'll be home soon, though. Hopefully."

"Is that Taq?" Martha said pointing at a large picture of him on the wall.

"Yep. That's him."

Martha was baffled. "Oh my God. That man reminds me so much of your father. No wonder you love him. I mean everything about him screams your father. Tall, handsome, rich. As a matter of fact, all of this is what your father and I dreamed of."

"What did y'all dream of?"

"Well. I don't know what Taq does, but your dad was a big time dope dealer. His name was

Sherman Robertson but everybody called him "Shake." He was flashy, charming, and ambitious. I was just the prettiest girl in the neighborhood. Everybody wanted me but I wanted your father. We had plans to get married together. To live in a huge mansion like this. But of course, it didn't work out that way. The federal government had been following him for the longest and then they eventually did a huge drug bust and took him down for cocaine, homicides, and a whole bunch of other shit they said he had done. He got life in prison. I was never the same."

"Wow. I never knew that story, Martha. Thank you for sharing."

"Of course, baby. There's a lot of things that I never told you when you was younger. Look, I have had a hard life. For the longest time I hated my mom, Betsy. I was in the streets at a young age, so once I got on drugs, I started treating her like shit. She didn't want me around at all. And she made it clear. So, I didn't come around."

"I know. Grandma Betsy told me. She knows she was in the wrong. But do you forgive Grandma Betsy? That's the only way that you'll be free from these mental chains."

"I forgive her. I know she did her best... that's all I could really ask for. What about you. I know that you still feel some type of way about me since what happen with Leah. All I can say is that I have felt a pain so deep that it has been eating at my soul ever since that night. I know you are hurting. Imagine your hurt times 100. I ask that you find it in your heart to forgive me for my wrong."

A tear traveled down Latoya's face. "I still love you, Mama. I forgave you a long time ago."

They hugged.

"Now that you're here. Feel free to make yourself at home. I want the best for you, Mama. As long as you're looking for jobs and looking to make yourself better, you will always have a place to stay here. We have plenty of space. Let me show you your room."

38. Side Peace

LA Fitness

Latoya has to keep her body tight. It's a part of her brand to keep a nice figure. She was working out at the LA Fitness in Buckhead. All she needs is her headphones and then she gets in her zone. She was on the treadmill. Getting it in. She finished her run. Then she went to the water fountain. Someone taps her on the shoulder. Ugh. She hates to be bothered while she's working out. She figured it was probably some thirsty guy trying to holler. She turned around.

"Yes?" She said turning around taking one of her headphones out of her ear.

She found herself face-to-face with a 6'2" brown-skinned man, clean cut, well-built. Six pack. Nice chest. Nice arms.

"I'm sorry if I startled you. How are you?"

He had some amazing teeth.

"I'm good. Can I help you?"

"Since you came in the gym, I'd been contemplating on if I should approach you or not. But I finally got the courage to do so. I'm Samuel... Samuel Patrick," he held his hand out.

She looked down at it for a second. Then shook it.

"Nice to meet you, Samuel. Latoya."

"Now, I'll be 100% honest with you. I don't have any game. And I'm sure you probably think its awkward to try to hook up with someone in the gym. But, I just had to come and at least introduce myself to you and let you know that I think you are the best looking woman that I've seen in my human existence."

He was fine. But corny. "Well, thanks. I look a mess. My hair is a mess, and I'm all sweaty and stinky, so I sure as hell don't feel like it."

"Well check this. I'd love to connect with you and maybe take you out sometime. Maybe for coffee or tea? How does that sound?"

"Ummm. That sounds ok, I guess." She grabbed his phone and gave him her number.

"Got it. Well, I'm not going to hold you for any longer. I'll let you finish your workout. I'm looking forward to connecting with you!"

"Me too."

Mbar Atlanta

"Wanda, have you ever been in a love so deep that you feel like you're borderline insane?"

"Of course. Why do you ask?"

"That's how I feel right now. I've been holding Taq down. He's been locked up for almost a year now. I have no idea when he's going to get out. And now

I'm here waiting and hoping that he gets out soon and we'll live happily ever after."

"Have you spoken to him?"

"Yes. We write each other. We talk on the phone. All that."

"I mean every girl has her tipping point. And every girl needs some occasional dick, if you know what I mean," said Wanda.

"A part of me wants to hold him down. I mean he really could get out soon, but another part of me wants to believe that I'm stupid for staying."

"Just go with your gut. I say there's nothing wrong with dating around to see what is out there. He can't do shit for you behind bars, I don't care how much money he has," says Wanda shrugging.

"You're right. It will be impossible to replace Taq though. Let's be honest."

"Don't look to replace him. Just look to find someone that will be right for you. Maybe you don't need a drug dealer. Maybe you need someone totally legit. Just for peace of mind," said Wanda.

"Well, there is this guy that I met recently. He's an attorney. He's been hitting me up like crazy to go out with him. I met him at LA Fitness.

"See I knew it! There's your answer. Maybe it's time for a change, Toy. This might be God trying to tell you something. How does he look? He's fine ain't he?" asked Wanda.

"Oh, he's fine," said Latoya.

"If he's fine, then stop wasting time. Because I'll find him and make him mine," said Wanda.

They laughed.

Piedmont Park Picnic

Samuel had been trying to take Latoya out for the longest, so she finally decided to give him a chance. She knew this was going to be something different. He invited her to Piedmont Park to have a picnic. He brought all types of food. Sandwiches, mac and cheese, BBQ chicken. It was as if it was a picnic for five people.

"You brought a lot of food!" Latoya said.

"I wanted to make sure we had options, go ahead and eat up," said Samuel. "Soo what type of work do you do? I never asked you this before."

"Ummmm. I'm into real estate."

"Oh, a real estate investor, or are you an agent?"

"I'm in real estate. Let's just keep it at that."

"Discreet about your business. I respect that."

"Yep. I didn't ask you what type of attorney you were did I?"

"I guess not. And I won't disclose if I don't have to."

"Good. Do you like it?"

"Yep. I enjoy it. It pays the bills. No complaints on my end. So, tell me about your last relationship."

"Oh wow. Past relationship? Um. It was fine."

"Fine? If it was fine why aren't y'all together."

"Long distance. He was just. Far. And I needed that physical intimacy in my life."

"Yoa. Long distance is tough. But judging hy the ring on your finger, he must've really loved you. Long distance or not."

Latoya looked at the ring, "Oh yea. He was a little gaudy when it comes to taste. How about you? What does your past relationship look like."

"Ummmm. Well my ex fiancée and I broke up because she just didn't appreciate me. She said I worked too much and that I didn't give her enough attention."

"Really?!"

"Yes really. See the problem with her was that she didn't want to work. Which was fine with me because I made enough money for the both of us. But all she would do is spend all my money, then complain about me not being around. This was when I was fresh in my career field, so I worked long hours. So, she left me."

"I bet she regrets it now."

"Regret? Oh, she hates her decision. To this day she still tries to get back with me. At the time I was devastated. I thought I couldn't live with myself.

But that was one of the best things that ever happened to me. I dodged a bullet."

"I see."

"And now I'm just waiting for someone that I can build something great with. Something everlasting that isn't fake. Someone that understands me. Someone that understands what sacrifice is."

"And you're looking for that in me? Already?"

"Not necessarily looking. Just waiting for God to show me. Maybe it's you, maybe it's not. Only time will tell."

"Ok. Yea I definitely think we should take everything slow. I'm not trying to rush into anything yet."

"I respect that," said Samuel.

Samuel's Family Get-Together

Although Latoya said she wanted to take things slow, a couple weeks had passed and Samuel and Latoya started hanging out. A lot. To the point where he wanted to introduce her to his family at a small get-together. She's socially awkward when it comes to gatherings like this. Samuel introduced her to his mother.

"Mom, this is my friend Latoya. Latoya, this is my mom, Evelyn."

"Oh, Latoya! You are so beautiful! How did you end up with my son?!" she said jokingly.

"I know. She's a super lucky girl, isn't she?" says Samuel.

"No, but seriously. My son is a great man! You all are a perfect couple. I'm patiently waiting for him to find a good heavenly girl like yourself to settle down with."

"Well she's not my girlfriend officially, yet. I'm working on it."

"Well, you're not working hard enough," she mentioned.

"Ok, Mom. Let me go introduce her to Everett."

"Ok. Yes, Everett, he is a surgeon at Northside Hospital. We have a super successful family as you can see. Nothing but the best."

He took her over to meet his cousin, Everett. He stood in the corner with glasses. He looked very distinguished.

"Everett, this is my friend, Latoya. Latoya, this is Everett."

"Nice to meet you, Latoya. Wait, you look very familiar. Where have I seen your face?"

"Ummm. Not sure. I know a lot of people, and I'm out and about."

"No, I've definitely seen your face before. What line of business are you in?"

"I'm just in real estate."

"Oh. Ok. Maybe I've just seen you out and about somewhere."

"Maybe so," said Latoya.

During the awkward silence. Someone's phone began to ring. Everyone checked their phones. It appeared to be Latoya's. She looked at her phone and saw that it was a call from Pat. She ignored it.

They continued small talk and Latoya checked her phone again and saw a text from Pat.

"Good News! Taq is coming home! Call me ASAP!"

Immediately Latoya turned to Samuel. "I have to go."

"But, honey, we just got here."

"I have to leave right now!" she said in a stern voice.

"Ok. Well, I'll walk you to your car, hold on," Samuel said.

"Nice to meet you," Latoya said while walking away and towards her car. Samuel followed.

"What's the problem?! Is everything ok? Talk to me Latoya!"

Latoya got to her car and opened the door. "Nothing's wrong, Samuel. You're an amazing guy and all, but I can't be with you. I need some space."

"Is there someone else that's in the picture that you want to tell me about?" asked Samuel.

"Yes. My ex. So, I suggest you don't contact me anymore. At all. You have a beautiful family, by the way. Goodbye, Samuel."

Latoya closed her car door and drove off.

39. Too Legit to Quit

Taq had one of the most successful attorneys in Atlanta. His attorney managed to find a discrepancy in Taq's criminal case, which allowed Taq to be released early. He would be home in a month.

The anticipation for Taq's release was unbearable. Atlanta rappers shouted him out and spoke about his return in songs. Promoters had welcome-home parties in his honor, even though he wasn't even out yet.

Although the city was excited, the stress had been mounting for Latoya. It was days before Taq was coming home from prison and she, Patrick, and Poison where planning a coming home party for him. From the guestlist, to the decorations, to the food, to the liquor, to the valet; everything was stressing her out. It was Pat who came up with the idea, and she loved it, thinking that her, Pat, and Poison would put it on together. Until she found out that she was going to be planning the whole thing, by herself. She wasn't going to do anything subpar, and she knew that Taq wouldn't want anything below standards that had his name on it. And that's where Latoya's frustration came from.

She tried to delegate but that failed miserably. All Pat did was came up with a list of people who he said MUST BE INVITED. A list that kept growing and growing as the date got closer because Pat would forget to add certain names. Latoya tried to get Poison to help but that was an epic fail. Poison's lack of accountability made Latoya so mad that she cursed him out and told him that he was only good for killing people. Although he didn't take it personal, she apologized afterwards.

She was also worried about Martha. She didn't know what Taq would think about Martha living in their home. She hadn't necessarily told Taq that Martha was going to be living there. She told him that she was getting out of prison and that was it. She just moved Martha in since the estate was so big. What if he doesn't like her? What if Martha doesn't like him? What if Taq kicks both of them out. Her mind wondered. Plus, Martha was still jobless, it had been two months.

Taq's Estate

Tonight was the night. The house was full of people. Not just any people, wealthy people: celebrities, politicians, doctors, executives, athletes. Of course, there were drug dealers there, but they didn't dress like it, they were suit and tie sharp. They blended in well. People even flew in from out of town. Bentleys, McLarens, Rolls Royce, any high-end car you can think of filled the lot.

The house was full and Taq was on his way. He arrived in style. He pulled up in a black Bentley truck right up to the front entrance of the mansion. He got out of the passenger seat with an all-black tailored suit on. Black was his favorite color. He had a huge smile on his face. Latoya had it set up for Taq to get picked up from the prison then taken to a high-end clothing store to put on his custom-made suit. Once Taq arrived at the party, Latoya greeted him with a long kiss and hug, then they walked into the party together. Once he made his entrance, everyone's head turned and they started cheering. Pat got the microphone and gave a quick introduction.

"I hope everyone is having a great time! I want to thank everyone for coming out, on behalf of Black Wall Street Inc. The man of the hour has finally arrived. We missed him so much that we threw him a party to let him know how much we appreciate him. I must say, I love this guy with all my heart, and if it wasn't for him, I don't know where I would be. So, without further waiting, introducing my boss, my friend, my mentor—even though I'm five-years older than him—and the leader of Black Wall Street Inc, Taq Taylor!"

Everyone applauded and cheered.

Taq took the mic from Pat. "Wow. Thank you, Pat. That means a lot to me. Great intro. First of all. I want to thank every single one of you for coming out! Y'all are my closest friends and I have no idea what I would do without you. You know, let's face it, jail time is no fun for anyone. But sometimes you just have to make the most of every situation. Good and bad. I want to give a special, special, special shout out to my fiancée, Latoya aka Mrs. Black Wall Street. She's been holding me down since I got locked up. When I tell you that she is the best thing that ever happened to me, I am not kidding. Without her, I'm nothing. I love you baby. Thank you for sticking by my side. Also, to Pat and Poison. Thank you for putting this event together and for many, many, more things that you do for me. I owe you all my life. With that being said, let's keep this party going!"

Everyone bombarded Taq with hugs and handshakes.

After five minutes of greeting everyone, Latoya tapped Taq's shoulder. "I'm going to introduce you to my mom, Martha, really quick. She's here too. I want you to meet her."

"Of course, where is she," said Taq.

"Hold on. Let me go find her. I'll be back," Latoya broke off from Taq.

While looking around, Latoya see's the back of Poison's head. She thought maybe he had seen Martha. He's speaking to a man and woman. She taps on him; he and the couple turn around.

"What's up, Latoya," asked Poison.

"Have you seen my ma..." she stopped mid-sentence. She stared at the man that Poison was talking to in disbelief.

"Have I seen your mama, Martha? No, I haven't. But, let me introduce you to two of our fine guest. Latoya, this is Marvin Maples and his date Vicky."

Marvin held his hand out. "Nice to meet you...Latoya," he said with a smile.

Latoya looked at his hand. Denying the handshake.

"Is there a problem?" Poison said looking confused.

"Oh no. I ummmm, just came from the bathroom and I didn't wash my hands that's all. Um. How did you find out about the party and how do you know Taq? I'm the one that sent the invites and I don't remember seeing your name?"

Marvin giggled, "Oh Taq, we met a while ago. He's so successful now he probably doesn't even remember me. I just came to show my support that's all."

"Good. Now that you've done so. You can leave the premises," said Latoya pointing towards the door.

"Excuse me?" said Vicky.

"You heard me. I did not stutter. I said that you both can leave the premises. Poison, please escort Mr. Maples and his date out immediately.

"Was that an order from Taq?" asked Poison.

"No, that's an order from me, speaking on his behalf," said Latoya.

Poison looked towards Marvin.

Marvin shrugged. "It's ok. She's right. We just wanted to stop by. We didn't have plans to stay too long anyway. Mr. Poison, thank you for the hospitality, I'll be in touch. Come on, baby, let's go," he said. As they made their way to the exit.

Poison looked at Latoya. "What the hell is your problem?"

"Nothing. They weren't on the guest list that I sent out. Mind your business, Poison."

"I am minding my business. Those were my guest that I personally invited. He's a very powerful business man and you just disrespected the shit out of him. Do you know him?"

"Nope. I don't know him," said Latoya.

"Come on. Latoya don't lie to me. How do you know him? It seems like y'all have history. Do you have something going on behind closed doors with him too? Something that Taq doesn't know about? You got another secret you want to let me in on? You know I can keep secrets. I got your back."

"I know of him, that's all. Marvin used to date a friend of mine. He's just a snake. An old low down dirty snake in the grass. I know he's cheating on that dumb bitch Vicky. Poor girl. Ugh! Everyone that is here should have been on that guest list. Because if I would've saw it I would've crossed his name out with red ink."

"He's just a successful businessman that came to network. Just like everyone else. And don't let your emotions get entangled with possible business partners. Keep them separate. Now let me go escort our guests out properly," said Poison before walking off to catch Marvin and Vicky.

Latoya then hears an obnoxious, but familiar laugh over all of the noise and wonders where it came from. She hears her mother's voice and then she turns and sees her and her so called boyfriend, Eddie, laughing very hard by the bar. Eddie was about 50-years old but he dressed like he was in a time machine. He had on a big chain and a vintage, Michael Vick Falcons jersey on with saggy faded FUBU pants. He stood out like a sore thumb. Martha's mouth was wide open with a cup in her hand.

Latoya was embarrassed. So, she approaches her mother.

"Mom, you're kind of loud over here, is everything ok?"

Martha looked at her. "Oh Latoya, did you meet my new boyfriend, Eddie! Eddie this is my daughter, Latoya."

"Oh! Yeaa! Nice to meet you, Latoya. Your mama been telling me all about you. I heard you got it goin ooonn. I'm just trying to be your future stepdaddy," Eddie slurred his words and giggled with Martha as they tickled each other.

Latoya looked at Martha. "Is Mr. Eddie helping you find a job? Because you managed to find a new boyfriend every week but you can't manage to find a job. You've been living with me for two months now. All you do is sit around the house all damn day, but when you do leave you just bring home a boyfriend."

"Latoya, don't start that shit today. I'm looking for a job, ok. I'll find one when I find one damnit. Don't try to talk to me like I'm your child. I'm your mother. Don't forget that. I raised you."

"No, Grandma Betsy raised me. You just used to get drunk and high and pass your pussy out to old broke down raggedy negros like this one. And that's why Leah is dead now."

Martha reached back and slapped Latoya. The slap sounded off through the whole party.

Everyone's head turned towards them. "Now listen here! You watch your damn mouth! I deserve some respect!"

Latoya grabbed her face. She points towards the entrance. "Get out of my house. Both of you!"

"You don't have to tell me twice. I'm out of here. Come on Eddie."

They both stormed towards the front entrance.

Taq came up to Latoya.

"What was that all about?" he asked.

"She has to go. I'm through with her. They don't belong here."

"Why not? That's your mother?"

"She's just here embarrassing me. I was about to introduce her to you and ask if she could stay here with us, but she's just a mess and I know you wouldn't tolerate that type of behavior around you."

"Wait what? Of course, she can stay here. She seemed fine to me. She's just having a good time. I saw the whole interaction Latoya. Don't ever talk disrespectful to your mom like that. Do you know what I'd do just to have the opportunity to tell my mother I love her? I'd do anything to have my parents back. Your family is all you got. That's your blood. Your family isn't perfect and neither are you. Go apologize. Call, find her right now and apologize."

"Ok. I will. Just give me a second to cool off."

"No. Go now!" Taq pointed their way.

Latoya headed towards the entrance looking for her mother. Her mother had already left the party.

The day after his homecoming party, Taq scheduled a meeting with Pat, Latoya, and Poison. Latoya was afraid that Taq had somehow found out about her actions while he was locked up. They all gathered in the back conference room. Taq sat at the front of the desk while everyone sat around.

"Man, that party was crazy last night. I had a ball! You all did a wonderful job. And I want to thank you all for being there for me when I couldn't be there for y'all. It really means a lot to me."

They all nodded. "I'm just happy to have you back home. You don't belong in that cage," said Pat.

Taq continued. "You're right, Pat. That cage is like hell. But during my time locked up, I met some amazing people. Did a lot of reading, and most of all, I did a lot of reflecting on my life in general. I must say that I am not the same person that I was when I went in. With that being said, I have a huge announcement to make. After many talks with Latoya and doing some soul searching, I've decided to leave the drug business. For good."

"You're fucking with us, right?" said Pat fixing himself in his seat.

"I'm dead serious," said Taq.

Latoya had a sigh of relief, "I'm soo proud of you baby. This is the best news I have heard since forever!"

"So, what are we going to do for money?" asked Pat.

"We're still the Black Wall Street Inc. Is *whatever it takes* not our motto? We'll figure it out. We still have millions of dollars to invest in whatever businesses we want. The possibilities are endless. Car washes, barbershops, restaurants, real estate, car dealerships, the stock market. We can buy up the whole hood. We can invest in our communities. We have wealthy friends and friends in high place. We just have to think strategically and work hard."

"How long is all that going to take to make a profit? Look boss, I understand you are a changed man and you had a revelation and all but how are we just going to stop cold turkey? You can't just quit the drug game cold turkey. There's huge repercussions to that! You put food on a lot of people's plates, and money in a lot of people's pockets, including mine. This is going to send shockwaves through the whole industry. People are going to be upset. Somebody like Musa may look at this move as a surrender which is a sign of weakness, people are going to come after us," said Pat.

"Pat, it may take some time for us to turn a profit and some adjusting but it will all be worth it in the end. That's what sacrifice is all about. I have ruined lots of families and I left kids fatherless, and mothers crying over their dead son's bodies. Drugs are simply bad business. It's time for a change. I'm going legit. Plus, I've already planned to increase our budget with security. I have full faith in Poison protecting us while we make the transformation. If we have to go to war, we can go to war with whomever. Do you think you can handle that, Poison?"

"Of course, boss. I got your back," said Poison in agreement.

Pat responded. "Ok, boss, how about this? Why can't you start a business now, stay in the dope game until the business takes off, then slowly transition out?"

"I'm out for good, Pat. No more turning back. I will not sell an ounce of any type of drug for the rest of my life. This is not up for debate, it's final."

"Excuse me, I need some fresh air," Pat gets up and storms out of the room.

"He'll be fine. He'll adjust. He has no choice but to. Poison, I need you to hire some more street soldiers to protect us while we make this change with our business. Stay ready for war at all times so that you don't have to get ready." Taq then looked over and held Latoya's hand. "And I need you to protect my queen like you've been doing. Keep her safe. Anywhere she goes, you go." Taq turns to Latoya. "Baby, don't go anywhere without notifying Poison or myself. There was one thing that Pat was right about. When people see that we're trying to make a change for the good, they might try to attack us because they think we're vulnerable. So be alert. Stay focused. Do you understand?"

"Yes, I'm with you, babe," Latoya responded.

"Good. Did you ever get back in touch with your mom last night to apologize?"

"Unfortunately, no. She had left before I could catch her."

"Well, call her now. Check up on her. You still need to apologize to her," Taq said.

Latoya dialed her mother. Her mother answered.

"Latoya! Thank God you called. I was just about to call you. I need you. I need you now. Where are you?"

"What do you need, Ma? More money?"

"No. It's Eddie. He's mad at me. And he's going to try to hurt me. Really bad. I need you to come. Hurry! I'm at this house on the corner of Piedmont and MLK Blvd. He's coming in the room now!"

"Call the police, Ma!"

"I can't! It's dope everywhere. I'd go back to prison!"

"Never mind! I'm on the way!" said Latoya. She ended the call.

"Where are you going?" asked Taq.

"I'm on the way to my mom. She's in trouble."

"Trouble?! Where is she?!"

"On the corner of Piedmont and MLK. I'll take care of this myself though. I don't need back up. This is my family," said Latoya walking out the door.

"You don't listen do you. What did I just say? Your family is our family!" said Taq to Latoya as she walked out the door. "Poison, get some ammunition. We're going to follow her and meet her there."

Latoya rushed out the house and hopped in her car. She was doing 100 miles per hour. She went so fast Taq and Poison lost sight of her car. She got to the house. Went to the door and knocked. Tried to open it. It was unlocked. She tiptoes in. The house was filthy. Martha was right. There were dirty needles and drugs everywhere. It smelled like gym socks and burnt wood.

"Is anyone here?!" Momma, are you here?" Suddenly, she heard something move in the backroom. She headed that way. The door was cracked open. She opened it wider. There Martha was. Laid out, with nothing but a shirt on, lying on a mattress on the floor. Face down. Latoya ran to her and turned her over. She had a black eye. And a swollen jaw.

"Mama, you ok?!"

"Yes. I'm ok," moaned Martha.

"Where is he?! I'm going to kill him!" said Latoya looking around.

"He went to the store to get cigarettes, he'll be back any minute."

"What are you doing here?! Why did he do this to you?!"

"Last night, we left your party and came here. We were still drunk, and I was still mad so I told him I wanted to get super high. We got high then we got into an argument. That's when he started punching and kicking me."

"Martha!" someone yells from the front door.

"Shhhhss. That's him. Hide," said Martha cringing.

"I ain't hiding from that piece of shit."

"Martha, who you talking to?" he says right before walking in.

"Oh. It's your rich-ass, fine-ass daughter. What you doing here?!" He has an open bottle of liquor in his hand.

"You made a huge mistake by putting your hands on her. You fucked with the wrong family."

He walks up to Latoya, "Now, Toya, don't come in here trying to fix some shit that has nothing to do with you. That's my woman. I do what I want with my woman. Now, leave before I give that pretty face a black eye just like your mama."

Latoya pulled Mace out and sprayed him right in the face. Then she punched him square in the jaw and kneed him in the nuts. He fell to the floor on his knees. He dropped his liquor bottle and it shattered everywhere. She had heels on so she took one off and started beating his face in with her heel with all her might. He screamed for help.

"You're going to learn who not to put your hands on!" she said after giving him one last knee to his nuts.

Seconds later, Taq and Poison run in. They had guns.

"You ok, baby?!" asked Taq.

"I'm fine," said Latoya catching her breath.

"I thought that was you screaming." He looked at Poison. "I guess she didn't need a bodyguard after all. My baby can kick some ass too," said Taq with a chuckle.

Sirens came.

Taq looked at the scenery. "We have to get out of here now! If the police catch me even near a place like this, they are putting me under the jail. Let's go, now!"

Martha looked at Latoya. With a squeaky weak voice, "You're not going to leave me here are you? They may take me to jail too. I can't go back to jail. I'd rather die."

"Martha. I love you, however, I cannot harbor you in my house again. If the police find you at Taq's house, they're going to arrest you and Taq. I came and saved you from Eddie. Now, it's time to save yourself. And it's time to find yourself. You may not realize it now, but this may be the best thing for you right now."

"Don't leave me here Latoya! I'm begging you!" she said with her hands held out.

The sirens grew louder.

"Bye, Martha."

Latoya was aware of the fact that would possibly be the last time she saw her mother.

40. Leader Shift

Latoya had never seen Taq so alive. He was more enthusiastic as he had ever been. Day in and day out he had been running around the city and making moves. His first focus was to buy some more real estate properties. He wanted to buy duplexes, triplexes, and apartment complexes to create a consistent cash flow. He even put Latoya to work. Her job was to go around Atlanta looking for foreclosures and properties that appeared to be cheap. She was told to contact realtors to see if they knew of any good real estate deals for Taq to invest in. She enjoyed it. While she was filling up her tank at the gas station, her phone started ringing. She saw that it was Lisa Smith. She ignored it. She figured it was her just trying to apologize again. Then she had another incoming call from Poison. She answered.

"Where are you?" asked Poison.

"I'm at the BP gas station off of Buford Highway. Why?"

"Ok. Don't panic. This is not a drill. Taq's in trouble. Someone has him hostage as we speak."

"Really?! How?! What's wrong?!"

"Remain calm! Do not call him, someone has his phone and is trying to set you up next."

"Oh shit! I'm scared Poison, what should I do?"

"Just stay there! I'm coming to get you now! I'm not too far. Do not move!"

"Ok! I'll stay here."

Latoya sat in her car and locked the doors. She was terrified. Ten minutes passed and she was getting a call from Taharq. She knew it was a set up. Poison said not to call him, he didn't say anything about Taq calling her. But what if he escaped? She answered.

"Hello," answered Latoya in fear.

"Hey baby. Did you eat already?"

"Everything ok?! Thank God it's you! Are you still a hostage?!Did you escape?!"

"What the fuck are you talking about? Escape what?!"

Knock. Knock. Knock. Poison knocked on the driver side car window.

"Poison said that you were in trouble... Wait a minute he's hear now," Latoya opened the door.

Poison grabs Latoya and yanks her out of the car. Four guys hop out Poison's car dressed in black with ski masks. They had on gloves and carried a rope. Latoya tries to escape Poison's grasp and she tries to scream. "No!! Stop! One of the men punches Latoya in the face and she passes out.

Latoya eventually wakes up dreadfully in fear. Her hands and feet are tied together. She's in a warehouse. The heat had sweat dripping profusely from her pores. It smelled like something had died. Panting. She looks to her left and sees a dead body with his hands tied, slumped over. She recognized the body. It was Pat. She screamed! She looked to her right and saw Farren, tied up sitting next to her. Farren was still alive but she looked defeated.

"What is this all about?! Are you responsible for this too?! Another set up. You and Poison?! Which one of y'all murdered Pat?"

Farren shook her head. "You're right. It's my fault. I'm sorry Latoya. I'm sorry that I brought you into this life. I'm sorry that I introduced you to Poison. I'm sorry that I created Black Vanity. I always knew that you'd be the shit when I first met you. Deep down inside I envied you because I knew you'd become bigger and better than me. I'm sorry that I talked shit about you behind your back. I'm sorry that I jumped you in the Dreamville parking lot. You didn't deserve this, I love you, Latoya."

With tears of fear running down her cheeks, Latoya said, "Now is not the time to apologize. We're going to make it out of this. We're going to be ok. Right? Where the fuck are we?" Latoya said.

"I have no clue. Somewhere in one of Musa's warehouses. But I do know one thing. If I make it out alive, I'm done. I'm done with it all. I'm going legit. I swear to God, I'm going to stop. I'm done with the naked hustle."

"I am too. I'm done with it all."

"I'm going to mentor little girls to not take this path. I'm going to start my own beauty and skin care line. Make-up, Eye-lashes, Hair, all that shit!"

"What is it going to be called?" asked Latoya.

"Vanity-Kisses Inc. My name and your name put together. We can launch it together too."

The warehouse doors swung open and the guys that kidnapped Latoya walked in. They still had their ski masks on. They then took them off. Three of the guys, Latoya didn't recognize. One of the guys was Poison.

"Poison, why are you doing this?!" yelled Latoya.

Poison smiled and walked over to Latoya. "Latoya, aka Black Vanity, aka Mrs. BWS. You know I was in love with you. I would've spared your life if you would've just gave me a chance. I protected you from dangers that you didn't even know existed. Not Taq. I did! You and I could've lived happily ever after. But you didn't appreciate my service to you. You overlooked me. So now, it's time for you and Taq to pay the price. With your lives."

"Poison! You know this shit is going to cost you your life too! This is like suicide. You and I go way back. You're smarter than this. Don't go through with this," said Farren.

"Shhhhh. Hush up!" said Poison. "The real boss is coming. Musa doesn't want any squealing from y'all. He wants everything to be done quickly and quietly. Y'all both lived a fantastic life. Sorry, it won't end the way y'all would like it to."

Moments later. A dark shadow came from around the corner. It was the devil himself. Latoya was dumbfounded.

"Surprise, surprise. Well look what the tide brought in. Latoya. My crush from awhile back. From working in construction to the stripper pole. You are a multifaceted young lady aren't you. How's that bitch, Tina, doing?!"

"Wait Marvin? You're Musa?!" said Latoya.

"Ding. Ding. Ding. Marvin Maples aka Musa. You got it! In the flesh. The one and only. The legend himself. The guy everyone loves to hate. Now, you're probably wondering why we're all gathered here today. My money is the one thing that I don't play about. The streets have spoken, and they are saying that y'all robbed me. About two years ago, $75,000 of my money was stolen from me. And my accountant Booker was found dead. Y'all remember that? It was all over the news."

"We don't remember," said Latoya.

"I thought you'd say that. Well, I remember. See my friend, Poison here, told me how everything went down with Booker. So, I know EVERYTHING. He was hired by Taq to rob me. Along with you two. But see, I like Poison. He's the best in the business. It's hard to find a good hard working hitman like Poison. That's why I decided not to kill him. I actually decided to help him switch teams. Now he's with the winning team. I can use a killer like him. But you two, y'all are disposable."

"Musa, please. Spare us. Latoya had nothing to do with this. It was all me. I forced her to come," said Farren.

"Quite frankly, I don't give a fuck about who did what at this point. All I know is that my money is gone and somebody will pay the price, plus interest. And when I mean pay, I mean with your lives," he looks at Poison. "Fire her."

Latoya looked at Farren, she looked confused. Poison pointed his gun at Farren and pulled the trigger. The loud pop of the gun startled Latoya and she screamed at the top of her lungs. She looked at Farren's body as it pulsated, pumping blood from her like a waterfall making a lake around her.

Poison ran up to Latoya with the gun and pointed it at her head. "Shut the fuck up! Shut the fuck up! Before I blow your brains out next."

She was quiet but still whimpering in horror.

"Let her be. Let her be. Let me talk to her for a second before she is fired," Marvin walked up close to her and made Poison back up.

"Latoya. Or better yet. Black Vanity. You know I liked you. Like, I really did. When I first saw you when Tina had you in my house, I was amazed at how beautiful you were. Fine as wine. If I would've had to choose between you and Tina, I would've chose you. You had some bomb-ass coochie. I mean, damn.

Whoever taught you how to fuck should be proud of themselves. But when Tina found out about our little secret, it was all ruined. And I thought I would never see you again. But, see how destiny works. We were meant to run into each other again. Different circumstances of course, but either way, we're together. So, I get one more chance. One more chance to make love to you. To fuck you like it's our last time. Which it will be because you'll be dead afterwards. And the fact that you're Taq's fiancée now is even better. If I fuck you on tape, then send it to him, it's like a fuck you message to him. You get it? Knocking two birds out with one stone. So that's exactly what we're going to do. I'm going to fuck you, my men are going to record it, and then we're going to send it to him as a message not to fuck with us. I crack myself up. Then you'll be fired just like your friend, Red Kisses." He smiled and gave her a light kiss on the lips. "Alright, Teddy, go take her in the room and let her undress. Bring the gun and watch her closely, so she don't try no funny shit. If she do, shoot the shit out of her."

They took her in a room. A big black fat dude name Teddy with a big gun stood and watched her. He was like 6'5" 300 lbs. She sat there, still sobbing and in disbelief. Knowing that her demise was near, she reflected on her life. Thinking about what had all transpired to bring her to this point. She thought about Martha's life. She thought about her grandma Betsy. Then she started crying again. She couldn't stop.

"Baby girl, Musa said you gotta get undressed. You can't just sit here. No crying." Said Teddy.

She thought to herself. She can just sit here. Her life is over. She had given up. They can just kill her at this point. There was no way out of this one. Until she remembered something. She looked at Teddy's leg and saw that there were two rectangular objects in his pocket. Teddy had her phone. That was a sign not to give up. She looked at Teddy with the big gun. And she thought of a plan. She was going to do whatever it took to escape.

"Ummm. Teddy. Are you going to be the one who is going to kill me?"

"Nah, baby girl. Just get undressed, like Musa said."

"Because you're too damn good looking to be killing people," said Latoya looking him up and down.

"That's how you feel huh?"

"Uhh yea. If I survive this. I will fuck the shit out of your big black sexy ass."

Teddy Laughed. "I feel you, but it won't happen."

"So, you wouldn't want to fuck me? Be honest? It's just me and you here."

"Maybe."

"Good. Because I would do you for sure. As a matter of fact, if I don't survive, I want you to remember me. I want you to masturbate to me when I'm gone."

"Jack off to a dead bitch? Nah, I'm not that freaky."

"I bet you I can change your mind. Hand me my phone and I'll show you something."

"Fuck no. Why do you need your phone? It's off," he said pulling it out and showing her that it was off.

"I'm going to send you some naked pictures of me. It only takes a second for me to send them. The same pictures that I send to my man, Taq."

He hesitated. "I can turn your phone on and send them for you."

"No! I have them hid in my phone. I don't keep my nudes in my gallery. They're in a secret place."

He didn't say anything for a second then he handed her the phone. "Hurry up and send them."

She turned the phone on. "Ok, I will. Just give me a second. What's your number?"

"678-458-7835."

"Ok. Sending them now." She had her phone and she attempted to send her location to Taq. Right before pressing the send button, Teddy snatched the phone. "Bitch!" Then slaps her upside the head. "You must think I'm stupid."

"Teddy, bring that bitch out," yelled Marvin from the other room.

She came out with just a towel on. Teddy escorted her to Musa's room with a gun pointed at her. Musa was in a robe. There was a camera on a tripod. The room had nothing in it but a mattress and a shelf. There was an empty glass and a bottle of some type of liquor plus a red pill. Musa poured the liquor into the glass and picked the pill up. Take this to the head. "You're going to need a little motivation," Terry held the gun to her head.

Latoya then lays on the bed with the towel on. Musa proceeds to take his robe off. Suddenly shots are fired from the other warehouse room.

Musa peaks out the room and sees a tall figure with multiple guns in hand. He sees two of the his men shot dead.

Musa grabs Latoya by the neck, points a gun to her head and slowly escorts her out the room.

"Hey! Hold fire! Is the what you want?!" yells Musa walking into the main room. The gunshots stopped. Teddy and Poison, have guns pointed at Taq and he had guns pointed at them.

"Poison you know better. I trusted you. You know that you just committed suicide by betraying me." Said Taq.

"No. No. No. See, Poison is smart. He joined the winning side. He knows that you're weak now. He knows where the biggest opportunity is, unlike you," says Musa.

"Drop your gun, Taq. The game is over for you, three on one, you lose," said Poison.

"No, you drop your gun! I trusted you with my life, Poison. Whatever happened to loyalty? You were like a little brother to me. You could've stepped to me like a man if you weren't happy with me."

"My son! Oh my son, I see you haven't changed one bit! You don't know shit about loyalty. Because if you knew anything about loyalty, you would've stayed working for me and we wouldn't be in this mess now. But you're still stubborn and ignorant just like you were growing up," said Musa.

"I'm not your son, anymore. Don't call me son!" said Taharq.

"Oh really? Who taught you everything that you know! Who raised you?! Who took you in when you were homeless? Who put food on your plate? Who gave you your first million?! Huh?"

"I earned my first million!" said Taq.

"You earned that million because I put you in a position to win! And this is what I get in return? You leave my organization to start your own little operation. Then you rob your own father?!"

"You're not my father! My father's dead, just like you'll be soon. And I robbed you because you tried to kill me three years ago, Musa. That's why I robbed you!"

Marvin chuckled. "Ok. Ok. I will admit that I did try to wipe you out. Because you were dealing in my territory. And you know better, not to fuck with Musa's money! So how about this. I'm going to give you an offer you can't refuse. How about we settle all of this and you just join my organization and shut down your operation. Be smart like Poison. Just like the good ole days. Or I blow your girlfriend's fucking brains out all over this dusty warehouse floor."

"Fuck you, Musa," said Taharq.

"Wrong answer."

Shots rang in the air. Latoya closed her eyes in terror. However, she felt nothing. Musa stumbled and appeared disheveled. Latoya escapes Musa's grasp, runs and ducks for cover. Musa looked down and saw that he was shot in the leg. Then immediately another shot in the chest. He fell to the ground. Poison looked at him confused from where the bullet came from. Then fired shots at Taharq, hitting him in the arm and leg. Taharq stumbles and falls to the ground. Poison then gets hit in the chest by another bullet. Poison then realized that Teddy was the one that had shot him and Musa. He turns and fires at Teddy, killing Teddy. That's when Taharq fired a bullet right through Poison's head. And he was killed instantly.

Wounded, but determined, Taq managed to get back on his feet. He limps over to Teddy. Teddy laid on his back with his eyes wide open in a puddle of blood. Taq whispers "Thank you," in Teddy's ear and closes his eyelids. He grabs Teddy's gun then he limps over to Musa.

Struggling to stay alive, Musa is laying on the ground, gasping for air with a mouth full of blood.

"Now, looks like I'm not the only one that doesn't understand loyalty," says Taq.

Taharq shoots Musa in the head. Latoya ran to Taharq's arms.

41. Ride or Die

Taq's Estate

That night, Latoya and Taq were home watching the news.

"A massacre has occurred in the city of Atlanta today. The assassination of the CEO of Maples Construction, Marvin Maples has shocked the city. Marvin Maples' body was found alongside four other bodies in an abandoned warehouse off of Candler Rd. Investigators have identified the other four bodies as Farren Hernandez, Patrick Williams, Peter "Poison" Porter, and Teddy Henderson. Investigators believe that this could've been a drug deal gone wrong that turned into a bloodbath. Although Marvin Maples was a super successful business man in the community, some sources say that Maples may have been one of the most successful drug lords in the country. Estimating that he had a net worth of over 100 million dollars. Investigators believe that there is one suspect by the name of Taharq "Taq" Taylor, a rival drug lord that is still at large. If anyone has any tips that can lead to the whereabouts of Taharq "Taq" Taylor, they will be awarded $100,000."

Taq's arms and legs were wrapped firmly with clothing and bandages from the bullet wounds. But that didn't stop Taq's arms from being firmly wrapped around Latoya. They laid on the couch naked, inhaling and exhaling deeply. The sweat from their bodies dripped onto each other. They had just finished making the most passionate love they had ever made as if it was there last time. Escaping the reality of what they had just been through; temporarily releasing the stress and the worry of what the near future held. With the remote in her hand pointed at the television, she wished she could turn the channel of their life to something more pleasant and peaceful. Instead, their present circumstances were painful. Latoya couldn't turn on the television or even stroll through her phone without seeing Musa or Taq's name.

"What are we going to do? Shouldn't we be leaving the country right now? We have our passports," Latoya said looking up to Taq.

"There's no need to run. I'm going to turn myself in. Then you're going to bail me out."

"You sure? I'm scared Taq. What if there isn't a bail?"

"Don't be afraid. Worry is a waste of imagination. I'm going to beat this case. I'm determined. As long as I have you on my side, I'll be fine." Taq shifted himself on the couch and turned to make sure that they saw eye to eye. He continued. "I do ask one thing from you. Poison turned his back on me, Pat's dead. It's just me and you left. We all we got. Just me and you. I need you to hold me down. It's going to get rough, but that's why I need you more than ever. You are my rock, I can't do this without you. Can you promise me that you'll have my back?"

"Baby, I'll do anything for you. You saved my life. I got your back. Because I know you got mine."

"You promise?" he asked.

"I promise."

They locked hands. He kissed her on the forehead. Then he got up and limped away into his room. Five minutes later he limped back with a duffle bag and dropped it on the floor in front of the couch.

"In this bag, there's 2.5 million dollars. I need you to hold this for me, some of it will be to bond me out. The rest of it, well, I know you're not dumb enough to spend it. Use your own judgement. You're a hustler like me so, do what you have to do. Flip it. I trust your judgement. I trust you with my life."

Latoya looked at the bag with big eyes. "Ok. I got you baby. You can count on me. When will you turn yourself in?" she asked.

"Tomorrow morning. That will give me enough time to get my affairs in order."

"You don't think that they're not going to come looking for you before then?"

"Of course, they will. But trust me, they won't be able to find me. I'm the best at hide and seek," said Taq.

42. Fed Up

That day, with a sense of urgency, Taq and Latoya thoroughly cleansed the house of any evidence. Even though, Taq was meticulous enough not to have anything there in the first place to get him indicted. That same day, Taq met with his lawyer, his accountant, and his banker to put the money in Latoya's name. He also met with some unnamed powerful individuals that he wouldn't even tell Latoya about.

The next morning, Taq had turned himself in at 8:06 a.m. The news ate it up. His face was everywhere. CNN, local news, Good Morning America, you name it, his face was featured. Taq was officially a national sensation. Not only because he was labeled as a drug kingpin that had assassinated another drug kingpin. But because to the women, he was labeled as a fine-ass drug kingpin. His mugshots were going viral on social media. Although social media loved him, the judicial system didn't. Taq was being held with no bail. She had to wait on his directions.

Latoya was lounging on the couch watching the news when she heard the doorbell ring. She was perplexed because she wasn't expecting anyone. She got up and looked in the peephole and saw two white males with briefcases standing patiently.

"Can I help you gentleman?"

"Yes. We're with the Fulton County Police Department. We're just here to speak with Latoya Robertson."

Latoya's heart dropped. She was clueless on what to do or say. Not wanting to appear suspicious, she calmly opened the door.

"Hi Latoya. I'm detective Rupert Stinson and this is my colleague, Lewis Foster. We're here just to ask you a couple of questions. Do you mind if we come in?"

"Ummm. Yea sure. Why not. Come in." She let them in.

Detective Stinson looked in awe. "This is quite a nice dwelling you have here Latoya. Business must be booming for you and Taq."

"What are the questions that you have for me?"

"Well. You know why we're here. The night of Musa, Farren, Teddy, and Poison's death, where exactly were you?"

"Minding my own business, like I always do," answered Latoya.

"Ok. Let's start over. Let's cut to the chase. Latoya you and your drug dealing boyfriend Taq are looking at life in prison. We know where you were that night. We know everything about you. We know that Taq killed Musa. They were rival gangs. It was only a matter of time before one of them would kill the other. You're stuck between a rock and a hard place. You're in too deep. Do me a favor, don't try to protect Taq. It's over for him. He's not getting out ever again. But you on the other hand, you have a chance to keep your freedom. If you just tell the truth. The absolute worst thing you can do is lie to us. That would dig you an even deeper hole. We are really here to help you get out of this mess. But you have to work with us. With that being said, I'll ask you again. Where were you on that night?"

"Sorry guys. I'm not saying anything without speaking with my lawyer first. You all can leave now."

"Ok. If you want to make this difficult, then so be it. Just remember that I tried to help you. Can't you see, all of this is over. This huge house, your fancy cars, your fancy lifestyle it's all over. The game is over. Taq can't protect you. You are on your own now. You better protect yourself. Goodbye Latoya," said Detective Stinson as he and his colleague walked towards the door.

Latoya immediately called the number that Taq told her to call whenever she needed to get in contact with him. Somehow he had a personal phone while locked up.

"Hey, baby. The police just left the house!"

"Yea I knew they would eventually come. You didn't tell them anything did you? My lawyer should be calling you soon." said Taq.

"No, I didn't say anything. But now I'm nervous. What am I supposed to do? Just sit here and wait for you to get released?"

"Just be patient, baby. I'm probably going to have to take this thing to trial."

"Trial?! Taq they say you're looking at life in prison or maybe even the death penalty. They also said that there's a zero percent chance that you will beat this."

"Fuck what they say. I know what's possible. Stop listening to the news. Stop listening to the naysayers. I know I can beat this thing. Just have faith. You have to believe with me. Stay strong with me."

"I will try."

"Try?! Don't try. Do it. BWS for life, baby. Remember. You made a promise. My first court date is on January 27th at 2:00 p.m. I need you there front and center. I need you Latoya."

"Ok. Just let me know when. I'll be there."

After her conversation with Taq, Latoya called Wanda.

"Girrrlll! I'm seeing your boo's name all over the news for this mass murder," said Wanda.

"I know, Wanda. I'm tired. I don't know if I can do this anymore. I'm fed up. I can't hold him down anymore."

"Finally, you come to your senses. Get out of there now. He's a murderer," said Wanda.

"He's not a murderer. He's misunderstood. But it doesn't even matter. This is it for him. I feel it. But he doesn't know it. He's going to prison. And this time, he's not getting out. And I feel trapped."

"Nothing is holding you back from getting as far away from him as possible. I'm so confused. Why are you still with him anyway? You control your destiny."

"It's not that simple. There is something holding me back. Plus, I have his mone... I mean I have his trust. He's depending on me for everything now. It's complicated, I can't just up and leave him."

"It's very simple. Just leave. How can it be simpler?"

"I'm in love with Taq. Still. And I don't want to leave him hanging. He's counting on me. He has no one else. And plus, what if he tries to hurt me. He has the influence even while he's in prison."

"Well you have to. If you are serious about leaving this lifestyle, you have to cut all ties from the streets, including Taq."

"But, I made a promise that I wouldn't turn my back on him. I promised him that I would be there for his court date on Thursday."

"Court date?! You want to be seen supporting a murderer? Promises are meant to be broken. I wouldn't touch foot near that courtroom to support him. What if they try to attach your name to those murders? Then what?"

"You're right. I won't go."

"It's time to move on, Latoya. What you need is another man to take your attention away from Taq.

Like Samuel. What happened with him? He would be the perfect replacement to distract you and to get you away from this nonsense."

"Samuel is a great guy. I really like him. But I'm still in love with Taq."

"Toya, whether you like it or not. Samuel is your way out. He's an attorney. He's good looking, he has a future, he makes good money. You need a good wholesome guy that is going to take care of you. And that has no ties to the streets."

"So that's what you think? I should just cut Taq completely off?" asked Latoya.

"Yes! Duh! He'll get the picture just like any other guy. Life is all about growth and change. So what if he's salty? He's going to prison for life anyway. It seems like it's dangerous with him or without him. But at least you'll have your peace of mind."

Wanda convinced Latoya to leave Taq. She decided not to answer his calls anymore. Latoya hopped in her car and started driving. When she pulled away from the property, she saw at least 15 police cars pass her while she headed the opposite way. She looked at the passenger seat and thankfully she had the duffle bag that Taq had left her. Looking at the mansion in her rearview. She held her head up and sped off.

At first, she thought to go to Wanda's house. But she wanted to make a pit stop.

Ding-dong. She rang the doorbell.

Samuel answers the door. With a robe on.

"Wow. I can't believe this. I guess God does answer prayers huh," said Samuel. "Because the woman that I had been praying about just shows up on my doorstep. What a coincidence."

"Oh, stop it!"

"I'm corious! What brought you here? You could've called you know."

"Yes, but sometimes, I like to arrive unannounced to see if I'm always welcomed."

"Well, you're always welcomed here! Come in," said Samuel motioning her in.

She came in and took a seat on his couch.

"Do you need some water or anything? Some tea?"

"No, I'm fine."

"So, tell me. What's going on? You just went ghost on me. Was it something I said or did? Did you end up back with your ex?"

"No Samuel. It has nothing to do with you. You're a great man. I've just been going through a lot."

"Well you know you can talk to me about anything. We're friends first, remember?"

"Yea. I remember. I just want to come clean about something. I'm not the person that I've been saying I was."

"What do you mean?"

"I'm not really in real estate. I was a dancer. An exotic dancer."

"Wait. What?! You have to be kidding me!"

"I'm not. I was just so ashamed to tell you who I really am. Life is too short to be hiding the truth."

Samuel shook his head. "Well. At least you came out and told the truth. Even though I already knew the truth."

"Oh no! How did you know!?"

"I mean. You would never tell me where you worked. That was the biggest red flag. I assumed that you had a profession that you weren't proud of."

"Why did you pursue me if you knew that I was a stripper?"

"Why wouldn't I? You're one of the best people that I've ever met. You're cool, you're gorgeous, you're smart, you're down to earth, you're an entrepreneur, you're ambitious. Who wouldn't want that in a woman?"

"You're joking, right? You're a lawyer and you wouldn't be ashamed of me? Do you really feel that way about me, or are you just trying to butter me up?"

"I'm serious. Your past wouldn't stop me from wanting to be with you. As long as you're not trying to continue being a dancer. Are you?"

"Of course not."

Samuel replied. "Exactly, I can help you find more work that will fit your skills. That's what relationships are about. Accepting someone for who they are, flaws and all. Loving them unconditionally, and just trying to bring the best out of them."

"So, what about your family? How will they react when they find out that I was a stripper?"

Honestly, they may be taken aback by it. But at the end of the day, it's really none of their business. it's what matters to me, not them. And I think you'ro fabulous," said Samuel.

He knew the right things to say. She got emotional and gave him a hug. She held him tight. He leaned down and gave her a kiss on the forehead. She looked up into his eyes, then he kissed her. He kissed her neck and then they started undressing each other until they were fully naked. He picked her up and carried her into his room. Upstairs.

He took everything slow. The foreplay didn't exist, and she didn't care. She needed to be sexed passionately, immediately. And he did just that. While they kissed on the bed his dick eased inside of her. It was shockingly big. It felt right. She didn't feel guilty. It felt like innocence. He stroked inside her, slowly but surely. After 25 minutes they both had an orgasm. They got up, took a shower together then cuddled up and fell asleep.

7:00 a.m. Samuel's House

"Good morning, baby girl," said Samuel standing bedside with a robe on and holding a cup of coffee.

Latoya, still sleepy, responded, "Good morning."

"So. What do you have planned today?" Asked Samuel looking at his watch.

"You're trying to kick me out?" Latoya rolled over and looked at him.

"No. Just asking. You can stay here if you want. Or you can come to work with me."

"No. I have somewhere else to be today. I promised someone that I would be there for them."

"Ok. Just checking."

Latoya got up, got dressed and left Samuel's house.

After much thought and consideration, despite Wanda's advice, Latoya decided to show up for Taq's court date. She made her way to the courthouse. She got there a little early so she was there patiently waiting. She was in the front row. Taq entered. He saw her immediately. He smiled and waved. He held his head up high. She smiled. Then waived back.

Then Latoya felt someone grab her waist from behind. She swung around as a reflex, ready to knock someone's teeth out. Her eyes were as wide as Texas when she saw who it was. It was Samuel.

"What are you doing here?! I guess you wanted to surprise me at work!" said Samuel with a big smile.

"Uhhhh yea I did," Latoya said petrified.

Taq watched closely, trying to make sense of what he was seeing.

"Come over here and sit with my mom. You're sitting over there on the defendant's side. You don't want to sit over there. You don't want to be associated with a murderer, do you?"

"Ummm. I think I should just... go," said Latoya looking towards the exit.

"Go?! It hadn't even started yet. Why leave?"

Samuel's mother stands up and starts waving her arms, "Come sit with me."

Not knowing what to do, Latoya listened and took a seat right next to Samuel's mother and right behind Samuel. She avoided looking in Taq's direction. She was terrified to look him in his eyes.

Once the trial session began. The judge gave Taq the opportunity to speak.

Taq stood up.

"You know it's funny. I had never been in love before. Never in my entire life. My heart didn't have a place for love since my parents' death. I had hidden myself from love because the one time I decided to love someone, they were taken away from me forever. But there was this one time, I decided to love again. I took a chance and I decided to love someone again. This woman that I took a chance with... I loved her because she was like a reflection of myself. For some reason it felt like she was an extension of me. And I trusted her. I trusted her with the only love that I had left within my heart. And I would do anything to protect her, because I didn't want that love to leave me like the one time it did when I was a child. Because that pain was unbearable, excruciating pain that I wouldn't wish on my worst enemy. Unfortunately, today, my biggest nightmare has become a reality. And the love of my life, is now dead to me. And that's all I have to say." Taq took a seat.

Latoya hopped up out of her seat and started walking towards the back door.

"Latoya!" Samuel yelled as he followed her out.

"Where are you going?! Come back! Order in the court!" yelled the Judge.

"One second your honor!" Samuel continued to follow Latoya.

He caught up with her outside the courtroom. "What's going on here?!"

"Why didn't you tell me you were a prosecutor?!" asked Latoya.

"Why, is that a problem? I told you I was a lawyer. You never asked me what type. Just like you didn't tell me you were a stripper. Remember?"

"Well. I've never told you who my fiancé was either."

"Who?" asked Samuel.

Latoya shook her head and paced back and forth. "This is bad. This is soo bad."

Samuel looked worried. He pointed towards the courtroom. "Wait. Please don't tell me your fiancé was that man right there? Taharq Taylor?! Taq!? The leader of the Black Wall Street Mafia?!"

Latoya nodded in agreement.

Samuel threw his hands in the air. "Oh, that's the deal-breaker for me. I can't believe this shit. So that explains everything! If the media knew I had relations with you, my whole career would be ruined!"

"I don't care about your career! This is my life! Taq trusted me. He trusted me with his whole life. I made a promise to him that I would never turn my back on him. And now he just saw me sitting with the person that is trying to put him in jail for the rest of his life. Now, I don't know what to do."

"I know exactly what you should do. You better get as far away from town as possible because if Taq thinks that you snitched on him then there is no doubt about it, he will kill you. He has the power to kill you even if he's locked up. Hell, he might even think about killing me at this point. I strongly suggest you leave town. Like, immediately. But hey, I have to go back in to do my job so I'm saying goodbye. I'm sorry that us two couldn't make things work between us. But, I wish you the best. Good luck." Samuel gave her a kiss on the forehead and went back into the courtroom.

Latoya went to the parking lot and got in her car. She had no idea where she was going but she just started driving. She wanted to get as far away as she could.

Best Western Hotel, Montana

After driving for awhile, Latoya ended up at a hotel in Montana. It was one of the quietest places that she had ever been to. The people were very nice. She spent most of her time in the hotel room pondering on what her next move would be. She thought about what her life would be like hiding out in a rural place like Montana, or maybe Kentucky. She could grow old there and probably marry a farmer. Or maybe she should move out of the country and lay low there. Taq's reach would never find her there.

Two days had past and she was still in Montana. Latoya was bored. After sitting and staring at the duffle bag on the hotel bed, she came to a realization. The thought of her living in fear for the rest of her life scared her. Latoya hated living in fear. To her, that was like a mental prison. She wanted to choose faith over fear. She didn't want to hide, she wanted to thrive. She then asked herself where she would go if she wanted to pursue her wildest dreams. She closed her eyes. After a moment of silence, she opened her eyes and smiled.

43. Pursuit of Happiness

New York, New York

Latoya made it to Manhattan. A month after she had got settled in New York, she was at restaurant dining by herself and she saw that CNN was on one of the televisions. The headline read, "Well known mafioso in Atlanta, sentenced to life in prison without parole," Latoya didn't know how to feel about Taq's conviction. A part of her was sad and felt sorry for Taq. She felt like she had a lot to do with his arrest. The other part of her felt a sigh of relief, knowing that she was at least safe; for now.

Three years later at the Women's Empowerment Awards Ceremony in New York City

"I am so pleased to be the host of the 5th annual, Women's Empowerment Banquet in New York City."

Everyone clapped for the lady as she smiled and blushed.

"For those of you that don't know, let me explain to you what this magnificent occasion is all about. The Women's Empowerment Banquet is an award ceremony that honors women from all across the country that exemplify excellence in their chosen careers and have been a positive influence on the communities that they serve."

Latoya sat at the banquet style table with the other guests. She sat there alongside her assistant Karen, who she had hired a year and a half ago. Everyone was dressed eloquently. The men had on tailored suits and the women had on long fancy dresses. Everyone talked and laughed amongst themselves. There were six more people around the table that looked very sophisticated. They looked well-polished and put together. They looked like success. They looked rich. Five years ago, she would never had imagined sitting alongside such people. And if she did she would have felt inferior to them; as if she was lesser than them and she didn't belong. But now, she felt like she had earned the right to sit at the table. Especially since Latoya was one of the women being honored.

The award presenter spoke, "This next woman exemplifies what it means to be a true hustler. A relentless entrepreneur, a business mogul. And she came out of nowhere. Just three years ago she drove from Atlanta, Georgia to New York City to pursue her dreams. You may not know her, but you may have heard of her make-up brands like Vanity Kisses, which has become a multi-million-dollar brand in less than three years. But some people don't know that she's also a real estate tycoon. She is the perfect example of a rags to riches saga. Her story will absolutely blow your mind. She's what the American dream is all about. I am honored to present this Mogul of the Year Award to Latoya Robertson, aka Black Vanity. Congratulations!"

Everyone clapped as Latoya got up and made her way to accept her award on stage. She grabbed her trophy, waved at the crowd, and made her way back to her seat. She looked at the golden heart shaped award with her named engraved on it and started reflecting on her journey.

"The next award is probably the most important award of the night. This award goes to a woman that has made a huge difference in her community. Her story has inspired millions of people. She has turned her life's devastation to determination. Determination to plant seeds of hope and faith for little troubled girls that have been broken. As a motivational speaker, she is based out of Atlanta, Georgia but she has touched lives all over. The Ultimate Fighter Award goes to Martha Robertson!"

Latoya almost broke her neck when she heard the name. It couldn't be who she thought it was. She was flabbergasted when she saw her mother, Martha, walking up to receive her award.

"Wow. Thank you all! This is truly an honor! But I will not be standing here if it wasn't for Lisa Smith, and the TEA CUP organization for believing in me and taking me in when I was at my worst. Stand up, Lisa, so they can see you."

In the crowd. Lisa stood up briefly and waved at everyone.

"The TEA CUP organization helped to bail me out of jail when I had lost all hope for my life. Not only that, but they helped to mold me into a woman, that for the first time in my life, I can honestly say that I am proud of. If it wasn't for Lisa, and TEA CUP, I don't know where I would be. This is a dream come true. Thank you all!" The crowd cheered as she left the stage.

Latoya got up out of her seat and began to walk to the table where Martha and Lisa were sitting. Once she got close, Martha saw her and looked at her with the biggest smile. To Latoya's surprise, Grandma Betsy was sitting at their table as well. Latoya opened her arms with tears rolling down her cheek. Martha embraced her and they both wrapped their arms around each other tight. Grandma Betsy got up and joined the hug as well. All three of them began crying hysterically in joy. Lisa watched and teared up as well.

That night the TEA CUP received a $1,000,000 donation from an anonymous donor. The organization also added a new board member. Latoya Robinson.

Knock, knock, knock. Latoya knocked on the door of Martha's and Grandma Betsy's hotel room door. She wanted to join them in her hotel room to catch up after the ceremony. Latoya had a visitor with her. She held him in her arms.

Martha opened the door surprised. "Who are you babysitting for?" asked Martha.

Latoya laughed. "I'm not babysitting for anyone. Say hello to your grandson."

"What?! I'm a grandma! You have to be kidding me! He's so cute! What's his name?" asked Martha.

"Emmanuel. But just call him Little Manny."

"Uh oh. Looks like we have a lot more catching up to do. Come on in and have a seat next to your mama and your granny. I made some tea, grab a cup." said Martha.

Naked Hustle

The End

I want to give a huge Shout out to Desiree McGowan and Mia Graves for assisting with the book!

If you enjoyed the book, leave a review on Amazon.com or reach out through email douglastparker@gmail.com or via instagram @Treyparker_

Made in the USA
Middletown, DE
18 March 2022